Samuri and Jewel:

The Forbidden Friendship

Kimily Kay

Samuri and Jewel: The Forbidden Friendship

©2023 by Kimily Kay Duffield

Printed in the United States of America

Published in the United States of America
by Kimily Kay Books

Hardcover: 979-8-9892470-1-1
Paperback: 979-8-9892470-0-4
Ebook: 979-8-9892470-2-8
Library of Congress Control Number: TXu2-381-024

This book is a work of fiction. As such, all people, places, and events depicted are strictly fictional.

Cover design by Faille Schmitz
Map by Heidi Morgan
Wrens and Compass Artwork by Kimily's husband, Bob
Interior design by Inkling Creative Strategies
Editing by Lindsay Cornett

Dedication

*To each brave one on this Samuri and
Jewel journey of true friendship
and freedom . . .*

*. . . may you always, always
have help.*

The Township

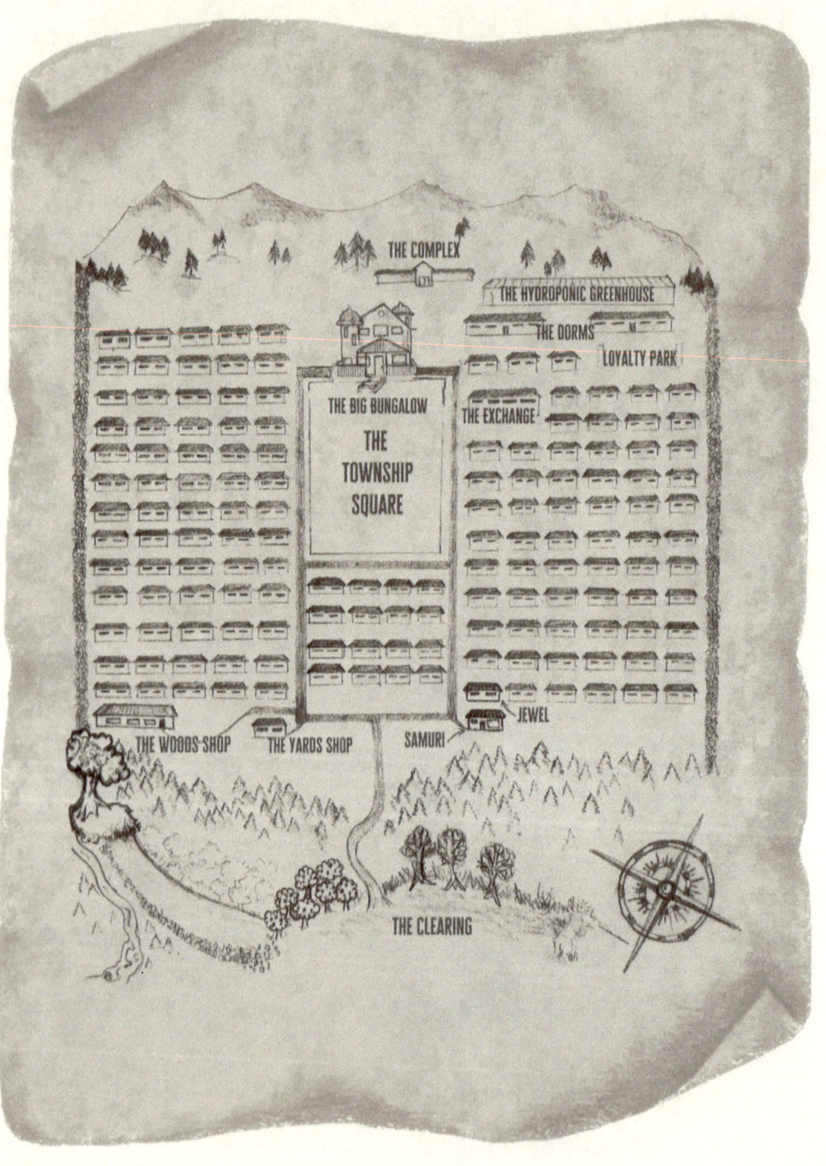

The Promise

Samuri,

Be brave and be true. You have many things to do in your life. You will do well, and you will have help.

Even when we cannot be with you— you will always have help.

Name Pronunciations

Samuri: *Sam-uh-ri* (rhymes with sky)

Para: *pair-uh* (rhymes with Sarah)

Daro: *Dar-oh* (rhymes with car-o)

Tuckit: *Tuck-it* (sounds like "tuck it")

Nyah: *Nigh-uh* (rhymes with "Hiya")

Dupree: *Due-pree* (rhymes with "see")

Cree: *Rhymes with Dupree*

1

samuri

"Loyal-Township-folks, one-and-all!" Town Master Edward forced the words out in his best staccato voice. "Welcome-to-the-thirtieth-annual-Celebration-Day!" The pain in his chest and stomach made it hard to smile, hard to speak, but he was determined to push through. He could rest after today.

The Ceremony of the Bungalows had gone smoothly, but the Naming Ceremony was terribly slow. Three sets of paras had not shaved their tinys' heads yet. That meant Official Nyah, the Township's oldest official, must shave those tinys right in the middle of their Naming Ceremonies. Oh, how those tinys wailed! Town Master clenched his teeth and took a deep breath. Though he despised Nyah, he was glad she was in charge of the Naming Ceremony. She could handle the worst situations safely, pleasantly, *and* without his help.

The last set of paras came forward, whispered, "Bungalow seventy-six" to the official, and settled their tiny into the official's arms. Nyah parted the blanket and sighed with relief. This tiny's head was smooth and neatly shaven.

"Samuri," the official announced with significance. "His name is Samuri."

Two paras in the middle of the crowd muttered, "Hurry up" under their breath. Why should *they* care? Another Naming only meant another bothersome tiny.

Samuri opened his eyes, gazed at the official, and cooed. When Official Nyah handed him back to his paras, she was struck with the fierce, determined pride in this he-para's eyes. Samuri's she-para glowed with joy. These two, so like the paras decades ago, might give this tiny a life truly worth living. Nyah swallowed the lump in her throat and dared to speak again. Her lips barely moved. Her voice was hushed but rich with meaning.

"His name is *Samuri*."

Neither the crowd nor Town Master Edward heard Nyah. Even Samuri's paras, Chloe and Patrick, wondered if they had imagined it. Why had the official spoken just to them?

Suddenly the wind stirred, and a quintet of wrens swept above the crowd, bursting into delightful melodies. All eyes dropped fearfully to the ground. All except for Town Master Edward, whose disapproving scowl went unseen by flying creatures and Township folks alike. Para Chloe gasped—folks assumed it was from fear, but Para Patrick knew better. The flying creatures' song was a sign.

The song of the wrens shook Town Master Edward back to reality. He glared toward Nyah, but her face was lowered obediently, reminding him of her lifelong devotion to the folks of the Township. He too would carry on and wipe out the memory of the wrens' intrusion.

Town Master Edward shouted as joyfully as he could. "Township Folks, I present to you this year's four new tinys!" He motioned dramatically with his arm and nearly stumbled from the pain. "Let us help our tiny folks be pleasant to all and loyal to the Township, so they may live safe, long lives."

The Celebration went on as if nothing had happened. Only Official Nyah felt the pain of Edward's hard heart.

Para Patrick sheltered Samuri in his slender, muscular arms, following Chloe as she made her way through the crowd. After she knelt on their blanket Patrick bent, handed her their tiny, and whispered, "Samuri." When he turned to sit beside her, he saw an official had passed them seconds before. Patrick's heart skipped a beat as the official plunged into the crowd ahead of them and pulled a he-para to the side. How many points would that bungalow lose?

Finally, dark crept in and the apprentices lit the torches surrounding the Square. The ceremonies and the scrumptious Celebration Day Feast were done. Folks rushed to gather their blankets and get a spot behind the apprentice who was leading them to their bungalows. Small clusters of folks followed the torchlight of the apprentices into the moonless night.

Para Patrick and Para Chloe gathered their belongings slowly and followed last in line. The stream of folks in front of them thinned out quickly. Sputtering sparks burst into the air dangerously near Patrick, but Samuri slept safely under the edges of the blanket.

"Which bungalow?" the frightened apprentice asked, holding the torch as far away from herself as she could.

"Our bungalow is number seventy-six, the last one," Chloe said pleasantly. "It's okay if you'd rather stay here with the torch. Please just give us a moment to reach our door."

"Pleasantness to each and loyalty to the Township." The apprentice's voice trembled sarcastically.

"And a safe, long life to us all," Para Patrick returned in the proper Celebration Day farewell.

Safe? No, the apprentice could not feel safe so close to the woods. She stood loyally, holding the torch high and counting to fifty to push away the frightening stories raging through her mind. She would not fail these paras lest they drop their tiny

right by the woods. Who knew what terrifying creature would rush out to claim it?

"Look, Chloe," Patrick whispered when they passed the bungalow before theirs. "A light. Maybe we'll have friends."

"Shh! That's impossible!"

Patrick laughed at Chloe's attempt to be stern. She looked like a fourteen some days, not like a para with a tiny.

The memory of life before his dear Chloe choked out his laugh. Patrick thought back to the unbearable silence in the apprentice dorm. By the end of the forty-second week, he'd felt himself slipping toward hopelessness. But what could he do? The Laws of Loyalty required that Patrick wait two more years before he could request a bungalow. So, with only eight weeks before the annual Celebration Day, Patrick had plotted to escape. Of course, the Township's mandatory horror stories about the woods concerned him, but he'd always doubted they were true until the most recent one. Wild creatures had killed and devoured an escaping she-para not quite a year ago. Patrick's greenhouse supervisor had been terribly upset.

Patrick decided to risk it, anyway, planning and preparing each detail precisely. He'd wait until the night after Celebration Day and slip off while the dorm directors were preoccupied with new apprentices. Hopefully, he could be far away before anyone noticed.

Then, two mornings before that Celebration Day, the dorm director had instructed Patrick to report to the Complex before tasks.

The official at the Complex greeted him stiffly. "Pleasantness, Apprentice Patrick." Patrick remembered how his stomach had churned with fear, thinking they'd caught him.

The official had shut the door and continued in hushed tones. "An *unusual* need has arisen. You will be bungalowed at this year's Celebration Day. Come forward the moment the Bungalowing Ceremony is announced. Afterward, proceed to bungalow seventy-six. The dark, gray tunic and matching trousers of a para will be on your cot. Wear them when you report to the greenhouse for your usual tasks. This is official Township business. Not a word about it to anyone."

The "unusual need" turned out to be Chloe, a second-year apprentice. The elderly master weaver who had been training Chloe had died four weeks before Celebration Day. The Township Officials insisted Chloe stay in bungalow seventy-six where she had been living with the weaver. But she would have to be bungalowed. Why? No one said. And why did they choose Patrick, who was two years too young? That was an even greater mystery.

No matter what the reasoning, it had changed everything. Patrick's life with Chloe was indescribable—more pleasant than Patrick imagined was possible. Chloe was conversation, light, loyalty, and love in every part of Patrick's life. And now, only a year later, they had a tiny. Yes, Patrick had reason to believe impossible things were possible.

Now, Patrick reached their doorstep. "We're safe," he called out to the apprentice. The light of her torch quavered and then dipped in a hurried path back to the dorms.

Chloe turned toward the pines and gazed up. Impossible was more believable under the vast starry sky.

"Samuri," Patrick spoke with a quiet strength. "It's a brave name."

"And true-sounding," Chloe whispered. She hadn't said "true" since five years ago when Town Master Edward made the List of Forbidden words. But tonight, in the safety of the dark, she just had to say it. "Brave and true."

Soon Samuri was tucked-in on his cot, and his paras sat against the gathering room wall, shoulder to shoulder on the floor. Chloe and Patrick talked late into the night, reliving each detail of Samuri's Naming and dreaming about the days ahead.

The day after Samuri's Naming, Patrick returned from tasks and found the bungalow empty. Samuri wasn't on his cot. Chloe wasn't weaving in the task room. Could they be outside at this time of day?

One look toward the yard sent chills up his spine.

Patrick strode impatiently past four giant pines and grabbed Chloe by the shoulders. "What are you doing out here?" His voice was rough, and he pushed her toward the back door. Samuri, who had just fallen asleep, woke and began to wail.

"Chloe, can't you keep him quiet? Come on, hurry."

Inside, Patrick reached for Samuri so Chloe could prepare last snack like usual, but Chloe, pale and shaking, drew away from him. Could she trust him to hold Samuri now?

Patrick slipped his hands around Samuri and spoke gently to him. "Here you go, lil' tiny. Don't cry. We'll keep you safe and sound."

By the time Chloe had last snack ready, Patrick had Samuri wrapped snugly on his cot, fast asleep.

Chloe avoided Patrick's questions and small talk, knowing she was about to burst into tears or yell. Suddenly she did both.

"Why did you do that Patrick? There haven't been guards by the woods for a year now. What are you so worried about?"

Though he hated to do it, Patrick knew what he had to do. "Chloe," he said, "I have to tell you about the Township. It's the only way to keep us safe." He shut his eyes tightly, covered his mouth with his fist, and held his breath much too long, thinking of how to begin.

Chloe peeked at him, and her heart softened. Something

must be terribly wrong. She scooted closer and laid her head against his arm.

Patrick began to speak, slowly and grudgingly. "When I was first assigned to the greenhouse, there was a para who was forced to give his tiny to another bungalow."

Chloe frowned. Was Patrick making this up?

"Of course, none of us knew it. Then one day, the rest of the crew was away, and that para broke into tears. I held him while he sobbed and told me the whole story."

"The Township wouldn't do that." Chloe scoffed, afraid to believe him. "The Township is here to help us."

"Yes, they help in some ways. But why are we forbidden to share our stories with our neighbors or our task crew?"

Shock swept across her face as the saying came to mind. *Your story is your story, and their story is their story. Sharing stories makes trouble for everyone.*

"They wouldn't." She shook her head stubbornly in disbelief and protested loudly. "They can't. We can't let them!"

"Exactly, but we must be smart . . . and safe." His intense blue eyes begged her to trust him and agree. "And . . . the Township couldn't find anyone to guard the path anymore, Chloe. So, the Officials take turns watching from the high window of the Big Bungalow but I don't know how far they can see."

The reality of it hit her in waves and she wept, sobbing on his shoulder. When her tears were all cried out, she raised her head, and he wiped away the last of her tears. Her eyes were red and puffy, but he saw trust in them again.

"Okay," she said. "So . . . what can we do?"

Patrick leaned back with his elbows on his knees, his mind searching wildly as he began a mental list. "Well, the Township has folks convinced the woods are deadly, so they fear our bungalow, too. That's one."

Chloe's hand flew to her mouth in shock. She understood for the first time how wrong this was.

"Two—" Patrick shrugged his shoulders, and looked down,

like he was in trouble. "I think I overreacted, Chloe. The Officials shouldn't be able to see the east side of our yard or the trees beyond our bungalow."

"And . . . three. They gave you this bungalow because of the weaver's task room and its large window. The lighting is perfect for designing, right? You can watch the shifting colors of the woods and the sky and dye exquisite threads. But—that's not all." Their eyes met and a spark of understanding passed between them.

The two of them leaned forward, secretively, with their foreheads together. "But that's not all," Chloe's whisper echoed him.

"When Samuri gets bigger," Patrick continued in a promising voice, "he can play outside while you weave. No one will see him."

"Only me." Chloe spoke with resolve. She closed her eyes to imagine it and a picture of the wrens swept before her. "The creatures in the sky yesterday, Patrick."

In one swift motion Patrick stood, pulled her up, and twirled her.

His voice was full of wonder. "Chloe, you and I have been blessed from the start in impossible ways!"

"And my weaving!" she said. "Town Master Edward depends on me for his linens, for all of the flags, and most importantly, for the Scarves of Remembrance. He says I learned from the best weaver the Township has ever had." Chloe laughed whimsically.

Patrick did not laugh with her. His solemn eyes looked distant for a moment. "I forgot to tell you . . . an official found Town Master Edward dead on the stairs inside this morning."

Chloe bit her lip. Neither of them actually knew him, though he had talked to Chloe occasionally. But he had been the only Town Master in their lifetime.

"There's no saying how it will affect things." Patrick shrugged. "When my director announced it, he also mentioned the officials were meeting today. It sounds like they may have someone in mind." He straightened his shoulders with resolve. "But we still need a plan to keep Samuri safe. The Laws of Loyalty rule us more than the Town Master."

Sadness darkened Chloe's eyes. Her voice sounded defeated as she offered her meager suggestions. "I can . . . stop using forbidden words? Though I will miss them." Favorite words drifted through her mind like friends saying farewell. *Special. Impossible. Blessed. Trust.* So many more. "Oh, it's been lovely being hidden away here by the woods."

"Watching your words is a good start. I already get a lot of practice at the greenhouse, but I'll stop here, too. And . . . I'll start calling you Para Chloe so Samuri will have the advantage of thinking that's your proper name. It will prepare him for errand-going. We have to think ahead and be smart in every way."

"Oh, Patrick, I want him to be *free*. How do we follow the Laws without limiting him?"

"Forbidden word." Patrick spoke gently, his eyes apologizing. "We're going to teach him to be safe. Like letting him play outside, but never going in the woods."

"Yes." Her voice was bright and determined. "I'll do whatever I have to."

There was a hush as the last grains of sand trickled to the bottom of the hourglass.

"Chloe! I mean, *Para* Chloe. How long will it be until Samuri can talk?"

"Um, I don't really know. At least a year. Maybe longer. Why?"

The candle burned out as Patrick whispered a gentle plan of defiance. Chloe lifted her eyes toward the stars in the high window, considering what Patrick had said. Slowly, breathlessly she mouthed each word.

"What if Samuri remembers one of the forbidden words?"

"Those words will get replaced with new words, but his heart . . . his heart will know."

Chloe bit her lip and breathed in this hope. "Yes. A thousand times, yes."

In the morning Para Chloe gazed into Samuri's dreamy, pale blue eyes and spoke the exact words Para Patrick had given her.

"Samuri. Be brave and be true. You have many things to do in your life."

Tiny Samuri cooed back at her sweet smile and peaceful, intentional voice.

"You will do well, and you will have help. Even when we cannot be with you—" She paused to kiss his soft, shaved head. "—you will *always* have help."

Samuri cooed a delighted sound like a giggle, and Chloe couldn't help giggling, too.

Each day Para Chloe knelt early to speak over Samuri before the messengers came. Then she settled him by her loom in the task room and began weaving until he needed fed or soothed to sleep. Quicker than she'd expected, he was crawling.

By the next Celebration Day, Samuri was into everything. He drummed on the large scrubbing tub when it sat empty on the floor. He climbed up the stack of smaller tubs, sometimes falling, sometimes not. The empty looms got pulled out from under the shelves again and again. But best of all, he spent hours on his tiptoes, reaching up, determined to pull the brilliant-colored threads down from the rafters.

When Para Chloe was breathless from trying to keep up with him, she would call out, "Window time, Samuri." Plop! She sat him down by the huge window with a wooden tumbler of snack bars. Samuri munched away, gazing out at the sun-sparkled pine boughs while Para Chloe told him stories and continued to weave.

Eight weeks before the next Celebration Day, Samuri blurted out his first word, "Ahways".

The next day, Para Chloe went about her tasks without stopping. Samuri came to her and waited. "Ahways?" he asked in his funny little voice, raising his eyebrows and smiling expectantly.

Something *had* gotten through. Para Chloe knelt and placed her hands on his shoulders, beaming with pleasure. He gave her head a quick pat and toddled off to play, giggling. The song of the flying creatures echoed in Para Chloe's memory. Yes, it was time to trust and move forward.

Para Chloe was relieved how naturally life went on. She watched for ways to teach Samuri everything the Laws of Loyalty required her to: good listening skills, pleasantness, and daily tasks. He helped outside handing her wet laundry. He roamed through the bungalow "reorganizing" shelves and cupboards to make them *better*. But a Township life was simply too dull to keep an active tiny occupied.

On the hardest days, he tugged at her tunic, anxious to go outside, until he gave up and sat blankly in front of the window. Para Chloe tried to remain cheery, but his silent disappointment wore on her as much as his pestering.

The day after Samuri became a five, Para Patrick said, "It's time, Para Chloe. Samuri needs more time outside. Just keep an eye on him while you weave. And remember the song of the flying creatures."

"Yes." Chloe sighed sweetly. That night Chloe dreamed of the graceful flying creatures circling Samuri as he played outside. Their song whispered, "Remember. Remember." Yes, it was time.

"A pleasant daystart to you, Samuri. How would you like to go outside by yourself this morning?" He ran swiftly to the door and began fiddling with the handle.

"Wait, wait, wait!" Para Chloe said. "Not yet. We have to shave, eat, do our bungalow tasks, and wait until the messengers are gone. And remember—not a word about this when the messenger comes."

Samuri's intense blue eyes searched her face for understanding. Maybe she should have avoided that; after all, he'd never spoken to the messengers before. *No,* she thought. *No, there is no taking chances.*

Finally, it was time. "Samuri, you have to stay where I can see you, at all times." Her voice wavered between cheer and warning. "Be as silent as a secret, and . . ."

"And we must *never* go into the woods," he interrupted. "I will remember." His intense blue eyes, so like Para Patrick's, shone with adventure. One brisk push on the door handle and Samuri was out.

He wandered and explored, exhilarated to play unhindered, as long as he stayed within their boundaries. Games like the pinecone toss came alive in his mind. Those same wind-blown pinecones worked perfectly for building miniature bungalows. Soon a Township of bungalows connected by tiny pebble paths sprung up near the weaving window. Samuri led Para Patrick out each evening to approve of his new construction.

Soon, that small corner of the yard was full and Samuri was bored with building. After that Para Patrick whittled toy gardening tools, explaining how the greenhouse used each one. But Samuri's bright mind, alive with thoughts of a real garden and real plants, lost interest when he realized it was all pretend.

Samuri was growing desperate for something more. He just didn't know what.

2
jewel

The yearly Celebration Days flew by until Samuri was a year away from becoming an errand-goer. The long, warm days ahead were perfect for getting ready, for getting strong.

Samuri flexed his thin arm and winked to himself. Strength and life pulsed through his body as he pulled his arm back and threw a large pinecone higher and farther than ever before. The pinecone went crooked midflight and landed by the front doorstep. *Oh no*, he thought. The doorstep was off limits.

Hmm. If loyalty is our highest goal, and safety is our greatest strength . . . He pondered how to do both. Loyalty to his paras meant staying within the boundaries they'd set for him. Safety meant moving the pinecone, so a messenger didn't see it and question his paras. What should he do? He crept closer.

I could tiptoe to the edge, get it, and come right back.

He moved forward, keeping his eyes on the pinecone, listening carefully for signs of messengers or neighbors on the path. His hand was just closing around the pinecone when he heard a small, delighted gasp.

"Ooo."

There, just a few meters beyond him, stood a surprisingly petite someone in the yard next door. The sight of her wiped every thought of loyalty and safety out of his mind.

The breeze tousled the hem of her dull, squash-colored tunic, filling it like a balloon one moment and whipping it gracefully against her sides the next. One of her hands reached to the sky, her thin fingers gracefully drawing the shapes of the clouds. Then, her hand stiffened as if to take command and push some clouds aside while calling others to come near.

Samuri watched spell-bound, unaware of his slow, still movements forward. He took in every detail of her glowing, curious face with its luminous blue eyes.

A parade of dazzling creatures suddenly skimmed across the sky, dipping and darting with iridescent purple wings that whirred and sparkled just for her. Her sweet, rosebud lips puckered in awe.

"Ooo! C'mere." Her delighted voice beckoned to them, and she stretched as high on her bare tiptoes as she could.

A gust of wind in the treetops drew her attention to the woods. She saw Samuri and froze. Who was this? Would he force her back inside? She clenched her fists and scowled at him. Then, her eyes of the deepest, brightest blue, gazed toward the door of her bungalow.

Samuri misunderstood the look. *No, no, no.* He willed her silently. *Stay here. I'm safe.*

Then without thinking, he walked cheerfully toward her, holding his tan hand out to her smaller, pale hand. "Greetings."

At the sound of his pleasant, confident voice, she flashed him a smile like daystart bursting over the rooftops and grabbed his hand. An odd feeling of bravery and responsibility filled Samuri. Why was she out here alone? Where were her shoes?

I will keep you safe. Samuri vowed silently. *I give you my word of loyalty.* His heart did not understand why, and it did not ask him. It simply decided for him. Hand in hand, he led her to her door and pushed it open, expecting she would go inside.

She merely stood on the doorstep, staring at him with those sparkling eyes. Hmm. What should he do now? A miniature pinecone still rested in his other fist, so he pressed it into her empty palm. She cradled the curious little thing in her hands, inspecting it from every angle. Samuri nudged her through the doorway and shut the door between them.

The instant the door closed Samuri was sorry he had shut it. He *must* see her again.

"Jewel! Stop wiggling," Para Madeline scolded as she shaved Jewel's head the next morning. "It's not going to be *my* fault if I cut your ear."

But Jewel didn't stop. Jewel didn't even hear her para's complaints. The only thing on her mind today was the someone she saw yesterday. Was that someone always outside? She must find out.

"I'm goin' owside!" Jewel exclaimed delightedly, tugging away, despite the sting of the razor cutting her skin.

"See? This is exactly what I told you would happen," Madeline fretted, quickly wiping the drop of blood away. "You are a townshipful of trouble. It's a good thing we kept you home from the Celebration Day last week. And it's 'go-ing', Jewel, not 'goin'. I'm going out-side. Learn to speak properly. The Township frowns on lazy speech."

At the thought of the Township, Para Madeline bowed her head slightly, proclaiming in a sugary, sing-song voice, "Pleasantness to each, loyalty to the Township, and a safe, long life to us all."

Jewel was glad to try again, "Pweasantness . . . I'm—going—out-side—Parwa Madewin." Her voice was sweet but determined.

"No, you are not going outside. Oh, you are the worst little ever. I suppose dealing with you is my opportunity to display loyalty to the Township." Madeline spoke dramatically, chin up, and shoulders straight, wearing an expression as noble as the Town Master himself.

While Para Madeline and Jewel squabbled inside, Samuri wandered in circles in the yard. How could he see that small someone again? The metal bell on the door was only for Township business. He must not ring it. Entering any bungalow other than your own was forbidden, so he could not open her door. As Samuri's circles neared the doorstep, Jewel ran to the door handle inside and tugged swiftly, but the latch was locked today.

"Jewel. Whatever are you doing? It is not safe to go outside, especially not alone."

"Not alone," Jewel replied cheerfully. "Safe."

She waited confidently for Para Madeline, but she refused to open the latch, so Jewel pounded on the door. Was anyone out there waiting for her?

A sudden pounding on the other side of the door startled Para Madeline.

"See? Not alone!" Jewel chirped, patting the door and pointing up for her para to unclasp the latch.

Para Madeline eyed Jewel suspiciously. Then she tidied the light gray tunic worn by all bungalow paras, ran her hands along the smoothly shaven sides of her head, and turned to the door, composed and noble once more. She grabbed Jewel's arm to stop her from darting straight out, then pulled the door open slowly.

There stood Samuri, tan and healthy, his calm, serious blue eyes looking at them with hopeful expectation.

"Pleasantness, Para." It was the greeting he heard every day from the messengers.

Jewel held out her hand to go with him, but Para Madeline stepped between them glaring at Samuri. "It is not safe to be outside! What bungalow are you from and why are you here?" she asked rudely.

Samuri was not easily put off. "Bungalow seventy-six, just next door, Para." He replied so pleasantly she couldn't help liking him. "Can your little come outside with me?"

Para Madeline shuddered and looked in the opposite direction of his bungalow, keeping a firm grip on Jewel, who continued to tug against her. She shuddered again. How could anyone stand to live in that bungalow by the woods?

Just when she was about to quip "Absolutely not!", a thought occurred to her. What would it be like to have a few moments to herself? Jewel was terribly distracting lately. Honestly, it was hard enough for Madeline to think, let alone keep up with her quota of knit hats. Maybe she should consider it. This Samuri was pleasant enough. No! Being outside was never safe. But still . . .

"Do you know the Laws of Loyalty?" The tone of her voice was skeptical, even accusing.

"Uh-huh," Samuri said. "Don't go on the Township path alone until you're a young. Stay out of other folks' bungalows. Never go into the woods."

His attitude was impressive. Para Madeline's heart swung back and forth between safety and having time to herself. That was when Jewel gave her biggest tug yet and escaped her para's grasp.

"I'm going out-side now!" Jewel exclaimed lightheartedly and reached for Samuri's hand.

"Of course," Para Madeline agreed in her sticky-sweet voice. She acted like it had been *her* idea all along. "You may go outside, Jewel, but do let go of his hand."

"Take care of my little," Para Madeline warned Samuri. "Or this will be the only time she comes out. And—" She stepped out, pointed to the north corner of the yard, and made a small circle with her finger. "Stay there, only there. Keep away from your bungalow. I will be watching you. And one more thing. Jewel must be in before the afternoon messengers come by. I'll set the hourglass."

Samuri smiled confidently and nodded. Jewel yanked his hand, pulling him off the doorstep into the yard.

"Jewel! Let go of his hand or I will bring you back in now."

Para Madeline watched until Jewel let go of Samuri's hand, then stepped inside. Immediately Jewel took Samuri's hand again and pulled him toward his bungalow.

"No, this direction." Samuri said brightly, pointing toward the far end of her yard. "Watch. It's fun."

"Fun? What is *fun*?"

Samuri led Jewel across the dirt and gathered an armful of stones from under bungalow seventy's water pump. Jewel followed him without question, watching curiously as Samuri dropped the stones in a pile and built a tower. After all the boring days she'd spent inside, even this simple game impressed her. Her words spilled out jumbled and excited. Then she slapped her hand over her mouth and looked at him with wide, anxious eyes.

"It's okay. Just talk quieter," Samuri whispered. "Quiet as a secret."

He handed her the three flattest stones; the best he had found. The sloppy tower she built toppled down before it was half as tall as his. Still, Jewel beamed at him, did a funny dance, and ran small circles around that corner of the yard.

"Samuri sky. Build it high! Samuri sky," she cheered him on.

At first Para Madeline checked on them every other minute. One time the small flags at the base of the door caught her eye and whispered, "Trouble, Madeline, trouble." What if the Township caught them? Would they simply put the warning flag up, or . . . ? She nearly called Jewel inside, but the luxury of having quiet moments to herself dulled her fears. She was content to believe all was well.

For the next hour, Samuri and Jewel built towers, tossed stones, and ran circles together. Jewel chatted away in inaudible whispers. Samuri listened and smiled. *This* was the something more he'd been missing.

Para Chloe sat in the warmth of the morning sun weaving peacefully. When the sun rose beyond the window and the room grew chilly, she wondered where Samuri was. She scanned the east yard. Where could he be? He knew not to leave their yard.

She hurried to the other door to check.

"Oh, how fun!" Para Chloe burst out. "Samuri has found a friend."

Then she frowned. Wait. Samuri should be in his own yard. She scanned the paths quickly. No, no one was there.

Para Chloe rushed back to her weaving room and out the task room door. *Whoosh!* She blew the breathy warning signal at the north corner of their bungalow, motioning for him to come inside.

Samuri nodded but pointed to the door of Jewel's bungalow with raised eyebrows, asking Para Chloe's permission. She winked and gave him the one-finger-one-minute warning.

Jewel caught on and was not about to go inside. Instead, she grabbed Samuri's hand tightly and tugged toward the woods. She was surprisingly strong, but Samuri was stronger. Jewel narrowed her eyes in a ferocious scowl, flung his hand aside, and clenched her fists.

Samuri laughed. "I'll come again tomorrow," he assured her cheerfully. He took her hand again, swinging it playfully.

Once they reached her door they knocked together, laughed, and waited. "You *better* come again!" Jewel threatened, but her eyes sparkled with joy.

Para Madeline was pleased with them and with herself. Their little venture had turned out quite safe due to her loyal ability to handle difficult situations. She bowed slightly to Samuri and whisked Jewel in for an early midday snack and nap.

"Jewel." Para Madeline's voice was sticky-sweet again, as she closed the door. "You must not tell Para Philip, or . . ." In a sudden shift her voice became rude and threatening. "Or . . . or you will *never* be allowed out again. Never."

Jewel nodded rapidly with frightened eyes.

"Good." Para Madeline's pleased, genuine voice reassured her. "If we understand each other, we can both get what we want."

Jewel had no idea what her para meant, but she would agree to anything if it meant seeing Samuri again.

Samuri marched boldly to his bungalow, shoulders straight, face set in determination, each footstep like the victory march of a hero. Jewel's voice rang in his ears cheering him on. "Samuri—sky—build it high." He would be back. Jewel could count on it.

Para Chloe rubbed her knuckles on his smooth scalp. "So, you found a friend!" she exclaimed.

She pushed aside the dozens of curious questions she wanted to ask him. Para Patrick must know before she said anything more to Samuri. Safety came first, and Samuri had broken both the Laws of Loyalty and their boundaries.

The afternoon dragged by. Finally, after Para Patrick was back and last snack was over, he wrestled with Samuri until the two of them were worn out.

Then, as they sat resting shoulder to shoulder against the wall of the gathering room, Samuri announced, "I have a friend, Para Patrick."

"A friend?" Para Patrick questioned Chloe with a troubled glance.

"Yes, um, a very small friend, Para Patrick." Para Chloe's calm excitement begged him to understand. "Remember the lonely days? A friend would be a special thing to have . . . wouldn't it?"

Para Patrick's eyes sprung open wide. His voice was a cross between shock and scolding. "Words?"

"I mean a friend could be . . . *pleasant.*"

The tension between them disturbed Samuri. He watched them intently.

"Yes, a friend is . . . uh . . . pleasant." Para Patrick put his arm around Para Chloe and took a moment to think. "But—let's talk about this later." The Township was the real problem.

In no time the conversation shifted to Chloe's first weaving project for the new Town Master, but that was a touchy subject, too. So, she asked Patrick about his experiments as the new Director of the Hydroponic Greenhouse. Samuri relaxed and scooted closer. Safe.

In the morning, after tasks, Samuri headed straight for the door, but Para Chloe stopped him.

"Wait a second! Samuri, it was not loyal to leave our yard without asking. You absolutely must stay where we tell you." She put her hands on his shoulders and paused to let the words sink in. "Para Patrick and I agreed you're safe near the bungalow on the north half of our neighbor's yard. But . . ." Para Chloe paused, and a few tears welled up in her eyes, "If you go any farther, you won't be allowed outside at all. *And* you must be so quiet that I can't even hear you from the door. Do you understand?"

First, he nodded, but Para Chloe shuddered when he answered, "Quiet as a secret." Then he shook his head. None of it truly made sense.

"Samuri, you know many of the Laws of Loyalty. The Township made those laws to take care of us and to help us be safe."

Samuri listened intently, never taking his eyes off her face.

"Laws like not going into other bungalows, because each bungalow is . . ." She paused, trying not to use any of the forbidden words.

"Special?" he offered.

"No," Para Chloe said. "*Different* is a better word. Each bungalow is *different* because they each have their own way of saying and doing things."

Samuri had a lot of questions, but he'd rather go see his friend. "I will be safe. And very quiet. And I'll teach my friend to be safe and quiet, too."

"Oh, and *friend* isn't a Township word either. You can't say it to anyone, not even to your friend," Para Chloe said warmly, smiling at him despite the butterflies in her stomach. She must be smarter, and more careful with words. She must think ahead. No trouble must come to their bungalow. "Can you do that?"

Samuri shrugged his shoulders, then nodded heartily. "Don't say *friend*. I won't Para Chloe. I won't." He would do whatever it took to keep this friend.

That morning, and every morning after, Para Chloe checked the hourglass often, listening, always listening. If anything seemed the least bit out of order, she peeked out to warn Samuri with the signal like the wind. Friendships *and* bungalows must be kept safe.

3
the hero and his girl

Jewel danced silently on her tiptoes while she waited by the door. At the sound of Samuri's knock, she stopped and stood straight and serious. Para Madeline came briskly from the task room, shaking her finger and warning Jewel. It was the same each morning. When the latch was unlocked, Jewel cautiously stepped out.

At the click of the door behind her, Jewel burst off of the doorstep, her eyes sparkling with adventure. "C'mon, follow me," she whispered as enthusiastically as a whisper could be.

Samuri watched and followed her to their corner, with a hint of laughter in his calm blue eyes. Weeks full of free days lay ahead for them.

Samuri showed Jewel every game he had ever invented, but with two of them to play, the games came alive. The only bother was that Samuri *insisted* they stay on the north end of Jewel's yard. Finally, Jewel learned to turn even that into a mystery and a game.

"The messengers are talking trees," she told him, her spy-eyes moving side to side suspiciously. "If I go out of my yard . . ." She gasped. "They'll grab me and carry me into the dark woods!"

She ran toward his yard, faked a look of fright, and raced back to hide behind him in mock terror. Then they both fell to the ground, stifling their laughter with their hands over their mouths.

Occasionally, Jewel's eyes blazed with an eerie determination, and her voice was strange and defiant. "I *am* going into the woods. Go with me," she commanded Samuri, and walked past him as if she couldn't care less what he thought.

"Jewel, if you go into the woods, I can't ever come outside with you again." His voice was sad, but stern. He knew you did what you had to for a friend, but this was too much. Jewel would have to choose.

Jewel inched slowly forward, watching him out of the corner of her eye. Surely Samuri would follow her, even if only to keep her safe. Wouldn't he? But when he neared the edge of his bungalow and turned toward Para Chloe's window, Jewel always sprinted back, grabbed Samuri's arm, and tugged him toward her yard.

"I won't." Her whisper was breathy and sincere. She was herself again. "Really, I won't, Samuri. Not ever. Don't go inside." She looked at him with a begging expression. "Okay?"

Every night, Samuri and his paras snuggled against the gathering room wall chatting about new snack flavors, greenhouse experiments, and best of all, past Celebration Days. One night, Samuri jumped up unexpectedly, made a sweeping bow, and exclaimed in an animated voice, "Greetings, Township Folks."

It caught his paras off guard. They laughed so hard that they rolled on the floor until their stomachs hurt.

"Maybe Samuri will be the next Town Master after this new Town Master Cree," Para Chloe teased.

"I think he could." Para Patrick was dead serious. "Samuri is pleasant, a loyal worker, a good listener, and . . . and now we know he's a great announcer. But I'd rather have him work with me."

Samuri moved over to lay his head on Para Patrick's shoulder, but Para Chloe frowned at Patrick. What was he thinking putting that idea into Samuri's head? The day would come, sooner than they wanted, when Samuri would become an apprentice. That would be the end of these sweet times. The Laws of Loyalty forbade contact between them after that. Oh, if they watched carefully, they might spot Samuri in the distance on a Celebration Day, but anything more was strictly outlawed.

Para Chloe shuddered at the thought and headed for the snack corner to hide the tears in her eyes. She whipped up a mug of frothy, sweet hazelnut milk for each of them and brought it out, becoming her cheery self again. They must tell Samuri eventually, but not now. The Laws of Loyalty would not ruin this night.

The next day, Samuri was first to burst out in whispers. "What do you like best about Celebration Days, Jewel?"

Jewel's eyes lit up, then went blank. "What are Celebration Days?"

Samuri started with the purple flag. Messengers made sure it stayed hidden under the other flags by each bungalow door. Jewel had never noticed them. What a wonder they were! One green flag. One yellow. One red.

"Green tells the messengers to come," Samuri explained proudly. "Yellow means something is wrong. Red means trouble. But the purple is the biggest, most pleasant flag, and it says, 'Get ready for the Celebration Day.' The messengers put it up twenty-one days before Celebration Day."

Samuri wanted to tell her his para made the flags, but Para Chloe insisted he must not tell anyone. He used big hand motions to turn bungalow seventy's bare, dirt corner into a model of the Township Square. Jewel listened in awe as Samuri tried to explain the Township Square, the Big Bungalow with its amazing turrets, the ceremonies, the grand Feast, and the applause of the crowd. But it was easier to do than to describe, so he showed her.

"Loyal Township Folks One and All," he announced in the grandest whisper he could muster. "I present to you this year's new youngs."

In a secretive voice he confided to her, "I like the youngs best of all. They wear tunics the color of the woods and they help keep our Township safe."

Then he lifted both hands up dramatically and swooped into a deep bow. Jewel gasped, dissolved into giggles, and pretended to clap her hands. Clapping made her want to chant. "Town Master Ri! Town Master Ri!" It was tricky to celebrate quietly.

Three days later Samuri had shared everything he could think of, and Jewel begged him to show her all over again.

"I want to be a young this time, Town Master Ri," Jewel exclaimed. She popped up off the ground abruptly. "How does a young walk? And where do I stand? Why can't we all have green tunics like the youngs?"

Samuri went through all the age groups and their colors. He didn't know why, but tinys, years one through four, wore light blue tunics and trousers. Littles, years five through eight, got mustard-colored sets like hers. Juniors, years nine through twelve, were given rust-colored ones.

"And youngs wear green," Jewel interrupted. "Will I get a rust-colored set like yours, Ri?"

"Um-hmm." Samuri smiled, pleased with the sound of the nickname, and continued to explain. "We'll both be juniors after the next Celebration Day."

Then, Samuri told her about apprentices and their beige

tunics. Now Jewel wanted to act out the tasks of the apprentices. She carried pretend trays, heaped with pretend food for the Feast. She couldn't quite imagine the torches, but they sounded dangerous and fun.

After another week went by, Jewel insisted on being the Town Master, but she was a loud town master. Samuri had to keep shushing her.

Suddenly he thought he heard someone approaching on the Township path. "Do you hear something?" a muffled voice asked.

"Whoosh!" Samuri sounded the breathy danger signal, grabbed Jewel, and pulled her toward the end of the bungalow.

Anger flashed across her face. She could be loud if she wanted. He couldn't push her around.

"Messengers," Samuri whispered, and got her quietly to the end of her bungalow before the messengers reached her doorstep and jingled the bell.

"Pleasantness, para," a dull voice droned. "Your yarn is ready, and the Exchange wanted you to have it immediately."

"Shh . . ." Para Madeline coaxed in a sweet whisper. "Pleasantness. My little is napping, and I want to start on this yarn right away. Set it here, quietly."

The messengers put the bulky bags inside by the door.

"We'll return for the empty the bags tomorrow," the first messenger agreed.

"Napping?" The second messenger raised her eyebrows. "I thought I heard a little talking." She thought she might check around outside, until she turned and saw the woods again. "Oh well, it must be one of the other messengers. Sound travels far on cool mornings. A safe, long life to us all."

Samuri and Jewel stared at each other wide-eyed and red-faced. Could they lose each other that quick? They stayed crouched against the far wall, unsure when or how to come out. Would the messengers be watching?

A few minutes later the door cracked slightly open, and they heard Para Madeline whisper, "Jewel?"

Jewel slipped inside silently, relieved her para didn't sound mad. Samuri stole cautiously to his own yard and waited awhile before he went in. If Para Chloe hadn't heard the messengers, it was probably better she didn't find out.

The following morning, a chilly breeze hinted of cooler days to come. Samuri watched from the corner of his bungalow until the messengers came for the bags and left. Finally, he went and lay near Jewel's bungalow, hidden by the doorstep. Would Jewel's para ever let her come out again? Soon, the door opened a crack, and Para Madeline peeked out. All was clear, and the junior from next door was surely hiding somewhere waiting.

"Only one hourglass today, Jewel." Para Madeline whispered. "And remember . . ."

Jewel stepped out solemnly, sat on the doorstep, and almost kicked Samuri in the face. Samuri pointed up. One glance at the clouds and Jewel was up and running graceful figure eights back and forth, imitating the patterns of the clouds. Her arms flowed behind her, and she ran until nothing else existed but her circular motions.

A quick turn, and tangled legs, sent Jewel sprawling onto the ground, staring into two beady, black eyes. A smooth caramel-colored creature lay before her on the dirt, looking like a small, enameled pebble.

Jewel held her breath as long as she could before bursting out, "Ooo! Look, Ri. What is it?"

The breath of Jewel's whisper sent the creature scuttling to the shelter of the nearest dirt clod. Samuri couldn't help laughing at the delighted, goofy look on Jewel's face.

"Find it. Find it." She urged him in a dramatic whisper, her wonderstruck eyes fixed on the dirt clod. Samuri rolled the clod aside and there it was. Jewel and the creature lay very still, but suddenly Jewel reached forward to touch the creature, and it disappeared for good.

That evening Samuri stood before Para Patrick, straight and tall, looking deeply into his eyes without speaking.

"Something new today, Samuri?"

"Um-hmm. Something small, like a pebble in the dirt, but it moved."

"That's a bug, Samuri."

Samuri nodded. He'd seen creatures like it before, but never paid attention. He repeated the word to himself to remember it for Jewel.

Para Chloe was about to mouth, "Words!" when Samuri spoke again.

"And Para Patrick, can you call me Ri? Jewel calls me Ri and I like it."

The paras glanced at each other. The Laws of Loyalty forbade nicknames, but would it really matter here in their bungalow?

"Next Celebration Day you'll become a ten and you'll begin errand-going." Para Chloe's voice was serious. "Then we *have* to call you by your given name. But . . ." Her eyes twinkled as she flashed him an *I've-got-a-secret* smile. "Until then, let's do it."

"How's that, Samuri?" Para Patrick caught himself and stopped. "I mean, Ri." The three of them winked all at once in an unspoken pact.

Para Patrick drew Chloe and Samuri closer. "There's not a more pleasant bungalow than ours." He gazed into Ri's intense blue eyes, so much like his own, and the burdens of Township life faded away.

Samuri was already asleep, mumbling something about bugs and Jewel, when Para Patrick came to kiss his forehead, and shut the door. The words *brave* and *true*, whispered through Patrick's mind. Not only did Samuri know what he wanted, he knew how to ask pleasantly. Para Patrick liked that.

Back in the gathering room, Chloe asked, "How did they find a bug with all the spraying the Township does?" She laughed at the thought, but then her voice grew hushed with concern. "Whatever you do, don't mention it to *anyone*, okay?"

"Chloe, I don't talk to anyone, anywhere, about anything other than tasks. It's miserable." His face seemed older and tired just thinking about it. "It's like I'm trapped in the Laws of Loyalty. One wrong word, one wrong conversation, and they'll start taking away my points at the Exchange, maybe even take away my new assignment as Director of the Hydroponic Greenhouse. We'd have enough food, but no extras." He eyed her solemnly. "Chloe be sure to remind Samuri that *bugs* and *nicknames* are only for *our* bungalow. And for Jewel . . . I guess. But Jewel must not tell her paras."

Patrick's eyes clouded over. *Loyalty should start in your bungalow.* It bothered him to make Jewel keep secrets from her paras, but who knew what kind of folks Jewel's paras were? This friendship thing was messy. Had they made a mistake allowing it?

The next day Jewel turned dozens of stones and dirt clods over searching for that bug. "Bug, bug, bug." She popped each word on her lips in different tones and liked the sound so much she wouldn't stop.

"You can't tell anyone." Ri had warned her a dozen times, but she didn't hear him until he blocked her path and said it as serious as a para. "You can't even say it in your bungalow."

A shiver ran through her body like she was only now hearing him. She squinted her eyes and peered around. "Bug," she said mysteriously and added it to her list of forbidden words.

I'm sure I can trust her, Samuri thought. *Still, I wish she'd take it seriously.*

The cold, cloudy Brave Days were coming. Keeping secrets would be tricky during the long hours shut inside. These unusually mild days wouldn't last.

The gentle night winds whistled in the pines, lulling Jewel to sleep. Those same winds kept Para Madeline awake, tossing and turning. She shuddered to think of Jewel shut inside all day, every day. The temperature did drop slightly, but oddly enough the sun shone strongly, day after day.

Early one morning, Para Madeline called out in an unusually welcoming voice, "Jew—el. Get up."

Jewel stumbled into the gathering room, rubbing her sleepy eyes.

"Here, let's see how this looks." Para Madeline's voice was tender and genuine. In her hands she held a lovely, dark green stocking hat that she'd made specially for Jewel because of the many pleasant days they'd had that year.

Jewel shook her head and turned toward the freshening room. She didn't want a hat.

"Jewel, the air is chilly," her para coaxed. "You've never been outside in the Brave Days before. The hat will keep you from getting sick."

Para Madeline reached out to slip the hat on Jewel, but Jewel ducked. The chase that followed left Jewel laughing and her para exasperated.

"Fine!" Para Madeline bluffed. "Don't go out. That's simply fine with me." And she turned to go back to the task room.

Jewel scowled and insisted defiantly, "I am going out, Para Madeline. And I am not wearing that hat."

Para Madeline walked away, straight and tall, seemingly indifferent. Jewel sat by the door smiling, thinking she had won. But Para Madeline didn't come when Ri knocked.

"Ri is here," Jewel chimed happily. "Come unlatch the door."

Ri knocked again, and Para Madeline replied from the task room, "No hat. No going outside." Her words were blunt and matter-of-fact. "And don't ever say that name again. It's not his given name. Nicknames are forbidden."

Para Madeline walked into the gathering room, unraveling the hat one row at a time in slow, exaggerated motions.

"No! Stop." Panic rose in Jewel's voice as she realized what Para Madeline was threatening. "I'll wear it. It's very pleasant, Para. I will. I'll wear it!"

Para Madeline's narrowed eyes and set jaw told Jewel it would be safer to go to her cot and wait it out. Time passed. Her para did not call her for the midday snack. Jewel stood on her cot and lifted her face to the high window.

"Samuri! Come get me." She called toward the yard. "Can you hear me?!"

Next Jewel clenched her fists and yelled toward the task room. "I–will–wear–the–hat. And I'll never use a nickname again. Let me go outside."

Para Madeline shut the door, stuffed tufts of yarn in her ears, and continued to knit.

Jewel yelled and pounded on the cot until her voice was hoarse. Exhausted and miserable she laid down and whispered, "Ri?"

Jewel's eyelashes fluttered, splashing little drips of tears down her cheeks. "Ri. You are my Ri. *My Ri*." She didn't know how long the Brave Days would be, but even a week without Ri was surely more than she could bear.

Their bungalow was unusually quiet that night, but Para Philip was not about to ask why. Para Madeline held her tongue, horrified by the thought of saying something careless about Jewel and the neighbor next door. Para Philip must never find out. *Never*.

The Brave Days stayed sunny, relatively dry, and just warm enough to be out . . . if you wore a hat. And Jewel did, whether she needed it or not.

4
count the days

Shortly before daystart, twelve apprentices went silently into the dim light to raise the purple flag on each bungalow. By the time they gathered back at the Township Square, wee pink clouds had appeared, sprinkled across the luminous sky like confetti. The twelve messengers, three of them at each corner of the Square, counted together "5-4-3-2-1", then shouted toward the bungalows in perfect unison.

"Township folks, one and all, preparations for our Celebration Day have begun!"

Para Chloe gasped with delight when she slipped outside to slide the new purple flag up beside their door. A perfect daystart shimmered above her. One hundred and seventy-five perfect, purple flags shimmered throughout the Township. She giggled and snuck back in without making a sound. The door was latched again by the time the messengers shouted and Samuri stepped out of his room. Beaming, he glanced at the door and raised his eyebrows asking silently, *may I?* She nodded and moved to unlatch it.

He pointed to his bare feet, and she nodded again.

"Greetings, you two," Para Patrick's voice boomed as he came out of the freshening room.

"Come out with us. Hurry," Chloe urged him. "You can grab your daystart snacks and eat on your way to the greenhouse."

Samuri's bare feet tingled with the chill of the morning as he stood on the doorstep with his paras. His heart soared. Purple flags, made by his own para, fluttered everywhere. *And* the messengers had not forgotten to raise their purple flag this year. He and his paras gazed back and forth between the confetti clouds and the myriad of purple flags fluttering joyfully in the spring breezes.

"Get ready! Get ready!" the flags proclaimed. "Celebration Day is on its way!"

Later that morning, Jewel ran out and announced, "Look Ri." She opened her fists and revealed small piles of yarn pieces.

Samuri shrugged. What was so exciting about scraps of yarn?

"We can count the days," Jewel explained breathlessly, pushing the scraps into his hands. "My para said there's enough for you and me. But I can't count. Can you show me how?'

Ri was baffled. Of course, he would teach her. But why couldn't she count?

Jewel clapped silently, jittering with awe and anticipation. The real Celebration Day was coming.

Para Chloe felt jittery, too, but not the fun kind. Town Master Cree wanted her to send him both Scarves of Remembrance before the end of the first week, and one wasn't finished. Para Chloe couldn't help it. Town Master Cree had insisted Para Chloe make new, brighter, purple flags for each bungalow in the Township and several for the Big Bungalow. And she had. The flags had turned out gorgeous, but Para Chloe would have to hurry to finish the second scarf even if it was not her typical perfect scarf. A perfect scarf was no good if it wasn't ready.

The clerks at the Exchange hurried, too. Everyone had unreasonable orders. The cooks from the Big Bungalow demanded unreasonable additions to their already large, preordered lists. The Feast must be the most pleasant ever. Paras who were busily making cookies for the annual cookie contest, had long lists now, as well. Their cookies would be tested on the second day of the second week before Celebration Day.

"We must have more tomatoes!"

"I need dried raspberries!"

"Send me as much hazelnut oil as you can!"

The paras in the contest must keep up their daily quota of tasks, too. The contest was optional, task quotas were not. Para Madeline had skimped on her regular orders for weeks to save points for special cookie ingredients. It was all she thought about. If her cookies were approved, the Exchange would fill her order for a Township-size batch of her cookies. For free. She dreamed of it all year long.

Jewel breathed in the delicious smells of hazelnut, nutmeg, and honey wafting through the bungalow. She couldn't remember Celebration Days, but she remembered cookies. Some days the hazelnut gave way to the smell of tart, dried raspberries. The tempting aromas lured Jewel back inside day after day to test cookies.

"What do you think, Jewel?" Para Madeline asked and handed her a cloth with three cookies, each made from a different recipe.

"Mmm." Jewel closed her eyes and scrunched up her face in delight. "Tasty. So tasty."

"Yes . . . but which one tastes the best?"

Para Madeline presented her with variations of the same three recipes each day and Jewel chose the berry cookie every time. What a wonder to have a full stomach and the smell of sweetness in her nose and on her tongue all day long! Even her blanket smelled like a big, delicious cookie. So, she buried her face in it, saving up every sweet smell to remember through the year.

Para Patrick had thought of entering this year, just for fun. Then the water pumps in the greenhouse broke down, sending the chefs, who needed more tomatoes, into a panic. By the time Para Patrick got home each evening, he was too exhausted to try.

Para Madeline's berry cookies were accepted, and the atmosphere in their bungalow changed. Now Jewel had to be silent and stay out of the way. No more cookie testing. Every cookie was needed for the Feast. Jewel lay on her cot, raspberry sweetness swirling through the air, listening to Para Madeline talk tenderly to each cookie as she shaped them. Jewel's stomach gurgled, hungry for more. She fell asleep, wishing with all her heart for a life of cookies and a pleasant para.

Town Master Cree was taken with Para Chloe's enchanting Scarves of Remembrance. Could she come up with a similar scarf or pocket kerchief for him by Celebration Day? Para Chloe burst into another flurry of activity.

And so, the twenty-one days that seemed like forever to Jewel and Ri flew by for others.

In the soft light of daystart, Samuri's eyes opened to Para Patrick standing by his cot lightly shaking his shoulder. It was Celebration Day. Would his para get to come?

Para Patrick had good news. "Last night we worked by candlelight to finish everything. Today we only have a few routine tasks. I'll be back." Samuri grabbed his hand, squeezed it, and nodded, then Para Patrick left.

Ten apprentices stood on the south, west, and north edges of the Township. They walked toward the Township Square ting-a-ling-tinging bells. There was no need to shout today. All ears were listening for the sweet bells of Celebration Day—all but Jewel, who slept soundly, like usual, until Para Madeline called loudly from the freshening room.

"Jew—el! Are you going to sleep right through Celebration Day?"

Jewel popped up and opened her fist to find the last little yarn had made it safely through the night.

36

"Greetings, yarn number twenty-one," she whispered to it excitedly. "Today is the day." She tucked it in the pocket of her other tunic and ran to let Para Madeline shave her head. "I won't wiggle at all today and maybe my paras will sit by Samuri." There was to be no more calling him Ri; whispers were not even safe. His paras had said so.

By the time Para Philip and Para Patrick arrived back at their bungalows for the midday snack, the bells were ringing again. One hour to go. Hourglasses were reset. Folks grabbed snacks and ate while they gathered blankets and filled bags with plates, cloths, and hats. Finally, the bells rang out one last time, calling folks to the Township Square.

The Township Square was surrounded by paths and bungalows on three sides. The paths converged on the east end past the bungalows and led into the woods. The week before, crews of youngs had packed the ground down to prevent dust. It was cleaner, but unfortunately harder. The Big Bungalow, a beautiful three-story building on the west end, was the glory of the Square. The splendid turrets on its southeast and northwest corners gave it the appearance of being much more than a bungalow.

However, Town Master Edward had hinted at tearing the Big Bungalow down, in his earlier days. "If we hold on to this display of inequality and materialism, we will defeat our attempt to change the whole culture," he had told his officials insistently.

The Officials had flat out refused. None of them had the heart to destroy the last remnant of the Township's glorious past. So, the Big Bungalow remained the showpiece of the Square, its noble turrets pointing to the sky and its breathtaking white porch spanning the entire front overlooking the Square.

Today, fourteen tall torches, not yet lit, were well-secured in a long row between the grand porch and the Square. Ten more torches were secured along each of the other three sides of the Square, forty-four torches in all. Long wooden tables, covered in plain dark cloth, were placed here and there between the torches on the north and south sides. Other than that, the Township folks and a few purple flags were the only decoration. The matching grays, squash, rust, lavender, and forest green of folks' tunics were splashes of beauty in an otherwise dull gathering.

Folks streamed out of their bungalows, heads down, only acknowledging one another if they accidentally bumped or made eye contact. An apprentice waited at each table to greet folks and check them in according to their bungalow number.

"Greetings," Para Patrick said, bowing slightly. "We are bungalow seventy-six."

Para Chloe and Samuri bowed as well, keeping their eyes down like they had practiced. The apprentice placed a small pebble on a framed grid and replied, "Pleasantness and loyalty, bungalow seventy-six."

Para Patrick found it difficult to avoid conversation even on typical days, but today, the only combined gathering of the year, it was nearly unbearable. His imagination was stirred by vague memories of paras laughing and chatting joyously while littles ran and played freely. What a Celebration Day that would be! Patrick shook his head as if to shake away the exasperation he felt. The back of his hand sprung to his mouth like he was wiping off some crumb from midday snack. How else could he stop himself from saying some simple nicety he would regret? Who was this apprentice? What was his name? What did he long for in the days ahead?

No. Para Patrick knew he didn't dare. Wasn't one day of celebration better than none? Today Samuri would be celebrated as an errand-goer. So, Para Patrick would play by the Laws of Loyalty for the sake of his dear Para Chloe and Samuri. Unfortunately, he had hesitated a minute too long.

"Eyes down, Para. Move on." The apprentice spoke sharply warning Para Patrick from behind his forced smile. "Loyalty."

A shiver went up Samuri's spine. No one should talk to his para that way. He reached to take Para Patrick's hand, but Para Chloe blocked him discreetly. She moved Samuri in front of her and used her shoulder to inconspicuously bump Para Patrick toward the *front* of the crowd. Her eyes caught his for a moment, briefly questioning him.

Para Patrick nodded and searched for a smooth spot to lay their blankets. What a relief to have her help. They settled themselves, and then he glance around discreetly. Would they see the neighbors from bungalow seventy? Would they even recognize them? Probably not, but it *would* be pleasant if Samuri's friend, Jewel, could be close.

As soon as all bungalows were accounted for, the apprentices carried their grids to the porch of the Big Bungalow and placed them on the round, white table. The Director of Apprentices bowed to them and rang the porch's grand bell.

The Director of Apprentices shouted out with twice the volume of the bell. "All bungalows are present. You have counted the days well, loyal Township folks. Let the Celebration Day begin!"

5
celebration day

Town Master Cree emerged from the door on the porch, breathed in invigoratingly, and lifted his head high as he strode grandly toward the stairs of the porch. Stopping at the top, he extended his arms toward the crowd dramatically. His broad shoulders, strong frame, and charming smile created a striking effect.

"Loyal Township Folks, One and All, Welcome to the Annual Township Celebration Day Ceremonies!" Town Master Cree's loud, bright voice carried the length of the Square.

To some folks, his enthusiasm seemed out of place in the barrenness that was the Township. Others felt rescued from the drudgery of Township life, if only for a day. He paused, leaning forward slightly, waiting for their response.

Apprentices and Township officials waited on the edges of the crowd, ready to correct any less-than-loyal Township folks.

The crowd stood and bowed to Town Master Cree, counting to three silently, before replying in perfect unison, "Greetings, Town Master. Pleasantness to each, loyalty to the Township, and a safe, long life for us all."

With a sweeping gesture Town Master Cree directed their

attention to the apprentices making their way forward for the Ceremony of the Bungalows. Four he-apprentices lined up on the left, in front of the unlit torches, while four she-apprentices took their place on the right. Apprentices were required to live in the dorms for a minimum of two years before submitting a request to be bungalowed. If a request was accepted, they were interviewed. Only those who passed the interview were standing here on this Celebration Day. Two apprentices had asked privately to be bungalowed with a specific apprentice, but the decision was up to the Town Master and the Officials. They considered each request, and ruled in favor of what was most beneficial for the entire Township.

A hush came over the crowd as Town Master Cree loudly and solemnly questioned the apprentices standing before him. "Have you chosen to begin in a bungalow of your own?" He paused as each of them stepped forward, one at a time, simply answering yes.

"Can you be loyal to the extra work and responsibilities of being a para and caring for a bungalow?" Again, each answered in turn.

Finally, Town Master Cree raised his voice even more, emphasizing to all present, the last and most important question of all. "Do you commit to remain pleasant to each in our Township, and to be loyal to the Township above all else, even as bungalowed paras?"

After commitments were made, Town Master Cree turned to face the apprentices, pointing to one on each side and motioning for them to step forward. Town Master Cree joined the couple's hands together with his hands over theirs, and then lifted them high for all to see. That was their one brief moment to be announced and celebrated. Their bungalowing was official. The Township folks clapped politely as the new paras were escorted away and directed to their bungalows. It was wise to send the newly bungalowed paras away immediately. The Township Officials expected these new paras to respond pleasantly no matter what they felt in the shock of unexpected decisions. The Township allowed them one day to pull themselves together before returning to their tasks.

Para Philip glanced at Para Madeline, remembering the second year of his apprenticeship. Oh, the embarrassment and fear he'd felt when the new apprentice first fluttered her eyelashes at him. Madeline, only a seventeen then, was daring, even disloyal, but she seemed sweet on him. It was irresistible. Philip waited a year and a half before boldly requesting to be bungalowed with her, hoping his tasks at the Complex would give him an advantage over others. Who wouldn't request Madeline? She was pleasantness itself, wasn't she? The night they were bungalowed, he saw the others walking away hiding their disappointment. Meanwhile, he walked away with Madeline, his heart soaring. Para Philip shrugged, remembering their faces. He now knew—time had shown him—that disappointment, though forbidden, was an inescapable part of life, sooner or later.

The Naming Ceremony followed the Celebration of the Bungalows. This was their day, the one and only moment tinys born in the past year would be celebrated by other Township folks. Today, each tiny would be given their name and would become a one.

After each tiny had been brought forward and named, Town Master proudly acknowledged them all.

"Tonight, we celebrate our newest tinys and commit to help them become pleasant to all and loyal to the Township."

He extended his arm to their paras, calling out winsomely, "Our best to your bungalows!" Then he directed them to return to their places.

An apprentice burst in with a high joyful voice, "The Celebration of the Years will begin."

A parade of sorts followed, beginning with the fives who would now become sixes. Paras throughout the crowd raised their hands, and helpers went out to find each five and escort them to the front. These small folks had not been up front since their

Naming Ceremony. Now they were led, or sometimes pushed, to the front, supposedly with their heads held high, which rarely happened with new sixes. At the front they paraded single-file to the center, bowed, and kept their heads down while they recited their first public Township motto.

Pleasantness to each puts loyalty within our reach.

After they mumbled through their motto, they received a new tunic set. Town Master Cree announced them as the Township's new sixes, and the parade of frightened littles wove its way back, while the new sevens came forward. Each age group was celebrated the same until finally it was time for the new nines.

Para Madeline's heart raced when it was Jewel's turn. The past two years, she claimed Jewel was too ill to attend. Really, she was worried about what unpredictable, unpleasant thing Jewel might do. This year, Para Philip insisted Jewel come. New nines were required to recite the Laws of Loyalty. Para Madeline breathed a smile of relief, thinking of the junior from bungalow seventy-six teaching Jewel the Laws. She smiled sweetly and gave Jewel a stout pinch of warning when Para Philip raised his hand.

"Loyalty paras." The helper bowed respectfully. "Excuse me, but this is the celebration for new nines." He felt sure they had missed the celebrations of the sixes or sevens. Could this small of a little become a nine?

"I give you my word of loyalty," Para Philip replied. "She is merely small for her year."

The helper nodded quickly and began to give Jewel instructions as he walked her to the front. "Stay with me, and when we get to the front, you must stand still. I'll be right there behind you. And absolutely no talking."

Jewel followed perfectly, with an air of refined posture, and her chin lifted just so. At the front, she lowered her head. When the new nines recited their Laws of Loyalty, her voice was clear, and sweet, but not loud. Everything went exactly as she had practiced with Ri.

Her toes begged to skip and dance on the calm walk back,

but she thought of Ri and refused to let them. Para Philip's eyes shone with approval when she reached him. Jewel slid close beside him. Maybe he would let her stand on her tiptoes if she was still and quiet. Oh, how she longed to see the entire Celebration.

The announcer had already called out for the Ceremony of Errand-Going, and most of the new tens were coming forward on their own. Samuri searched in the direction he'd seen Jewel come and go. Um-hmm. There she was, standing on her tiptoes at the very edge. Could she see him? He took a deep hero breath and came forward calmly and confidently.

Some of the paras of new tens were forced to raise a hand and request help for their hesitant junior. Once all of the new tens were lined up center front, Town Master Cree extended his hand toward them and proclaimed, "I present this year's new errand-goers. Welcome new tens. The time has come for you to begin the loyal task of errand-going." Here, the Town Master paused, and bowed toward them before exclaiming, "Loyalty to the Township."

"Loyalty to the Township," they echoed him, and filed back.

Para Patrick, fiercely proud of his junior's calm confidence, had to restrain himself from hugging Samuri. Hugs would have to wait until they were safe in their bungalow.

Next was the line of new elevens, and then the new twelves. They were celebrated mostly the same as they filed to the front, recited a few more Laws of Loyalty, and received their rust-colored tunic and trousers.

Now came Samuri's favorite moment, the Ceremony of the Youngs.

"Our loyal new youngs," Town Master Cree's voice was solemn. He leaned in addressing the new thirteens personally, almost secretively. "Tomorrow, you begin your years of preparation. Your pleasantness, or lack of it, will determine your future tasks. Your loyalty will keep the Township safe. Follow the Laws of Loyalty perfectly."

44

Samuri was spellbound. His ten-year-old heart wasn't sure what it meant, but he wanted to be part of it. He watched the new thirteens receive their bundled-up green tunic and trousers and return to their paras. One day he would wear the pine-colored tunic of a young. One day *his* loyalty would keep the folks of the Township safe.

The Celebration of the Years ended there. The new fourteens through sixteens were not celebrated; the officials thought it was unnecessary. Now previously bungalowed paras were acknowledged according to the number of years they had been bungalowed.

"Loyal Township paras who have been bungalowed ten years or less, rise and be celebrated."

Each pair stood in their places, keeping an eye on their tinys and littles. Town Master Cree bowed to acknowledge the group. They bowed in return and stood waiting as Town Master did the same for those who had been bungalowed for eleven to twenty years. Finally, those who had been bungalowed up to thirty years were acknowledged. Again, Town Master Cree bowed low while the Officials and apprentices applauded.

As the applause faded, a delicious distraction caught their attention. The grand bell on the porch rang out and a strong voice announced, "Let the Feast Begin."

The smell of sweet cinnamon breads and rosemary-spiced garlic potatoes wafted through the air. A long line of apprentices and older youngs approached, carrying platters heaped full of mouth-watering delicacies made only on Celebration Day.

What perfect timing! The hungry, wiggly tinys and littles need not sit still a moment longer. The Feast was ready. Folks' eyes sparkled with anticipation as they pulled plates from their carry bags and bustled to the tables lining each side of the Square. It was difficult to keep their eyes down and avoid contact with other folks, but they did their best. Even the Feast wasn't worth losing points at the Exchange. Officials and authorized apprentices watched carefully to make any necessary corrections.

Para Patrick and a few others who longed for friendship and laughter fought hard to focus on the food before them. Should they choose the sweet, berry-laden cookies or the delectable pumpkin bread with chewy hazelnut chunks? And what of the rich, gooey toppings? Were there any of those this year? The chance to fill an entire plate with your own choice of delicacies was almost too good to be true. Folks never had access to ingredients for special recipes, and lately the Exchange was out of even simple food, like potatoes and flour. But tonight? Tonight, folks lost themselves in the pleasure of one mouth-watering bite after another.

By the time plates were licked clean and stomachs were gloriously full, the mood shifted. The sun slipped below the horizon, casting a pinkish glow across the fading sky.

"Ooo!" Jewel gasped softly, her eyes wide with wonder, her mouth open like a baby bird waiting to be fed. The sky! She'd never been outside to see the sky do this. Para Madeline shook her head and quickly pulled Jewel over. Jewel nodded and put her finger to her lips assuring Para Madeline she would be silent. Madeline relaxed her grip but kept Jewel close.

Tinys nestled contentedly in their paras' laps. Littles gasped as the fiery torches lit by the apprentices burst into flame, shooting out sparks and loud popping sounds. An unusual, dreamy feeling settled over the crowd. Their full bellies seemed to numb their fear of the darkening skies and glowing torches. The timing was perfect for the last two ceremonies of this Celebration Day.

"The Ceremony of the Scarves of Remembrance," a large, loud official proclaimed more joyfully than any of the ceremonies so far. Two sets of paras came forward. Tonight marked their thirty-fifth year of being bungalowed. Town Master Cree stood to the side, motioning for folks to applaud. Jewel wanted to *shout* in the midst of the boisterous applause and blazing lanterns. She thought of Samuri, sitting quietly with his paras. It was ridiculous to be so quiet in the midst of such fun. They would laugh about it tomorrow.

Two officials approached with their arms slightly outstretched and their palms up, each carrying a thin, long piece of delicate cloth. Everyone watched in awe. At that moment two second-year apprentices chose to slip into the dark, hoping for a moment alone. They must be quick and wise. They could not be caught.

Para Chloe's heart raced at the sight of the Officials carrying her scarves. *Oh, let my scarves be perfect for each of these gran paras.* Para Patrick gave her hand a quick squeeze.

Town Master Cree and one of the Officials spoke privately for a moment before moving to stand by the first two paras. The official unfolded the first luxuriously woven scarf, handing one end to Town Master Cree. With an air of solemnity, they walked behind the couple, pulling the length of material across their backs and over their shoulders. The scarf was just long enough to "tie" the couple together loosely. It was a most heartwarming sight. The first official stepped aside, and Town Master Cree commended the paras for their many diligent years of pleasantness and loyalty. Then the ceremony was repeated for the other couple.

Finally, Town Master Cree and his lead official stood between the two couples, bowed their heads momentarily and stepped back. Full attention was given to the paras wrapped in their own unique, shimmering Scarves of Remembrance. Samuri reached to pat Para Chloe's arm, but Para Patrick shook his head. A hush fell over the crowd.

"Township folks," Town Master Cree spoke in a softer, more genuine voice. "These paras will never stand before you at a Celebration Day again. Starting tomorrow they will tie a silver band around the arm of their new lavender tunics. The silver band reminds us of the honor we owe them. You must always address them with the honored title of Gran Para.

"They live among us as daily proof that a long life of pleasantness, loyalty, and safety is possible. May *you* also live a safe, long life of pleasantness to each and loyalty to the Township until you receive *your* very own Scarf of Remembrance."

Town Master Cree scanned the crowd with serious eyes,

as if warning them. Then he led them in one last solemn bow, before releasing the gran paras to return to their places. Folks strained their eyes for a glimpse of the cherished scarves, but it was impossible in the dim torchlight and shadows.

Town Master Cree waited respectfully, until they were seated, and then burst forth triumphantly, at the top of his lungs, "And now, folks of our pleasant, most loyal Township, join with me in the Celebration of the Seventeens!"

The two disloyal apprentices timed their return perfectly, taking their places directly after an official passed.

The Celebration of the Seventeens was a bittersweet time. Each sixteen came forward with stories and hopes that would never be known. Most folks didn't care anymore, but Chloe and Patrick watched eagerly. If only they could know these new apprentices and help them through the unspoken hardships ahead. Would any of them be assigned to the apprenticeship tasks they had requested? Or had they been too shy to ask? An apprentice on the far south slumped, missing every prompt that was given. Did he even care? Could talking with him make a difference? Chloe and Patrick would never know. No one would if the Township had its way.

Your story is your story, and their story is their story. The very thought haunted Para Patrick. *Sharing stories makes trouble for everyone. So, don't listen and don't tell. Keep the Township safe.*

Town Master's voice rang out, again, bold, and pleased, "The Township welcomes you, new apprentices, as partners and paras-in-training through your loyal apprenticeship."

The voices of the new seventeens, or most of them, responded in unison. "We commit to be examples of pleasantness to each, and of loyalty to the Township above all. We pledge to keep the Township safe."

Folks of all ages bowed long and low, as was expected, replying, "And we know you will."

Each new seventeen received a colored armband indicating the tasks chosen for their apprenticeship, then tucked them into the pockets of the old green tunics they wore. Their new beige tunic and trousers waited on the cot assigned to them at the dorm.

Authorized second-year and third-year apprentices waited at the corners of the Square to lead folks back to their bungalows. The blazing, sputtering, torches they held were a thrilling sight, but the Township folks kept their eyes down, fixed on the path, trained by years of fear and caution. Two of the apprentices held their fiery torches bravely, emboldened with purpose. The other apprentices simply did their best to grip their torch and hide their fears of darkness and fire.

The new apprentices followed by torchlight as well, separated into two groups, that of the he-dorm and that of the she-dorm. At the dorms they were checked in, shown their cots, and commanded to stay on their cots after lights out. No talking, and absolutely no sharing stories. Training would begin tomorrow.

Once the lights were out their minds went wild with all sorts of thoughts.

. . . Dorms? Sleeping in a room full of seventeens? I'm not so sure about this.

. . . I'm ready. I will do my tasks with the utmost loyalty. Wait 'til they see me.

. . . Why didn't I get the apprenticeship I requested?

. . . I miss my paras already. Why can't I see them again?

Finally, though, they were swallowed up in the warmth of their soft, thick, new blankets. Few of them had ever had such a fine, cozy blanket. Now they slept, some dreaming hopeful dreams, some numb, but others in the nightmares of a life that could never be.

"Director Madge, I'm missing two of my new apprentices. Have you seen them?" Director Tony's low voice boomed from behind the outside door.

He was new and skittish from hearing the orientation information about *Accidents on a Celebration Day*.

"Mine are all here," Madge called back, "and I haven't seen or heard any others. Wait a few more minutes, then lock the door. It's probably shenanigans. If they show up, they'll ring plenty loud enough. If they don't show, they've probably chickened out. That happens. All you need to do is to take their bungalow numbers to office four of the Complex, tomorrow. That's Para Philip. He'll deal with it."

"I hope it's a misunderstanding, not shenanigans," Director Tony boomed through the door and left.

"Or an accident," Director Madge muttered, under her breath. That would be an awful way to end such a pleasant Celebration Day.

6
accidents happen

Town Master Cree sat silently, thinking through the events of the night. Smooth. Orderly. Folks seemed to respond a bit brighter than usual (or was that his imagination?). And no accidents. One of the best Celebration Days he could remember. In the dark of the Big Bungalow porch, he sat with his legs extended and his feet propped up comfortably. He was pleased.

Gazing out into the dark, he began to stare at the walls of the bungalow directly south of his, as if trying to see through the walls. "Come on, Brody, put the candles out," Cree muttered under his breath, clicking his nails against one another, nervously. "It's way past time, even for Celebration Day."

As if Gran Para Brody sensed Cree's watchful eyes and growing agitation, he drew Gran Para Rosie and Dupree closer to him against the wall of their cozy bungalow.

"Ah, my lovely girls," he whispered, and gathered them into his arms.

Thirteen-year-old Dupree nestled her face against his tunic, wrapping her arms as far around his stout, muscular waist as she could. After a long, snuggly hug, Gran Para Brody stood and pulled her up. He put his hands on her shoulders and stepped back to see her better.

"Ya know we're mighty proud of ya, don't ya? Yur the sunshine o' this here bungalow," Brody said with a pleased chuckle.

"If I'm the sunshine, then what is Para Rosie?" Dupree asked for the hundredth time, loving to hear him say it.

"Why Rosie, she be the fresh breezes blowin' through this stuffy bungalow, keepin' us all lively." His eyes sparkled, the lines around them bunching up in piles of splendid memories.

"Sounds like a perfect combo to me," Rosie said matter-of-factly, but her dark eyes shone despite her determination to avoid his silliness. "Don't you agree, my dear Dupree?"

Again, they hugged, but quickly this time, as Dupree still hadn't seen their Scarf of Remembrance up close.

"May I hold the scarf before I go to my cot?" Her eyes were the mellow honey brown of Brody's, but her face held the same dignity and reserve as Rosie's face.

"Mmm, I've never seen anything more beautiful," she said in awe, holding the scarf, shimmery and soft, in her hands.

"Just think, someday ya will have yur very own Scarf o' Remembrance. Look at ya, yur a new young already. Soon yur goin' ta be growin' up and leavin'."

His thought caught Dupree off guard, but her answer was steady. "I don't plan to leave at all. I'm going to ask Town Master Cree to let me apprentice with you and Momma. I mean, Gran Para Rosie."

She spoke with complete confidence, expecting life to be exactly as she believed it would be. That's the way it had been from the time she mustered her first sentence. Dupree knew her own mind, and always found a way.

A long, low whistle escaped Brody's lips. He raised his eyebrows, silently questioning Rosie. Had Dupree told *her* about this? Rosie shook her head slightly and mouthed "no" at him in reply. No, but the time was coming despite how much they had hoped to stop it.

"Every night on my cot, before I go to sleep, I pray and ask him." Dupree was as serious and full of faith as any young could be. "I ask to be apprenticed by you, both of you. And I ask him to give you long lives."

A hush fell, hanging heavily upon the room. Suddenly, distant voices broke through the silence, startling them back to reality.

"That's a big ask, Dupree," Rosie said wearily.

"And don't ya be talkin' about prayer outside o' this bungalow," Brody added, his voice stern, but tinged with sadness. "Us three must always remember the Township doesn't take kindly to prayer."

"No, Poppa. You mean it's forbidden." Dupree corrected his statement, straightening her shoulders and meeting his gaze with penetrating fearlessness.

"Enough, you two." Rosie's voice was firm. "Now, off to the cot with you." She enveloped Dupree in her arms with a soft, comforting hug. She frowned at Brody over Dupree's shoulder, warning him not to meddle. "We've had enough of beauty and chatter and speaking our minds this night."

A minute later Dupree was snug under her blanket and so soundly asleep she didn't hear Town Master's voice outside calling to the muffled voices nearing the Big Bungalow. Brody moved toward the door, his heart beating faster at the sound.

"Not our story, Brody," Rosie reminded him, grabbing his arm and tugging him in the direction of their room. They settled contentedly on their cots, listening to the rise and fall of Dupree's peaceful breathing.

"Are ya all right, m' Rosie?"

"Yes," she whispered as the voices faded away. "I'm grateful, Brody, so grateful. The Lord's been good to us. Yes, it's been harder than I thought I could survive, but there's been beauty, too. Can you believe our dear, quiet, steely Dupree? She's done well. Imagine, she's the perfect blend of kindness, sense, and determination. And we still have each other. I'm not going to let the mistakes and hatreds of other folks stop me from living the life I still have."

"And what about Cree?"

Rosie paused and Brody wished he could see her face, but the darkness was too thick. "Well, Maggie's been gone thirteen years, Brody. I like to think she'd be delighted how well her dear Dupree is doing. And Cree, too. She'd be pleased with both of them."

Her words, full of comfort and resolve, took him back to the joyous Celebration Day his daughter Maggie was bungalowed with Cree, the one they had all hoped for. He was kind, hardworking, wise beyond his years, and so good for Maggie. Paras Brody and Rosie had hoped Cree could tame the wildness in Maggie, could help her to forget her schemes for changing the Township. Then, she became pregnant, which only spurred her on in her pursuit of change. On her assigned visits to the bungalows of injured or ill folks, she urged a few of them to choose a day and steal away to the clearing with her.

"Life holds so much more for us. I practically lived in the clearing as a tiny." Maggie's confident, caring voice was compelling. "Truly. It's not scary or dangerous, and you can pick all the strawberries and lavender you want. Someday, I hope to help folks plant gardens in their own yards." She'd explain a garden if they'd let her, and finish with, "Our small folks deserve a more pleasant life."

With misty eyes she gazed toward the woods and patted her belly. Two of those paras listened willingly, letting the ideas take root in their hearts. The rest of the paras stopped her midsentence. They would use the ointments and follow her advice, but she should go. As far as she knew, though, none of them had reported her.

The day before her tiny was born, she went too far. The Exchange had been insisting there were no more potatoes, but she was craving them badly. What if a few had survived deep in the soil during the Brave Days? And . . . there was one last thing she could not do after her tiny came. So, one day when Cree left early, she slipped out seconds before daystart, tucking her garden spade safely in her carry bag. Soundlessly she snuck to the meadow, planning to be back after paras were at their tasks and before the messenger's rounds.

On the far side of the clearing near the hillside, she worked swiftly. Why hadn't she brought a cleaning cloth for her hands? Or cloths for the potatoes? Scanning the clearing for something to freshen her hands, she saw the lavender beginning to bloom, and simply had to have a bunch of that, too. Suddenly potatoes seemed unnecessary. The fresh air and woodsy scents breathed strength and peace over her, and she lingered too long.

When she finally emerged from the woods, she saw a messenger ringing the bell on a bungalow three rows away. *Oh, what was I thinking?* Maggie scolded herself.

What she didn't see was the startled messenger who caught a glimpse of her and hid behind a bungalow to watch where she went. After his first round, he reported her disloyalty, pleased to do his part keeping the Township safe. The officials visited Para Cree at his tasks, drawing him aside and warning him sternly.

The next day their tiny was born. Maggie's first look at the wee fingers and soft, sleepy baby eyes changed everything.

"Our bungalow is my loyalty now, Cree. You're the one better suited to change the Township, anyway. You'll change it slowly and steadily, and the change will last. But my place is here," Maggie vowed. "Look!" She spoke in a delighted, hushed tone. "She's a helpless wee thing. I won't risk going to the meadow—I mean, the clearing—ever again."

Celebration Day came four weeks later and their precious tiny was given the lovely name Dupree. They breathed a sigh of relief. The officials had given them a second chance, and all was well. Two weeks later Para Cree returned from his tasks to find the tiny Dupree asleep, wrapped snugly on her cot, and Maggie nowhere to be found.

An hour later, two Township officials arrived with horrid news. A messenger had reported seeing Para Maggie running into the woods, but when the officials went to bring her back, it was too late. They'd found her dead on the ground, swollen and puffy with a poisonous mushroom in her mouth and a swarm of killer bees surrounding her.

Para Cree turned up on Brody's doorstep after dark. Cree's eyes, wide in his pale face, darted back and forth crazily. Cree crumpled into Brody's arms sobbing and clinging tightly to a hungry, wailing Dupree.

"I can't do it, Para Brody. I can't bear this. It's not true. She promised me she wouldn't go anymore. It can't be true. It can't!"

"What's not true, Cree?" Para Brody asked, his brow furrowed with concern. "Here, here. Let Para Rosie take Dupree and feed her."

While Rosie warmed hazelnut milk for Dupree and peppermint tea for Cree, Para Brody eased Para Cree onto the floor. The soothing aromas seemed to give Cree a second wind, and he began to talk. First, he shared the facts as he knew them. "But it's worse than that, Brody." Cree's eyes went wild again. The Officials insisted the entire Township *must* be told in order to prevent further "accidents" and to keep other folks safe. They called it "a tragic accident that might have been prevented by greater loyalty." Brody's face grew angrier with each detail Cree shared. "Town Master insisted on finding a new bungalow for Dupree."

That was the last straw. Para Brody jumped up and strode to the door. "My girl—" He shouted and stomped angrily across the floor. "My girl knows her mushrooms! Town Master Edward will show me her body or else—"

Tiny Dupree began wailing, and Brody felt it like a slap in the face. He put aside his seething anger and marched directly to the Big Bungalow.

"Town Master Edward, I'll be taking my girl for a proper burial."

"The Officials are meeting in the office. Do I need to have them *escort* you home, Brody?" Town Master Edward's voice was cold and threatening. "Surely you've done enough damage teaching your girl to go against the Laws of Loyalty."

Brody gasped. "You—murderer!"

"No. I'm not like the folks long ago who started all the trouble. Your girl chose disloyalty. Now she's gone, and everyone is safe. What about you, Brody? Will you choose loyalty? The Officials will be watching you, Para Rosie, and Para Cree."

Brody's relief was so great he could barely stay standing. Maggie was alive, somewhere. He would play the Township game right, even convincingly. So, Town Master Edward agreed to let them keep Dupree *if* Brody kept quiet and followed certain terms. Para Brody agreed, bit his tongue, and left immediately. How sad that Edward had come to this.

Back at his bungalow, Para Brody told Rosie and Cree the terms without going into other details. Not that he really knew anyway.

Cree gasped and headed for the door. "Give me a candle. I'm going to go find her."

"Remember Cree," Brody said. "We don't ask to see her or to help bury her. We keep our story to ourselves. No blame, no explanations, not to anyone. No looking disappointed. We shrug our shoulders and say, 'Accidents happen.' That's all."

"With that story? How dare they!" Rosie had exploded, fire burning in her puffy, tear-stained eyes. Yet she knew there was no choice. If any of them demanded to see Maggie's body or to defend her memory, they would lose Dupree.

Cree crossed the room swiftly and bent his tall shoulders to lay his head on Para Rosie's shoulder. The grief they shared became the refuge they shared. Part of the terms were that Cree was never to visit Dupree. It was a knife in his heart, but he would do anything to keep Dupree with Brody and Rosie.

So, time went on, and eventually so did Cree. He was determined to change the Township. For Maggie. For Dupree. He lived loyally and pleasantly, applying himself in every task that came to him. When Town Master Edward died, the Township

Officials chose Cree to be the next town master, but change was not as easy as he had envisioned.

"Brody." Rosie's gentle voice brought him back to the present. "I'm done with lookin' back. Dupree is learning fast. You should see her when they call me to help folks who are sick or injured. She comes alive."

As pleasanter thoughts pushed their sadness away, a scuffling and a hushed voice sounded at their door.

"Greetings." The hushed voice beckoned them. "Pleasantness. Town Master Cree sent me. The he-dorm needs Gran Para Rosie's medic skills. An apprentice has burned his hand. Hurry."

Brody lit a candle as Rosie slipped on shoes and reached for her jacket.

"Momma," Dupree's sleepy voice emerged from her room. "I mean 'Gran Para'. Gran Para, may I grab your basket for you?"

At the door Rosie reached back to grab the basket, but her hand found Dupree's hand instead.

"Slip your shoes on. I may need your help."

Brody handed Rosie the candle and watched them rush into the dark.

Town Master Cree met them at the door of the dorm. "Pleasantness, Gran Para Rosie." He bowed respectfully. "I'm glad you've come quickly. The pain seems intense."

Junior Dupree bowed politely to Town Master Cree, and as she did, Cree's eyes shot over to question Rosie. What was she thinking, bringing a new thirteen for this kind of task? *His* thirteen.

"Town Master Cree, this is the Junior Dupree. She has a natural touch with medic skills."

"Loyalty, Junior Dupree." He responded with a quick nod, trying to think of some way to stall them. Dupree had grown since he'd last seen her up close. He longed for a few moments with her, but that would be disloyal to those inside. So, he held the door for them and was on his way.

Rosie wondered if she had made a mistake bringing Dupree,

but immediately it was clear Dupree belonged there. Dupree laid out the perfect antiseptic, cream, and bandages while Rosie examined the apprentice's hand. When Rosie began to clean the wound, he cried out as much in fear as in pain.

Junior Dupree was by his side instantly, with her head bowed to avoid looking at his eyes. "Take my hand in your other hand and listen to my voice." The calm command of her young voice startled him, but instantly he obeyed, and a measure of peace came to him. "If you breathe deeply and calmly, it will help. It takes air through your whole body, and air relaxes your muscles, and that helps it hurt less. Accidents happen, but you are brave and loyal. Your hand will be better before you know it."

Rosie stopped. Her heart pumped so hard she felt it would break through her skin. "Accidents happen." After seeing Cree face to face with Dupree by her side, this was the last thing she wanted to hear.

Dupree remained holding the apprentice's hand, speaking slowly of days to come when the pain would be gone. And she prayed without anyone knowing. Rosie worked away only needing hands-on help from Dupree at the end, when the burned fingers must be held apart for the bandaging. Even that did not unsettle Dupree.

While Gran Para Rosie and Junior Dupree were bringing skillful healing, Town Master Cree was settling himself in the porch chair again. Waves of relentless thoughts crashed over him from every direction. Which thoughts should he listen to?

An insistent voice from his past broke through it all.

"Cree, listen to me carefully." The sound of his momma's rich, purpose-filled voice was as clear as if she were there. And with it the memory of her holding his face still, cupped in her soft hands, helping him focus. "The Township will need a better Town Master when you are a para. Maybe it will be you. Never forget you're named after Uncle Creeander. He was always trustworthy and wise and kind to everyone. That's how he became Town Master. But we can't tell anyone." Her voice became a feather soft whisper. "Remember?"

Joy sprung up in his heart. Though he couldn't remember Uncle Creeander, they had been family in the days when there were families.

Suddenly a stern voice, weighed down with unbearable loss, broke in. "Catherine, what are you doing? Do you want to lose Cree, too?" Cree shivered and tried to wish the memory of his father away, but he couldn't.

"Tell me why, again?" his young voice questioned Para Catherine.

"Town Master Edward and his officials are convinced it's best to change how we do family. A lot of hurt can come from being so close." In his mind's eye he saw himself nod and turn to look at her with adoring eyes.

"But . . . ?"

"Family is good. Family is worth it." He could still hear, as well as feel her tenderness mingled with conviction. "We *will* speak of your brothers and Uncle Creeander, no matter how much it hurts."

He thought of his father, Para Corin. Para Corin had shown his love by protecting Cree but had kept his distance rather than risk the pain of losing another beloved son. A moan of mixed fear and longing stirred inside Town Master Cree. He had loved his difficult para and had wanted more than anything to help him.

Cree sighed. All his life he had tried to help. Did Brody and Rosie have to make it so hard for him? He'd done everything he could for them. He'd overlooked countless situations for them, and for Dupree and Maggie. Oh, Dupree. Every sight of her, every sound of her voice had made the pain worth it, up until tonight. And now, he saw that Dupree had both Maggie's brave ways and Rosie's healing touch. At only thirteen, she had the medic skills others were unwilling to learn. Folks had become weak and fearful, even the ones who thought they were brave. But not Brody and Rosie. No one could replace them.

"How I longed to protect them," he whispered to the dark. "But I might not be able to much longer."

Rosie and Dupree's footsteps pattered faintly back through

the dark, the flame of the candle leading their way until the door was closed behind them.

"Choose family," his heart assured him confidently. "No. The Township," a sterner voice demanded.

If only he had known that first Town Master. If only he could have saved Maggie. Was a safe Township really better than family and the risk of deep loss?

At that moment Cree thought of Para Corin one last time. "I choose to be strong like you, Para Corin. It is the only thing I have to give you."

Para Catherine's inviting voice beckoned to him again, but he refused to let her distract him. No matter how much he had loved her, protecting the Township was more important than protecting one family.

He would put the Laws of Loyalty first. He would beat the soft side of himself.

Para Brody was kneeling by the heat box early the next morning when there was a light knock on his door. The official, a man who Brody did not know, greeted him respectfully in hushed tones.

"Pleasantness, Gran Para. The Complex has summoned Gran Para Rosie to bungalow fifteen immediately. She is to take proper medic supplies and help a para with a newborn tiny.

"There's more. The Director of Tasks has a special assignment for your young. Rather than reporting to the Tasks Bungalow, she is to report to the Complex. An aging Gran Para fell last night. She needs ongoing care at least for the next week. Your young must pack her belongings and report within an hourglass."

Gran Para Brody's jaw dropped, and he stuttered to find words. The official looked down, bowed, and was gone.

Gran Para Rosie gathered up her supplies, tears streaming down her cheeks. The message was clear. Moments later, a sleepy Dupree was awakened to both of her paras kneeling by her cot.

"There's a bit o' a *special* assignment for ya, Dupree dear," Brody said in the bravest voice he could muster.

Dupree sat up in wonder. A medic assignment? This was too pleasant to believe! Then, she saw Rosie's tear-stained face. "Momma?"

"Imagine this, Dupree. I have a special medic assignment today, too. I have to go, but first let's pray?"

Sliding to her knees on the floor between them, Dupree reached to tuck a hand in each of their hands. Brody and Dupree took turns praying, but Rosie absolutely could not concentrate. The words "accidents happen" echoed through her head, drowning out the sound of their prayers.

7
growing pains

Ting-a-ting-a-ting-a-ting! The bell on the door rang loudly, frantically. The woods loomed dark and ominous beside the helper who came to take Samuri errand-going. He tried to be Township proper, with a hurried greeting and a half-nod, but a sudden gust of wind screamed eerily from deep within the woods. Dashing off of the doorstep, he motioned for Samuri to follow. Did he really have to tell the initiation stories?

Well, the quicker that was done the better. He spit out the stories of spooky creatures, and storms, and the deaths of disloyal folks who had dared venture into the woods. Finally, he began the regimen of questions for Samuri.

Samuri wondered how anyone could believe such stories about his pleasant woods, but he kept calm and answered correctly without arguing. It was a good thing his paras had warned him, but his calmness disturbed the helper even more. Was this junior one of the dull, mindless ones? Or was he crazy, like the para who was devoured by stinging creatures when she wandered into the woods? Hopefully he was a dull one. The answer lay in how well the junior from bungalow seventy-six could recite the Laws of Loyalty.

Samuri began pleasantly and with confidence, not missing a word, and finishing perfectly. The helper quickened his pace, putting more space between the two of them, hoping he would never see this junior again. Samuri thought nothing of it; he was busy staring ahead at the huge building on his right.

The Exchange building was impressive, standing two meters taller than any bungalow, and the size of eight bungalows together on the inside. Stepping through the door was like walking into a splendid new world. Rows and rows of shelves loaded with goods you needed, *and* goods you had never dreamed of. Samuri was stunned.

"Greetings," a quiet, insecure voice spoke to the left of the door. "Pleasantness . . . to each, and loyalty . . . to the Township." It was a new apprentice standing behind the checkout counter, timidly receiving instructions from the Director of the Exchange.

"Greetings. A long, safe life to us all," Samuri replied cheerfully, keeping his eyes down, but speaking with full confidence. "I'm the ten from bungalow seventy-six."

The Director of the Exchange stepped forward to introduce herself, and the junior Samuri looked up, as was expected, to return her warm, welcoming smile. She motioned toward the shelves of goods, inviting him to begin. Samuri scanned the shelves slowly, noting the items Para Chloe had asked him to get.

Again, the helper shuddered. How awful would it be if this junior forgot his para's list? The helper dreaded the thought of making two trips to the bungalow by the woods. But Samuri surprised them all. He walked straight to the shelf lined with boxes of scrubbing cloths, snack cloths, and freshening cloths.

"Six of these," he said, pointing toward each item as he listed it. "A large tin of cream for our heads, a portion of sweet potato flour, more walnut oil, a box of dried strawberries, and . . ." Para Chloe needed white thread, too, but it was on the shelves in the back, and he couldn't find it.

One by one, the helper handed the items to Samuri. One by one,

Samuri took them to the counter where he was allowed to choose a carry bag of his own. The new clerk forgot to show him how to pack items without spilling or bruising them, but he already knew how. The Director marked the points used by bungalow seventy-six on the tally sheet. The Director also made a mental note of Samuri's pleasant but intense eyes, sharp memory, and polite manner. Someday this junior might make a pleasant clerk.

On the way out the door, Samuri turned back to breathe in the delightful mix of smells. His helper was far ahead when Samuri caught up. Nothing was said until they neared Jewel's bungalow where the helper wished him farewell and turned to go.

I hope I can show Jewel this bag. It's her favorite color.

Samuri changed and hung his bag on top of this year's new rust-colored tunic. Then he greeted his para and rushed over to Jewel's. Tonight, after last snack he would answer his paras' questions, but for now he must see Jewel. He had made a plan to tell Jewel at least one new thing each day, starting with the Exchange building and moving on to the shelves overflowing with goods of all kinds. Jewel sat wide-eyed, hanging on every word as he described the color of the blue bag and the height of the Exchange building. Her eyes shone. Samuri had her full attention. He was the hero of a great story, not the ten next door doing typical Township tasks.

Para Patrick was right, Samuri told himself. *A friend is a good thing, especially my friend Jewel, who waits for me every day and always listens.*

Five weeks later, when Samuri's list was up to twelve items, the Director of the Exchange requested Samuri be assigned to a few small tasks at the Exchange. Samuri was given permission to walk there without a helper and to fill Para Chloe's list before he left each day. Slowly his tasks grew and so did his stories. He described with simple words the joy of being out and about with the messengers, walking the paths, ringing the bells on bungalow doors, and greeting paras around the Township.

The messengers were pleased to have his help on large deliveries. And though he didn't know it, the Director was pleased too. Samuri did everything well—odd jobs, organizing shelves, and even helping with inventory. In the Township's way of thinking, Samuri grew up overnight. One day he was just a ten errand-going, but only weeks later he was an eleven respected for doing the tasks of a young. No one said so, but he could feel it, and he was pleased, too. More tasks were fine with him, as long as he had time to help Para Chloe and to play with Jewel.

One day, Samuri still wasn't back after midday snack. *Where is he and why doesn't he hurry?* Jewel wondered. Para Madeline was knitting in the task room laughing and chattering away, caught up in one of her hilarious moods. Jewel was fidgety, and when she noticed the latch on the door was unlocked, she headed for the woods. After all, Samuri couldn't stop her if he wasn't here, and though she didn't want to upset him, this might be her only chance. The distant movement of a small creature rushing along the ground caught her eye. She would follow it.

"Greetings . . ." chirped a pleasant, loud voice, as Jewel skipped past the edge of Samuri's bungalow. "Have you come to help me?"

Jewel spun around, wide-eyed and nodding. The huge goofy smile pasted across her face was meant to hide any suspicion of her plan to go into the woods. Para Chloe, a laundry basket on her hip, was heading for the drying line. She showed Jewel how to grab one tunic at a time, shake it, and hold it up until she was ready for it. Twice Jewel dropped a snack cloth in the dirt, and shut her eyes tight waiting for a scolding, Para Chloe simply asked her to pick it up and shake it well. When the basket was empty Para Chloe walked to the corner of the bungalow, pointed at Jewel's door, and smiled. She watched until Jewel skipped back and shut the door tightly behind her.

Chloe was both relieved and disturbed. The Laws of Loyalty demanded that she report the para next door. She weighed the dangers and shuddered. Losing a little in the woods? The grief of paras having their only little taken from them? Samuri losing his only friend?

I'll do my best to watch for her, she thought, and checked around the corner before going inside.

Para Madeline was still knitting away and laughing hilariously. Jewel climbed onto her cot, unnoticed, and told herself a story about that morning. She failed to hear Para Madeline tiptoe up to listen.

When Para Madeline put the phrases "the para next door" and "laundry" together, she was furious. "You will stay on your cot for the rest of the day, and you will *never* help that para again."

This time there were no tears. Instead, Jewel sat on her cot with a whimsical smile and sparkling eyes, weaving a fanciful story of a brave para living inside a tree, hanging laundry on its branches, and doing whatever she pleased without being one bit loyal. Only this time Jewel kept the story inside, very pleased with herself. Para Madeline could not scold her for what she could not hear. Day after day the story grew, opening the way for new stories and making her days bearable.

The days were flying by too quickly. The Brave Days would soon be there, and before long Para Madeline would keep Jewel inside every day.

Quiet, attentive Samuri heard all the talk at the Exchange and around the Township. What he heard about the Laws of Loyalty began to make him uneasy. Did the Laws apply to yards and friends? Or were those the same as bungalows? He reminded Jewel more often now not to tell her paras anything they talked about.

She agreed wholeheartedly, nodding dramatically, her eyes bright and pleased. The last thing she wanted was for her para to meddle in Ri's life.

Jewel never wavered, not even during the long, boring Brave Days stuck inside. She guarded everything she said as she did her tasks and helped Para Madeline. Later, on her cot, her imagination went wild with stories woven from the new places, people, and ideas Samuri had shared. She made up story after story, sometimes merely in her thoughts, other times whispering so quietly Para Madeline could never hear. The quiet Jewel had once despised became a treasure. Being alone with whispered secrets felt safer than arguments and lost privileges.

Four weeks before Celebration Day, Jewel was allowed in the yard. She rushed out, jumping as high off of the doorstep as she could, ready for fun.

However, Samuri wasn't thinking about fun. He was thinking about getting Jewel ready for errand-going.

"Recite the Laws of Loyalty to me." Samuri's excitement was evident in his voice, but Jewel only shrugged her shoulders. No bright eyes today.

A week later, Samuri began to wonder if she knew any of them. After all, she couldn't count until he had taught her. So, he would have to bribe her to sit still while he recited the Laws to her.

"If you repeat the Laws of Loyalty after me, I'll bring you an armload of pinecones from my yard and a handful of pine needles. We'll build something new."

She couldn't resist. Spontaneously, she nodded and breathed in, remembering the sweet, piney smells. Later they built their own miniature woods made of pinecones, while he recited the Laws.

"Be pleasant. Don't go near the woods. Don't even look at the woods. Be loyal to the Township in every way, and today will be a perfect day." He paused and eyed her intensely. "The first day of every week your helper will insist *you* say them. And the tasks motto, too. *Loyalty is our highest goal and safety is our greatest strength.*"

The Laws were on Para Madeline's mind, too. The Township expected her to prepare her junior for errand-going, but it was too late. *Jewel is just too difficult,* she reasoned with herself. Yes, that was what she could tell Para Philip when Jewel got in trouble. Still, Para Madeline couldn't shake the nervous feeling she had about it. She was so nervous she thought she would explode. One day she eased the door open just a crack and heard Samuri reciting the Laws. Oh, was Para Madeline pleased with herself. Hadn't she known the first day she met Samuri that this was going to work out perfectly? Yes, of course she had.

Next, Samuri began teaching Jewel the more detailed Laws of Loyalty.

"We keep our eyes down. We are quiet except for greetings and answering questions. We look at Directors when they talk to us. We give our bungalow number, not our name. And, Jewel— *both of us* especially need to remember this one." He gave her an insistent look, then continued. "Your story is your story, and their story is their story. Sharing stories makes trouble for everyone. So don't listen and don't tell. Keep the Township safe."

"O-kay," Jewel piped in quickly, then jumped up. "Hey, let's race. Ten, oh, ten. I'm going to be a ten!" Jewel popped the words in proud whispers, like a rhyme, again and again.

What was Samuri supposed to do with her? Why did she have to be such a tiny? He wished she would grow up. Oh well, at least there were two and a half weeks left. He jumped up and ran with her, careful to stay where no one could see them. Every moment, he listened and watched for unexpected trouble. He must be safe, for Jewel and for his paras.

Each day he made her listen to his recitations, and a week later she joined along, pretending she was the leader of some lost township of woods folks.

"Oh, and the woods—" He stopped midsentence, not wanting to tell her, not knowing how.

He dove right into a story, a mild one at first, explaining she must act like she was listening, and she must not argue about the woods. Then he told her a horrid story but assured her it wasn't true. Secrets made Jewel come alive, and that was a good thing.

"Is it okay if I act afraid?" Her eyes darted back and forth mysteriously, then she giggled.

"I don't know. Not too much or they might figure it out. This is *serious* stuff. Listen, Jewel, most important of all . . . He paused, waiting for her to get serious. "No one can know about you and me. Okay? No one!!"

By Celebration Day, Jewel was ready. She knew the Laws and the warnings perfectly. She understood errand-going and was excited to begin. But the first week was a big disappointment compared to what she imagined it would be. Still, she managed to do okay.

The second day of the second week she returned to her bungalow, gulped down her midday snack, and ran out to wait for Samuri. Flopping down on the ground she stared up at the tall towers of white clouds, biting the inside of her lip, nervously.

"Ri? I mean . . . Samuri." She blew a big puff of air out, exasperated. "How could you ever like errand-going? How do you remember? Every day I forget something on my para's list." She did not tell him about Para Madeline changing the list three

70

to four times every morning.

"What do they say?" He was truly curious.

"They were pleasant until today. Uff!" Jewel's words raced out of her mouth. "Today . . . today I was disloyal." Her shoulders drooped and she dropped her head in defeat, unable to find words for what she felt.

It was embarrassing to admit she'd overslept, and her para had completely forgotten until the helper arrived. Her finger reached to touch the scab on her head where her para nicked her skin, rushing to shave her. A wave of insecurity mixed with anger washed over her as she thought of Para Madeline's fearful threat of the Township inspecting their bungalow if they saw that nick.

Jewel shook the whole way to the Exchange. She wore the hat Para Madeline insisted would hide the tiny scrap of cloth plastered to the nick, but the hat kept slipping. The helper, mad at being late, told her a terrifying woods story, even though it was the wrong day for it. By the time they reached the Exchange, Jewel had forgotten the list completely.

"You really need to listen better," the well-meaning clerk said kindly, suggesting they go back to bungalow seventy and try again.

That was when Jewel blew up.

"No! You can't make me!" She shouted angrily, with an ugly scrunched up face and clenched fists.

This shockingly disloyal behavior stunned the clerk and the helper. The dull-minded littles they could deal with, but this was unthinkable.

Jewel ended up in a back room, where the Director warned her that she would be sent home for a week the next time this happened. During that week, a gran para would come to her bungalow and . . . That was all Jewel heard. Panic seized her as Para Madeline's threats about gran paras echoed through her mind.

Right before she lost it completely, the oddest thing happened. A picture of a bug hiding under a rock came to mind. And with it came the idea that she, like the bug, must hide. But how?

Wobbly, but sweet words tumbled out of her trembling lips, "Pleasant . . . ness to all, and l-l-l-l . . . loyalty to the T-t-t . . . Township."

"Well, that's better." The Director sighed. "Let me think about what the Township would do with this."

A tall, perky young leaned in just then to get an order for the Big Bungalow. "Greetings. Pleasantness to each, and loyalty to the Township."

The Director looked especially glad to see him. She welcomed him to come in and wait a moment. One look at Jewel, shaky and pale, with a cut peeking out from under her crooked hat, and he asked tenderly. "She's so small, can't you let it go this time?"

"Sure, Young Tuckit. If that's what you think Town Master Cree would want us to do." The Director smiled in relief.

Young Tuckit sent Jewel's helper for a cup of water and a few strawberries. Then he knelt down at eye level with Jewel. "Try this," his kind, strong voice urged her. "Close your eyes . . . and try to hear what your para asked for."

Jewel tried, but instead of words, the feelings behind Madeline's words rushed in. Young Tuckit saw a shadow cross Jewel's face. The two sat together while she finished the berries, and Jewel's courage slowly grew, and with it, an idea.

What does Para Madeline like to get? I'll make up a list and get my helper to leave before Para Madeline checks my bag.

The scheme had worked, but she could not tell Samuri. Her embarrassment made her mad at Samuri for no reason. He sat there quietly, with a blank look on his face, wondering why she seemed out of sorts with him.

Suddenly she was sorry. "Ooo. Look," she exclaimed, pointing up, trying to distract him from the awful story. "It's a tree-giant stomping across the sky."

Samuri was tempted to ignore her, but he looked, and it was amazing. Her heart was asking him, "Friends?" even though her mind didn't know how to.

"Guess what I just remembered, Jewel? Since you're a ten we can go to Loyalty Park. Do you want to?"

"Sure," she chirped excitedly. "But what is it?"

Loyalty Park was Town Master Cree's solution for helping tens and elevens get in shape after years of being shut inside with nothing to do. Fearful, friendless, overwhelmed paras ignored their tinys, littles, and juniors, barely teaching them the Laws. Tens were coming to errand-going lethargic, weak, and dull. The Loyalty Park would shape them up.

"My para said yes," a triumphant Jewel greeted Samuri the next day.

"Okay. Count ten of my steps and then follow me."

"Huh-uh." She shook her head at him, pouting. "We walk together, or I don't go."

"It's different outside our yards, Jewel." Samuri made it sound perfectly reasonable. "No talking. No walking together. But you'll like Loyalty Park." He raised his eyebrows, nodding quickly. "And if you don't, we won't go again."

She nodded, obviously pleased, and followed when Samuri led her past the Township Square, and then north behind the Exchange. Loyalty Park was just ahead beyond the three bungalows on the side path. The long, high balance beam caught her eye first. That looked fun!

Suddenly a rush of movement startled her. It was Daro, a junior the same year as Samuri, but taller and broader. His shifty eyes and haughty up-turned chin mockingly demanded her attention. He'd seen Jewel from the doorstep of his bungalow near the park and felt determined to make her notice him. He'd never seen anyone like her. She walked lightly, popping up a bit on her toes with each step, trailing her fingers behind her as if she were wading in a shallow stream. Her eyes were down, as they should be, but she glanced up often. It seemed to Daro she was seeing something others did not see.

"Where do you think you're going?!" he challenged her with a smirky smile and an unspoken dare in his voice.

Then he stepped beside her, touching her foot with his toe, and threw himself on the path in front of her, screaming. Every supervisor at the park turned to look.

Daro stayed down, rolling back and forth clutching his knee, a drop of blood beading up on his trousers. Jewel stepped over him, speechlessly mad, hoping to escape from this crazy junior. Samuri was moving toward her when two of the supervisors passed him. One commanded him to wait in the park, while the other began scolding Jewel harshly.

"Oh . . ." Daro's voice was an odd mixture of pain and syrupy sympathy. "I don't think she meant to hurt me when she tripped me." He flashed his most genuine, kind smile at them.

The supervisor demanded Jewel give them her information, but she was not about to tell them her bungalow number in front of this junior.

"Pleasantness to each," Daro's smooth voice droned. "I think she's a new ten. Scared, you know? Can you let it go this time? After all, accidents happen."

His false pity made Jewel angrier, but just as she was about to shout out the whole story, she was given an unexpected choice.

"Pleasantness." The supervisor nodded sweetly toward Daro. Then she addressed Jewel with an edgy voice. "Fair enough, little. You're wise not to give out information." She looked at Daro again. "For his sake, we'll let you off easy. Here's your choices. One: If you bow and greet him, we'll let you stay. Two: You go to the Director of Tasks for making trouble."

Jewel was trapped. She detested both choices, but she had the sense to know anything was better than trouble. Her greeting was lame, but the supervisor accepted it because of Daro. The helper took Daro to get his knee checked and the supervisor walked

Jewel to the park.

"These are the Loyalty Park rules," the supervisor explained. "Greet. Nod. Eyes down. No talking."

Jewel was miserable, but she repeated the rules seriously, like she should. Soon she was scampering about happily on the equipment. When all the helpers had their backs to him, Samuri motioned for Jewel to leave. Once she reached the main path, he left nonchalantly, avoiding being noticed.

They tried Loyalty Park one more time, and Daro was outside again, watching Jewel every step of the way.

"You owe me," he accused her. The creepy sound in his voice trapped Jewel in a spiral of unsafe feelings, despite the fact that Samuri was ten steps behind her.

"Interesting you two arrive at the park together again," Daro taunted as Samuri passed. "What would the Officials think of that?"

Was he going to turn them in? Could a junior do that? Or was his para an official? Samuri didn't know those Laws of Loyalty and it wasn't worth the risk. Besides, they'd rather spend their times together talking and laughing. Soon enough, growing up would take even that away from them.

8
tasks and troubles

Jewel stood on the north end of Samuri's bungalow waiting. The sun dipped toward the horizon and the air grew chillier every moment. She kicked a cloud of dirt in the air angrily. Another day without seeing the "loyal" junior Samuri. Supposedly, the Exchange kept him so long because, in his words, there was a shortage of loyal help.

"Loyal?" she asked him, holding back a laugh. "That's funny. Look at us hiding over here like a couple of bugs behind a rock, breaking the Laws to see each other, sharing our stories. Loyal?"

"We're not disloyal, Jewel. It's a bungalow thing. Bungalows are different, and it's okay as long as we keep it here and keep it to ourselves. Just like stories." His earnest and unwavering voice matched the way his eyes met hers, clear and calm. He believed what he said. There was no deceit in him, not in his voice, not in his heart.

After that, she thought about it each day when she waited for him. She wanted to believe he was right. He always had been, but lately she wondered if they were being too daring and bold. What if they were headed for trouble?

Just then, she saw him leave the path and come around the corner, walking straight toward her.

"I have to go," Jewel said. "I told Para Madeline I'd scrub floors before last-snack today."

Samuri's head dropped and he sighed long and wearily. "The Director of Tasks found out I'm at the Exchange. I was supposed to be on crews all along. They've promoted someone new to be the Director of the Exchange. Tomorrow, they're assigning me to a crew of twelves." Then, his eyes brightened, and he looked as if he were finally seeing her. "Maybe I can start meeting you again. I'll try. Best and worst?"

"No, not today. I have to go. I'll try tomorrow, too. Get some sleep. Okay?" Her voice was kind, even hopeful. The anger in her heart had fled at the sound of exhaustion in his voice. She wasn't actually mad at him; she was mad at the Township. And worried.

Five afternoons later, Samuri still hadn't come. The Township Officials had insisted twelves do tasks more loyally and for longer hours. This year's thirteens and fourteens were practically useless at their tasks. The Officials were determined to change that before Samuri's group of twelves became youngs. But of course, Jewel didn't know that.

The minute she opened the door, her para pulled her aside.

"My nerves can't take anymore of hiding this from Para Philip," Para Madeline scolded in a distraught, accusing voice. "No more wasting time outside. And that's that! How did you talk me into this in the first place?"

The next morning, loneliness and disappointment clung to Jewel like a blanket she could not untangle herself from. Even the fresh air and brilliant blue sky could not cheer her.

Her task crew of juniors this week had been cleaning yards. Jewel was assigned to clean rocks and sticks away while another junior came two meters behind her to even out the dirt. Each time she reached the far end of a yard, Jewel was expected to wait silently, eyes to the ground, until the junior with the rake was finished.

She is so slow, Jewel complained silently, willing herself not to turn and look. *I'd like to rake. I bet we'd be caught up if I did.*

Poof. She heard the rake drop in the dust behind her. The raker stood there rubbing the palms of her hands, looking mournful.

"Slogger," Jewel muttered, turning to look. She had no patience with lazy, weak juniors. Before she knew it, the rake was in her own hands, swiftly smoothing out an overlooked patch of dirt.

"Junior! What are you doing?" the supervisor called out, striding quickly toward them.

Jewel assumed the supervisor was talking to the other junior and continued to rake. The powerful sensation of breaking through the crusty dirt and the faint piney scent rising from the dust overtook Jewel. She was unaware of anything happening until a hand much larger than hers snatched the rake away from her.

"I . . . I . . ." Jewel paused, trying to piece her thoughts together. Taking a deep breath like Samuri had taught her, she began again. "Pleasantness . . ." but the supervisor interrupted.

"Pleasantness? Seriously, Junior, that was the farthest thing from pleasantness. What are you thinking?"

"You see, I was being loyal. I—"

"Loyal? Do you know the Laws of Loyalty? Obviously, you don't. No speaking unless you are asked to speak, and—"

"You did ask. You—"

The supervisor did not take Jewel's challenge well. The raker was allowed to tell her story. She admitted she had dropped the rake, though only for a second, and when she went to pick it up this other junior called her a slogger and grabbed the rake right out of her hands.

The supervisor and his helper commanded Jewel to wait, head down, eyes on the ground, with her fingers interlocked over the back of her head. They stepped aside to discuss the situation privately. They decided against taking her to the Director of Tasks and gave her a yellow flag for the rest of that day instead. They would mention it in their report. A messenger passing by was ordered to escort Jewel to her bungalow.

This dull messenger explained the situation as if it didn't matter much. "Your junior was a bit unpleasant on the task crew today. The supervising apprentice recommends you review the Laws of Loyalty this afternoon and send your junior again tomorrow." Then he left with no thought of the yellow flag.

Para Madeline's sweet smile disappeared as the door clicked shut. She fussed horribly without any mention of the Laws and failed to ask Jewel what happened. By midday snack Para Madeline had completely forgotten it.

Jewel hadn't though. Anger weighed her down until late that night. Was there a way to sneak out and talk to Samuri? No, that could get them both in trouble. *Uff!*

The next day the supervisor watched how hard Jewel worked and added that to his report. The supervisors the next week let Jewel rake and were so pleased with her that they let her rake all week.

But trouble wasn't far away. On the third day of the ninth week, she glimpsed a pair of rust-colored trousers standing too close. Before she could peek to see who it was, she heard a familiar voice sneer at her quietly. "You still owe me."

Daro was on her task crew.

The first few days Daro concentrated on impressing the supervisors like usual. The last day, when the supervisors weren't looking, he hurled a dirt clod, hitting the junior in front of Jewel hard. The junior shrieked, grabbed his leg, and fell over. Daro humbly walked over to the supervisors and whispered politely, telling them Jewel had done it. That was how Jewel was given her second yellow flag. But Para Philip never found out about that either because Jewel dragged a stool onto the doorstep and took the flag down.

Now, not only was her sleep troubled, but Jewel began dreaming of strange dark shapes in her room pressing against her cot.

A stern voice announced, "A yellow flag for the junior from bungalow seventy."

A sneering voice joined it, echoing over and over, "You owe me."

Other voices pressed against her taunting louder and louder. "Unsafe, UnSafe, UNSAFE!"

A scream arose in her throat, but before it could escape, she woke up, pushed her pillow against her face and scrunched into a tight ball, with the blanket pulled over her head.

"Ri? I need someone to talk to," Jewel whispered into her pillow. "Could you come over? Help me, Ri. Help me." With her face turned toward the window, Jewel listened for the reply she knew would never come.

However, some kind voice deep in her memory called to her reassuringly.

"Here Jewel, you can come help *me*. It's safe here."

Who was it? Jewel searched her memory and caught a glimpse of the beautiful, brave para from her fanciful treehouse stories. The gentle voice carried her away from her dark dreams into the breeze-blown treetops where she slept safely until the light of daystart.

What a relief it was to be reassigned after that week! Jewel focused on her tasks with increased effort, repeating the Laws of Loyalty to herself throughout the day. She basked in the comfort of the Warm Weeks unaware the Brave Days were only weeks away. What would comfort her then?

Samuri breezed through his tasks those Warm Weeks, gaining favor with the supervisors on every task crew, without even trying. Some evenings he played Jewel's game "Pebbles & Pinecones" with his paras. Other nights he stretched out on the floor, dozing on and off, comforted by the murmur of his paras' voices and the pungent scent of the pines mixing together. At lights out he woke and went outside to return the pebbles and pinecones. The shimmering stars reminded Samuri how he and Jewel had laughed a lot about nothing. The dark beyond the stars whispered wild stories about living in the woods and cloud jumping and baskets at the Exchange coming alive after dark. He missed Jewel so bad it hurt. And her stories. Her stories had been a safe place to get lost in, promises of a better place and better life.

"Samuri, what 'cha doing out there?" Para Patrick's hushed voice floated through the moonless dark.

"Para Patrick," Samuri felt his para's arm come across his shoulder. "Remember when I found Jewel, and you said a friend was a good thing?'" His voice was strained. "Well, I want to be loyal to the Township and I want to be friends with Jewel, but . . . I don't know how."

Patrick stared into the vast dark of the woods. He knew what he believed. He knew what he wanted but the Laws stood in the way of it, and he couldn't see a way out. How much did he dare say to Samuri now? Or ever? What was best for Samuri? Or had he and Para Chloe already ruined that?

"I do remember, Samuri, and those are good thoughts. Give me time to think about it. Okay?"

One afternoon at the end of the Warm Weeks, the sky grew angry, and the wind picked up. Messengers dismissed task crews early so the Officials could meet with the supervisors to plan. They hadn't expected a storm this soon.

Littles, juniors, and youngs bumped into each other, dust stinging their eyes in their rush to get out of the wind. Samuri took his time, head down, searching out of the corner of his eye for rust-colored trousers in the blur of passing legs. The crowd thinned, so he risked a glance ahead of him, and there she was. Samuri changed his pace and got within two meters of Jewel before he forced a strong whisper. "Bug!"

Instead of looking up Jewel bug-poked the side of her leg and walked briskly until she passed her doorstep. "Quick," she whispered. "Best and worst?"

"Best: lots of new things. Worst: not seeing you. And yours?"

"Best: being outside. Worst: when Daro was on my crew. Uff. And of course, never seeing YOU."

The frantic wind whipped the flags at the bottom of the door around wildly, and Jewel burst out disgustedly, "I have to go in."

Then she poked Samuri in the arm and disappeared. It was the last time they would talk that year.

A season of Brave Days, worse than ever before, hit that night. Task crews younger than twelves were kept inside, and twelves were in high demand. The supervisors of the twelves relied heavily on Samuri aware he would do his best without complaining. Four weeks into the threatening weather, his crew was assigned to water yards. It was usually a warm weather job, but this wind was scattering the dirt, swirling it through the air and into bothersome heaps and piles. Samuri pulled his thick stocking hat tightly over his ears as he waited by the Yards Shop for instructions.

"Junior with the nice hat, grab that hose. And you, too." The supervisor commanded, pointing.

Samuri grabbed a section of hose, stood up and found himself face to face with Daro.

Wait, was Daro an eleven or a twelve?

"You two take turns at the nozzle," the supervisor growled. "When you start to get wet, switch. The rest of the crew will take turns pumping."

When it was time for Daro's second turn at the nozzle, he walked forward, glaring at Samuri, then grabbed the hose and tripped. Water sprayed everywhere, especially on Samuri, as Daro fell to the ground crying out for help. Finally, Daro limped to the side groaning, and Samuri was told to take another turn at the nozzle.

"Brave on, loyal twelve. Or are you okay with a red flag today?" the rough supervisor taunted him. "Situations like this are perfect preparation to become a loyal young. May the Township grant you the tasks you request."

To keep moving is to keep warm, to keep moving is to keep warm, Samuri reminded himself repeatedly, pushing aside the bitterness he felt toward the supervisor and Daro.

At the end of the hourglass, the supervisor gave up, sent the twelves to their bungalows, and headed to report "unsafe" conditions. The wind whipped around them so hard they stumbled away thinking only of themselves. Samuri sunk numbly to the ground, finding it difficult to understand or to move. A para from the Yards Shop noticed the others leaving, came to gather the hose, and found Samuri on the ground, sopping wet and shaking. Putting his arms under Samuri's shoulders, he lifted him up. Samuri's face reminded him of a kind-hearted Director he'd worked with when he was an apprentice at the Hydroponic Greenhouse.

"Not sure what to do with you," he said, and as he settled Samuri over his shoulder, tenderly, he heard Samuri mumble, "Bungalow seventy-six."

The para told Para Chloe how he had found Samuri, and carefully eased him onto his cot.

"I'm sure I've done tasks with your para," he said. "He's about the most loyal and pleasant folk I've met, but the Township is tricky, so I'd like to keep my part in this between us three. Pleasantness." The respect in his voice was evident as he said farewell.

Chloe worked fast to pull Samuri's wet hat, shoes, and socks off. Then she struggled with his jacket and trousers, rolling

Samuri first to one side then to the other, while he lay limp and shivering.

"Oh, Samuri. I'm chilled just helping you. Talk to me. How did this happen?" The disbelief in Chloe's voice was answered with multiple moans and the chattering of teeth. Was it that Samuri could not speak or that he could not even hear her? Then he lapsed into what seemed an unconscious silence.

The next hour was a rush of frantic activity. Para Chloe dried Samuri off the best she could, rolling him back and forth to remove the damp blanket beneath him and cover him with the only extra blanket they had. Panic fought to have its way with her, but Para Chole knew a calm touch was her strongest weapon now. She began the long task of massaging Samuri's hands, face, and feet, but even then, warmth stubbornly refused to return to Samuri's body. Finally, she went out and slid the yellow flag up.

"Don't avoid us. You *have* to come this time," she urged the distant messengers. "Remember your pledge. A long, safe life to us *all*."

Para Patrick was surprised to see the *thick* smoke rising from their heat pipe when he approached their bungalow. Inside by the heat box, he found the stack of dead branches Chloe had gathered from the woods. The bungalow was toasty warm and a bit smoky. An unfamiliar-smelling liquid simmered slowly in the pan on top of the heat box.

Before he could say anything, Chloe burst out, scolding him as she stirred the hot liquid. "Don't ask! I'm busy. I'm angry. And I'm scared. The liquid is a tincture of echinacea. Fortunately, I keep dried echinacea flowers hidden under a board in the snack cupboard. Samuri has a terrible fever, and he can't seem to speak. He just tosses on his cot moaning."

The following days were a nightmare. The wind howled, and a driving rain beat against the side of the bungalow. Para Chloe was up all night the first night, keeping the fever manageable. Samuri seemed oblivious to the cool, wet cloth on his forehead and the drops of echinacea placed under his tongue. The second

84

night, Para Patrick sent Para Chloe to bed. What would he do if Chloe got run-down and caught whatever Samuri had?

Even Chloe's most complicated instruction received Patrick's careful attention. Throughout the weary night he kept himself alert by talking to Samuri.

"You have many things yet to do in your life, Samuri. Be brave. And be true. You will do well, and you will have help." Patrick spoke the words slowly and with loving conviction, willing Samuri to respond. "Even when Para Chloe and I cannot be with you, you will always have help."

Tangled thoughts questioned Patrick as he gazed at Samuri's lack of response. Would Samuri always have help? Even without them? Para Patrick hoped with all his heart it was true.

No messenger had come by the third morning, so they slid the flag down. It would be best to be left alone now. Chloe had broken enough Laws of Loyalty to bring much trouble to their bungalow. So, they continued to treat Samuri, waiting, and hoping for some response, hurting with every rough cough that tore through his chest. Finally, in the pounding rain and the dim gray light of the fourth morning, Samuri spoke.

"Bra-a-v-e o-n-n," his hoarse voice mumbled weakly to no one in particular. "M-y-y mi-i-d-da-ay snack?"

Could he sense their presence? Was he asking them specifically or was he still in a semi-conscious state? Para Patrick stayed with him while Chloe ran to prepare something.

Patrick supported Samuri's limp shoulders and head, while Chloe spooned drops of a thin potato paste into his mouth. First Samuri mouthed the paste reluctantly, but then as if his tongue finally remembered, he swallowed and opened his mouth for more. A tear ran down Chloe's cheek and then she laughed. It wasn't much, but it was a start. Patrick was out the door seconds after throwing his warm clothes on and grabbing his day-start snack. He must get to the Tasks Bungalow early.

"Pleasantness to each and loyalty to the Township. I'm the para from bungalow seventy-six reporting our twelve is extremely ill," Para Patrick told the Director of Tasks.

"I know you, Para Patrick." The Director's voice was serious, but his eyes held a spark of appreciation. "Do whatever you have to. I'll order a free pass for you at the Exchange. I hope your junior recovers." The Director waved him away sadly. "There'll be no questions asked of you. There are already too many sick folks this week."

Para Patrick bowed low and headed to the Hydroponic Greenhouse, his heart full of thanks.

Most folks were back to their tasks by the last day of the next week. Samuri took twice that long to gain enough strength to be up at all. Town Master Cree discovered Para Chloe's special order was late *because* her junior was ill. He sent a messenger to the Director of Tasks immediately. The junior from bungalow seventy-six was not to be assigned any tasks until his health had returned fully.

Samuri's paras kept him inside until the breezes were warm, and he was his strong, bored self, again.

9
red flag

The air everywhere shouted "Sunshine!" Occasionally a few folks risked a glance upward to feel the warmth on their faces. The worst Brave Days of their lifetime was over. A handful of folks stumbled about in a fog, unable to cope with the tragedies they had endured, but everyone else moved on loyally.

Town Master Cree requested for the junior from bungalow seventy-six to be reassigned to the Exchange until after Celebration Day. Paras Chloe and Patrick were beyond grateful, not wanting Samuri to overwork until he was undoubtedly recovered. Samuri felt mixed. He preferred tasks outside, *and* he had worked at the Exchange far too much as an eleven. However, Town Master had told the Director to give Samuri "light" work until after Celebration Day. Could he finish on time and see Jewel some days? That would be more than worth it.

Instead, Samuri rarely saw daylight and never saw Jewel. The Exchange was a mess. In the months since Samuri had left, the tally sheets were badly neglected. On top of that, the Exchange was sending out the first full crew of messengers since before the storm. Each messenger returned several times a day with large orders to be filled and piles of handcrafted products to be counted and shelved. The new Director had heard what Samuri was capable of and was determined to catch up before Samuri was reassigned.

Each morning and through his midday snack, Samuri tallied the orders from individual bungalows. After midday snack, he added their incoming products to their tally sheets. When he finished with that, he did general inventory and stocked shelves. There was no end to Samuri's tasks.

The last day of the second week he overheard a messenger whisper that Celebration Day preparation was to be announced in the morning. Samuri was determined to tell Jewel himself.

If I have to, Samuri decided, *I will knock on Jewel's door.* It was a bold move, but Samuri was past caring about whether he got in trouble.

Jewel's task crew was cleaning and sweeping paths. The farther east they went the slower the other juniors worked. Jewel swept ahead pleasantly, breathing in the fresh air, loving the breeze tickling in her ear, glancing up now and then to mark her progress. Suddenly a movement by the woods caught her eye, and she shouted, "Look! Oh, look . . . !" as a dozen small flying creatures burst out of the treetops and pumped powerfully into the sky. She had never seen anything like it.

The excitement in her voice was irresistible. Juniors and supervisors alike followed her outstretched arm, only to drop their gaze to the ground again immediately. How dare she! The supervisors acted on it immediately.

"Red flag. You take her," the smaller supervisor demanded.

Within five minutes Jewel was standing in front of the Director's desk in the Tasks Bungalow.

"Greetings, Junior. I'm the Director of Tasks. Sounds like you're in trouble." He spoke seriously, but not unpleasantly, noticing how small and thin she was for a junior.

Despite her fluttering heart, Jewel remembered Samuri's years of advice and looked straight in the Director's eyes. "Pleasantness to each, loyalty to the Township, and a safe, long life for us all," she said.

"Pleasant, indeed. You sound reasonable enough. Maybe this won't be so bad. The Township Secretary is down the hall in the first door on the left. Talk to her, and then I'll join you. Eyes down now."

Secretary? What was a secretary? Jewel had never heard of it. Keeping her shoulders straight and walking quietly, she entered the room only to find a thick, tan screen that hid everything except the high window.

"Are you there?" an older, husky she-voice drawled. "And if so, what is your bungalow number?"

"Greetings . . ." The initial uncertainty in Jewel's voice was obvious. "I'm the junior from bungalow seventy." It felt odd talking to a voice behind a screen.

"Hmm? Now where is that?" Jewel heard a rustling like the tally sheets at the Exchange. "Ah . . . oh my! So, this is your fourth incident this year. That's against you. Ah, but only two were yellow flags." The voice brightened up. "Hmm, it is the first incident involving shouting or the woods, and *that* is good. So, tell me. Why did you shout?"

How could tally marks tell all that? Jewel wanted to ask if the secretary had all the records memorized, but her own answer was obviously more important. *Oh, help*, she thought to no one in particular, and then it came to her. Jewel told the truth, briefly, also pointing out that she hadn't meant to break any of the Laws. The secretary, an older she-para named Nyah, listened without interrupting and made a few scratching sounds.

The beauty of Jewel's storytelling touched the secretary's heart, and she replied with warmth and sympathy. "You seem like a pleasant junior—pleasant *and* honest, I think. I do hope you can be more loyal."

A bell tinkled behind the screen, calling for the Director.

"This is her fourth incident since last Celebration Day." The Secretary was sorry to have to say so, but she must. "It is a three-fold breach of loyalty. One, looking at the woods. Two, shouting. Three, encouraging others to look. After the supervisor's report today, I'll inform you if there is more, but I think not."

A messenger took Jewel from there to a small back room in the Exchange, where she sat at the rough table gulping down her first water of that day. Jewel did not know Samuri's tasks were at the Exchange now. Samuri had no way of knowing Jewel sat behind the closed door as he passed back and forth. The two friends were only meters apart but still with no hope of seeing each other.

Jewel fidgeted and fretted, thinking about her consequences. The low drawl of the secretary's voice wove in and out of Jewel's worries. Such a different voice and so kind. If only her paras would see her situation how the secretary seemed to see it.

At that exact moment, Para Philip was receiving a generic message to go to the Director of Tasks when possible. And a messenger was on her way to raise the red flag at bungalow seventy.

A clerk brought Jewel more water and an old snack bar for her midday snack. Then Jewel curled her feet under her knees on the chair, ate, and fell fast asleep with her head on the table.

Suddenly—or it seemed sudden to her—Para Philip was there. He'd left his tasks as soon as possible, confident he was about to receive the promotion he had requested. The news about the red flag was like a slap in the face.

They walked along the sunny path, Jewel ten steps in front of her para. There was an entire hourglass before the first shift of tasks would end. Suddenly, Para Philip let out a slow, loud breath of exasperation. There it was, the red flag, waving threateningly in the midafternoon sunshine.

Para Philip entered as quietly as he could and tried to question Jewel without disturbing Para Madeline. But when he burst out in frustration, "The *fourth time* since last Celebration Day? Seriously, Jewel?"

Para Madeline came rushing out. "*What* is going on?" she demanded to know.

Philip told her what happened. At the mention of the red flag Para Madeline threw her arms up in the air and insisted in a weary voice that Philip take care of it himself. Para Philip pointed Jewel toward the wall of the gathering room, where she stood listening respectfully, shoulders straight, head bowed, as he explained.

"No tasks for a week. During that time, you're to think over the seriousness of your repetitive unpleasantness and disloyalty. The fact that my tasks are at the Complex does not give you any special privileges. Next week a supervisor will be sent to question you. You must be ready to admit your disloyalty and to pledge to be a *completely* loyal junior from now on. Then and only then will you be allowed to return to a task crew. This is how I deal with the minor disloyalty of folks of all ages."

Jewel quietly sucked in her breath. So that was what her para did. She had never realized the importance of his position at the Complex.

"Look up, Jewel. I want to see that you are listening."

Jewel's eyes were piercing and serious, hiding how maddening it was to have folks make such a fuss over a few beautiful creatures.

Para Philip was startled by the depth and beauty of Jewel's eyes. Had they always been so gorgeous? Luminous? How had he not noticed?

"One thing, Jewel . . ." Para Philip asked. "Exactly what happened?" He tried to put his disappointment aside, wanting to trust her.

Jewel was surprised by the question. Could she hope that he cared? Cautiously, yet in the only way she knew, she retold the story. The wonder of how it appeared to her poured out, until, forgetting herself, she asked breathlessly, "What are they, Para Philip? Do *you* know?"

Philip paused, trying to pull his thoughts together, stirred by her beautiful retelling of the morning.

Para Madeline stomped in, accusation in her voice. "Surely, you are *not* going to tell her! Or have *you* forgotten the Laws of Loyalty, *Para* Philip, Officer of Corrections?"

A sly look rose in Para Madeline's eyes. "Go to your room, Jewel." It was the tone of voice Jewel feared most. Revenge hidden behind a calm, syrupy pleasantness. "No last snack. No warming stone. Your trouble costs us points at the Exchange. Less points. Less food. Less fuel."

"You can't, you—" Jewel burst out clenching her fists in a surge of anger and renewed energy.

Para Philip shrugged and shuffled toward the door to return to the Complex and complete his daily reports. No promotion this time, if ever.

Madeline locked eyes with Jewel, daring her to fight, but Jewel stomped off to her room and slammed the door. She threw herself on her cot and schemed how to get back at her para.

She doesn't care. She never has. She is so, so . . . Jewel fumed to herself, holding back a barrage of accusations too awful to speak. Both hands flew to her face and pressed hard against her mouth, willing herself not to scream.

Back at the Exchange, Samuri was shoving hard on the side door, pushing out into the dim, fading afternoon light. The air was chilly. If only he could have one minute with Jewel, even just one. Walking, head down, he rehearsed each step in his mind. I'll knock like I used to, and say "Greetings Para, can your junior come out for a moment?"

It felt flat. Where was the boldness he'd felt the first time he had knocked on that door? Five more steps to her door and then . . .

Samuri glanced up. The red flag caught his eye, mocking him. He kicked the doorstep, muttering against the Township under his breath, and moved on. When would he see her?

By the time Para Philip returned, the sun had slipped away behind him, and Jewel had made her plan. She would sneak to the heat box after they were asleep. They couldn't stop what they couldn't see. Even wrapped in her thin blanket, the chilly drafts and her hungry stomach tormented her. How long until her paras would sleep? Gradually Jewel's anger gave way to defeat, her eyelids grew heavy, and she slipped into a restless sleep of nightmarish dreams.

In the middle of the night a loud shout broke into her dreams, commanding them to stop. It was Samuri. At the sound, the menacing dream disappeared, and she woke sweaty and shivering with cold and fright. The loud snores she heard at the end of the hall reminded her of her plan and she slipped quietly off her cot, wrapped in her flimsy blanket. Without a sound she slid her door open, and settled herself nervously by the heat box, thinking of the after-dark Laws of Loyalty.

It's not unsafe to be out of my room in the dark. It's just laws for tinys and littles.

Still, she sat straight and tense against the wall, nervously peering through the dim room for any sign of her paras. The snoring faded and the dreamy warmth of the heat box enveloped her. Bit by bit she slid down the wall, until she gave in completely and curled up on the floor, fast asleep.

Para Philip found her there shortly before daystart. Lifting her gently so as not to wake her, he returned her to her cot. He was alarmed to discover how light and thin she was. Her baggy tunic and trousers disguised her small, underfed frame. He wished Madeline would stop withholding food from Jewel. Surely there were better ways to teach littles and juniors, but once Madeline got an idea, there was no peace until she got her way. Grabbing his daystart snack, he broke it in two and laid part of it under Jewel's pillow.

"Those are birds, Jewel," he whispered tenderly. "probably wrens, but not helpful for you to know." He pulled the blanket up and tucked it under her chin.

Moments later, the aroma of the snack teased Jewel awake. Lying in the dim light of daystart, she drifted in and out of sleep, her soft eyelashes fluttering open and closed. She was warm, and there was a snack under her pillow. A moist, sweet snack bar that melted in her mouth almost like cookies. Mmm, this must be a dream. She must hurry and eat this snack before the dream could end. Had she dreamt of the heat box, too?

Still too sleepy to figure it out, she dozed off until she heard the sound of the messengers shouting, "Twenty-one days to prepare for Celebration Day!" The thought of it cheered her until she woke fully. *Not me, though,* she thought to herself. *The red flag changes everything.*

The second morning her cot was toasty warm, and another

mouthwatering snack lay near her pillow. Had Ri found a way to sneak in? No, that couldn't be it. Then, what? The third day, Jewel woke in the dark and forced herself to stay awake. When she heard Para Philip rustling in the snack corner, she closed her eyes, and breathed as naturally as she could. After Para Philip left the snack and pulled the warming stone out of her covers, she peeked. It wasn't a dream; it was her para, her very own Para Philip. Mixed thoughts wrestled in her mind. *What pleasantness! But why? Oh, please don't stop.*

That morning Jewel scrubbed every floor in the bungalow. The motion of pushing and pulling the stiff brush back and forth helped her plot what she could say when the official came. By the time she had finished the floors and cleaned every shelf, her answers were ready. And Para Madeline was so pleased with Jewel's cleaning she let Jewel help make cookies that day. Jewel paid close attention. Someday she would make her own daystart snacks, snacks that tasted like these, not the dry, bland snacks that Para Madeline gave *her* each day.

Samuri passed Jewel's bungalow unseen. In the evenings he talked to his paras about the red flag, but they didn't know any more than he did. How long would the red flag be up? Would the Township make her miss Celebration Day? And why did the Laws of Loyalty forbid talking to others about important matters?

The first evening of the next week Para Philip called Jewel out of her room. "An official is coming to question you tomorrow."

"I'm ready," she assured him, bowed, and returned to her room. There was no glimmer in her eyes tonight, only steely determination. In only one week she'd lost the look of the fanciful junior she'd been the week before.

Near dawn, she woke, anxiously rehearsing her answers. *I give you my word of loyalty I will never be distracted again. I will not talk unless I am called on. I will never shout. I have thought through the stories of the woods again. They are unsafe.* Here she would act as if a shudder of fear went through her body. *Even looking at them is unsafe. I remember that now, and I will be loyal to keep my eyes far from them.*

The last line wasn't true, but she would learn to be perfectly careful when she did look. *Perfectly careful.* She liked the sound of that.

In the dim light of the next day, her para brought her part of his snack one last time. This time she gazed up into his eyes and reached to squeeze his hand lightly before closing her eyes again. How she hoped he understood. Even if he didn't, Jewel must have some way, no matter how small, to show him she appreciated all he had done.

"Please try today, Jewel. Try with all you have." His whisper was so soft, she might have imagined it. She nodded and rolled over. The best thing she could give Para Philip was to convince the Township to lower the red flag, and she knew she would.

The supervisor came early, questioned her, and escorted her to new tasks. From the start, Jewel *was* perfectly careful. That day and every day after, she thought through each Law of Loyalty as she walked to tasks. Any time her thoughts threatened to run amuck, she bit the inside of her lip to prevent trouble from bursting out unexpectedly. Celebration Day was coming. *Ri,* she vowed silently, *I will do whatever it takes to be there when you become a young.* Some days it took biting her lip all day long, but she kept that promise.

The second day of the second week the red flag was down, and Samuri saw Jewel leaving her bungalow. She only acknowledged him with a polite Township nod and walked away as quickly as she could. Though it unsettled him, Samuri didn't doubt her friendship. But something was definitely wrong.

That night Samuri sat down, his heart weary with worries, and buried his face into Para Patrick's chest. Was a twelve too old to act like this? He hoped not. Samuri wasn't sure he could take it if Para Patrick pushed him away. His need for Para Patrick's strength felt as deep as it had when he was a tiny.

Para Patrick drew Ri closer and left his arm around him, sensing the importance and tenderness of that moment. Samuri's worries, questions, and anger flooded out in a torrent startling both of his paras. Where was the strong, calm junior they thought they knew? How long had Samuri been holding this inside?

When Samuri finished talking, the three of them sat absorbed in the weight of it for a quarter of an hourglass before Para Patrick spoke.

"Samuri, I will never break a Law of Loyalty simply because I don't like that Law." Patrick's voice was genuine, both kind and bold, as he spoke. "But what we do matters. So, I will always look for a way around any Law that steals the life we were created to have."

"Created?" Samuri asked. He may have heard them use that word once or twice, long ago, but he didn't remember why.

Para Chloe rushed in to explain. "Like when I make a new snack recipe."

Para Patrick gave her a slight shake of his head. Though he hoped to discuss that with Samuri before he was an apprentice, now was not the time.

Para Chloe arched her eyebrows and finished with a perky "... only different."

Samuri lightened up, grinning at her mention of their old motto of bungalows versus the Township. He smiled, thinking of Jewel, the woods, and all the secrets he and his paras shared with her. The memory of anxious messengers standing at the door eager to get away came to him.

Yes, different, Samuri thought. And he could be okay with that. He felt much better.

If only Patrick had stopped there. Instead, he added what he saw as the final help for understanding the Township.

"Remember, the Township's greatest strength is keeping us safe."

"Is it?" Samuri burst out with intense emotion. "Are we safer when we don't talk with the folks around us? Are we ..."

"I think it's ... complicated," his para broke in. "The most important thing is for the three of us to trust each other, no matter what."

Para Patrick enclosed Samuri in a strong hug, knowing his answer was not enough to satisfy Samuri's deep need.

Samuri pushed him away. "And what about Jewel? And our neighbors? Or Town Master Cree? Are we supposed to trust him? What is loyalty, Para Patrick? Maybe nothing matters. Maybe it's all meaningless words."

Tears sprang into Para Chloe's eyes. She turned to follow Samuri toward his cot, but Patrick pulled her back and snuffed out the gathering room candle.

"Let him go. It's better for him to face all this while he still has us."

Together they walked through the dark until they were kneeling under the stars outside of the task room. "Help him to be brave," Patrick began.

"Help him to stay true." The sadness in Chloe's voice gave way to determination. "Help him to find *you*."

Their prayers swelled and dipped. They needed help. Was it time to tell Samuri about the only one who could give this odd life purpose? When? And how?

10
welcome youngs

Samuri kicked the corner. *She's not coming,* he fumed.

He squinted at Jewel's bungalow, calculating the distance from the end of his bungalow. Could he pitch a pincconc and hit her window hard enough for her to hear it, but soft enough that her paras couldn't? He had to let her know he was there.

He imagined Jewel on her tiptoes, stretching her short, thin frame up to the high window to search for him. He drew his arm back to throw the pinecone but turned and threw it toward the woods at the last second. It was no use; Samuri knew the window was too high for her to see out.

"Don't worry, Jewel. I haven't given up," he mumbled under his breath.

Suddenly it hit him. Jewel would never fit in the Township's way of living. The red flag was just the beginning. She would always be in trouble, one way or another.

And then what? The urge to yell surged through his body, but he fought it. What if the Township sent her to the dorms early? What if he never saw Jewel again?

A wild, irrational plan came to Samuri.

I will burst into her paras' bungalow and catch them off guard. I'll grab Jewel's hand and we'll get far into the woods as fast as we can.

Samuri didn't think twice before he dashed toward Jewel's yard.

Ring-a-ting-a-ting. Ring-a-ting-ting. The messengers' bells rang out, calling folks to come to the Celebration Day. Samuri was too late.

Samuri walked mechanically toward the front of the Township Square, numb with the memories of that morning.

"Welcome new youngs!" Town Master Cree's clear and compelling voice jolted him back to the ceremony.

Samuri fought the urge to scan the crowd on the north where Jewel's paras typically sat. He fixed his eyes straight ahead and caught an unexpected glimpse of her. Why was she in the middle? Was she seated with a supervisor as punishment? Or was her para hiding her from him? He guarded his expression so no one would question it, but the joy of having her there changed everything.

The next morning, Samuri busied himself doing extra tasks for Para Chloe. Despite the struggle of the past weeks, he was curious what tasks the Township would give him. And . . . could a new assignment give him a chance to see Jewel again?

At least they'd seen each other last night. Jewel's eyes had been fixed on him waiting for that brief moment when he'd see her. She'd raised her eyebrow in the goofy way only Jewel could. It made him laugh just thinking about it. What did folks do without a friend?

Ting-a-ling.

Samuri darted to the door but glanced at his para before he opened it.

"Okay!" Para Chloe's cheery voice spoke confidence into him like it always had. "Let's see what's next for you, Young Samuri."

The second Para Chloe opened the door, the squeamish messenger forced her words out rapidly. "Greetings. The new young from bungalow seventy-six is to go directly to the Woods Shop. Pleasantness to each and loyalty to the Township."

"And a safe, long life . . ." Para Chloe began, but the messenger left without listening or bowing.

"Busy day," Chloe said kindly, dismissing the messenger's rudeness and fear. "Stay here. I'll get your midday snack."

"The Woods Shop," Samuri mused. "I went there once on deliveries. Where is it from here?"

"Take the main path south and around to the Yards Shop. Behind it is a smaller path that keeps going south sloping toward the trees. Follow it to an even narrower path with a large building on the right. Go promptly."

Samuri saw the same messenger ringing the bell at Jewel's door as he left. This one time, he wished he could wait and listen.

Loyalty to the Township, he reminded himself, and quickened his steps.

A tall apprentice was standing in front of the building when Samuri approached.

"Greetings, Young Samuri." The freshness of the apprentice's voice, calling him by name, surprised Samuri. "You may call me Apprentice Tuckit. We'll need to wait here for one other young."

Samuri greeted him confidently, nodded, and stood a fair distance away, thinking. Was an apprentice authorized to call folks by name? And who would the other young be? Would they call each other by name?

The apprentice's voice interrupted Samuri's thoughts. "Are you ready to be a young? How did you like shaving yourself this morning? What a task!"

"Um, I think I'm ready. I started shaving myself two weeks ago," Samuri answered seriously and a bit hesitantly.

Who was this apprentice to ask about personal matters? He wore the bright blue band of leadership on his arm, but he acted strangely bold even for a leader. The confidence and sincerity shining from his dark, brown eyes eased Samuri's recent disgust with the Township.

Back at Para Madeline's bungalow, the hasty messenger was delivering another strange command.

"Your junior is to go directly to the Woods Shop."

Para Madeline gasped. "But—"

The messenger put her hand up, motioning for Para Madeline to stop, and replied in the same uncomfortable voice. "Further instructions will be given to her there."

The messenger was off just as quickly this time, leaving Madeline eyeing Jewel suspiciously.

Jewel stood there stunned. Her face was blank. She'd expected to report to the yard by the Tasks Bungalow, like she had in the past.

"What's the Woods Shop, Para?"

"Don't just stand there, Jewel. Hurry and ask *her* to show you the way," Para Madeline spit the words out impatiently, scowled, and flicked her hand toward Jewel, as if brushing a disgusting creature out the door.

Jewel caught the messenger just in time to get brief directions.

Look down. Jewel scolded herself, following the messenger's directions and pushing worries aside. *Remember the Laws. Smile.*

Look Directors in the eye. Why did my para look at me like that? Am I in trouble?

The thought of more trouble shook her to her senses. "Ooo. I don't know," she mumbled. "But I will be if I forget those directions on the first day of an assignment."

Once Jewel was on her way, her troubled feelings slipped away in the beauty of the short walk. The relief of walking on a path far from other folks poured over Jewel. She lost herself in the tall puffy clouds that floated across the perfectly blue sky above.

"Oh, I do hope I get a task with running back and forth," she confided to her wispy friends above. "I feel entirely sick of being inside so much! Maybe that's what makes me so difficult."

The narrow path was easy to find. The open space was refreshing, but when she rounded the curve and saw a tall apprentice in front of what must certainly be the Woods Shop, a pang of worry struck her. The apprentice's posture and arm band suggested that of a Township leader. She bit the inside of her lip hoping to keep quiet, or to be perfectly careful if she must speak. Then, she noticed the green tunic of the young standing on the other side of the apprentice.

It was Samuri.

What? What is he . . . Jewel pulled herself together and kept her words in before they saw her coming.

Samuri was just as shocked to see her, but he dropped his gaze to the ground as he would in any similar situation. What was going on?

Apprentice Tuckit held his hand out towards Jewel as if he were making a presentation. "Ah, we didn't have to wait long. Greetings young from bungalow seventy."

Jewel's thoughts were a swirl of confusion and questions, but she did her best to act in loyal Township behavior. "Greetings," she said respectfully. "Please excuse my speaking out of turn, but there's been a mistake. I'm only a junior."

"Ah yes, loyal one. But Town Master Cree agreed with me

that despite these circumstances, the assignment is right for you. So, we will consider you to be a young, though your size might pose a problem. I'll be sure to tell the Director of the Woods Shop not to send you on Township business this year." Then he reached in his carry bag and handed her a bundle with a new green tunic and trousers.

"Now." He clapped his hands together, speaking loudly. "I'd like to introduce the two of you. Since this is an . . . unusual assignment, you'll go by given names during your tasks. However, if your tasks should happen to take you into the Township, you must refer to each other by bungalow numbers. This is of the utmost importance."

Was he saying what they thought he was saying?

"All right let's get to the details. I need your full attention, so do look up." Apprentice Tuckit commanded with a quick clap indicating everything was settled. "This is the young Samuri from bungalow seventy-six. Perhaps the two of you have passed one another at some time. The Woods Shop will be his permanent assignment until next year's Celebration Day. If he does well, he will remain assigned to these tasks for several years. At the coming of his apprenticeship, he'll be allowed to request a change, but as always, the officials make the final decision.

"And this . . . this is the *Young* Jewel from bungalow seventy." The tone of his voice sounded amused, but his expression remained business-like. "Her assignment here is of a less permanent nature. The Director of the Woods Shop must verify Jewel is carrying out her tasks pleasantly, safely, and with the utmost loyalty to the Township, or she will be permanently assigned to caring for floors throughout Township offices."

Apprentice Tuckit paused, and his firm but pleasant voice softened as he went on. "Gran Para Brody prefers to work alone, but he's no longer able to fulfill all of the Woods Shop tasks on his own. Certain times he has allowed apprentices to help him temporarily, but this year Town Master Cree insisted Gran Para Brody have help on a daily basis. That's you."

The apprentice looked them over as he continued. "These tasks call for youngs with unusual qualities. They must be able to handle the frights of the woods, withstand extreme weather year-round, and fulfill difficult tasks loyally and pleasantly for long hours without help. The Director of Tasks and I talked at length and decided to overlook your years and give you a try, Young Jewel. Young Samuri, we think you may find the woods less intimidating than most folks." He glanced at Jewel with an odd expression, and she blushed. "And our daily reports suggest the Young Jewel may also be capable of handling these tasks."

Did Apprentice Tuckit know about her unsafe interest in bugs and birds and all things belonging to the woods? Did he know about her red flag?

"The Secretary at the Tasks Office was concerned with the Junior Jewel's past difficulties. It was she who affirmed my recommendation to remove Jewel from the typical tasks of a junior."

Jewel's hand flew to her mouth before she could stop it. He did know. The picture of the Young Tuckit helping her at the Exchange flashed through her mind. He was the one. His kindness had kept her out of trouble then, and now he was giving her a way out.

"Gran Para Brody will give you more details when you need them. Any questions?" Tuckit invited, holding his hands wide open, palms up.

"Hmm," Ri said, and thought for a moment, but shook his head.

Jewel felt quite awkward. Yes, she had questions, but she was afraid to ask.

"Wonderful! Come with me and I'll introduce you to your new Director," Apprentice Tuckit said with another quick clap of his hands.

The most intriguing smell hit them the moment he pushed the door open. Actually, it was a plethora of smells blending together in an aroma uniquely new to both of them. Jewel's eyes darted back and forth, up and down, taking in shelf after shelf filled with unfamiliar things. Above the shelves, hanging from strings, were bunches of dried flowers and leaves and herbs. Curiosity lit her face and she found herself suspended in wide-eyed wonder, oblivious to the two walking steadily ahead of her. Oh, the shiny, new metals interspersed with the old, dull ones! Wooden handles perfectly crafted for their own buckets, hammers, and spades. Dull, faded lavender hanging beside deep, maroon roses. The scents of rosemary and peppermint, dirt and oil, pine boughs and juniper wafting before her with each step she managed to take.

She failed to notice, forgot to even look for the Director of the Woods Shop. The stocky, old Director stood at the far end of the building with his back to them, his muscular arms straining to repair a broken shovel. Ignoring the squeaky door that signaled their entry, he continued his task.

Apprentice Tuckit paused, whispering down to Samuri, "Oh, and this wasn't his idea. It may take him some adjusting. Remember, pleasantness and loyalty."

"Greetings, Gran Para Brody. Pleasantness to each and—"

"I know, I know, pleasantness and all that stuff," Gran Para Brody grumbled.

He turned toward them, obviously disturbed by their interruption, but that changed when he saw Samuri's strong, earnest face. Gran Para Brody looked again, more carefully this time. The brightness of his sparkling keen eyes, set in his tanned, wrinkled face came to life as he smiled a most welcoming smile.

"Greetings, Gran Para Brody, pleasantness to each and loyalty to the Township," Samuri greeted him congenially, and the sound of it shook Jewel back to reality.

What am I doing? She scolded herself. *Uff! I've already messed up my chance to start well.*

However, the others seemed not to notice her absence. Gran Para Brody walked forward and placed his hand on Samuri's shoulder, finishing the greeting. " . . . and a safe, long life to us all."

106

A shadow crossed Apprentice Tuckit's face. The gesture was quite inappropriate by Township standards. He expected Samuri would pull away from the gran para's touch, but the young was completely at ease.

Jewel tried to make her way across the large shop quickly and noiselessly, before they noticed her, but Apprentice Tuckit had already turned to find her.

Oh no! Jewel thought. *I should have been paying attention. What if they send me back without even letting me try?*

But when Gran Para Brody turned his attention to her, he was chuckling warmly. "Aye, this must be m' other new helper. Greetings."

Quickly she bowed, using it as an opportunity to pull herself together.

I refuse to let them see me embarrassed, she thought with resolve. *I don't know why, but I want this place with this odd gran para. Maybe—just maybe—there is something I can do here other than scrub floors and get in trouble.*

Gran Para Brody and Apprentice Tuckit saw the bow and the brave, charming smile that followed it as a beautiful gesture. Jewel meant it as defiance against the Township. *I will not let them take this from me,* she vowed silently.

"Well, that's a good enough introduction," Apprentice Tuckit announced. "Time to go." Nodding to the two youngs, he added, "Do well at your new tasks. You were chosen for them."

Satisfaction welled up inside of Samuri, but Jewel heard it as a warning. Here they stood, awkwardly alone, in front of the unpredictable Director of the Woods Shop, who might not even want them there. For a moment no one spoke, while Gran Para Brody sorted through the thoughts running about wildly in his head.

He had expected the typical youngs, dazed and uncertain, like those the Township had brought him on other occasions. Mindless youngs with pasted on smiles, weak arms, and empty-looking eyes. But these two looked straight at him, their eyes shining with courage and curiosity.

"Well. It's good," Gran Para Brody said finally, crossing his arms across his chest, nodding. He glanced around the entire shop until his twinkling eyes came to Samuri and Jewel again.

"I see ya got no food with ya, Young Jewel. And surely a strong lad like the Young Samuri can eat a bit extra. Just what I was needin'. Like I always say, "Snackin' t'gether is a sure way ta get acquainted." So, the first thing I'll be teachin' ya is where I keep m' things for snackin' and how ya need to put 'em out."

Jewel pinched herself hard to keep from giggling at the funny way he spoke, but Samuri answered quickly, "Um-hmm," and moved forward to help.

It was one of the few days that Jewel felt a bit jealous of the way Samuri made good decisions without trying. In no time the three of them had drawn chairs up in front of the big stone hearth at the far end of the shop, and this gran para had a lovely little fire sputtering. Gran Para Brody placed a small bench in front of their chairs for a table and offered them delicious snacks unlike any they had tasted before. There was no room for jealousy in the togetherness of this cheery, warm place.

The rest of the afternoon, they listened to Gran Para Brody teach them about the tools and gear they would need for their tasks the next day. He demonstrated how to use each correctly, explaining how to clean and replace tools when they were finished. "In Brody's shop ya clean and replace what ya use. Right away. No excuses."

Samuri watched and listened intently. Every now and then he offered a simple "And?" asking for more details, but he took most of it in with his usual "hmm" and "um-hmm".

Jewel, despite her renewed determination to do well, found her mind wandering. Her eyes scanned back and forth, looking for beautiful novelties, daydreaming about the days ahead. Now and then, she caught herself and made more effort to listen to Gran Para Brody's instructions, but Gran Para Brody and Samuri didn't seem to notice either way.

The day ended well, though later than the usual time for youngs. Samuri sent Jewel ahead and they walked quickly and quietly back to their bungalows, pondering what the next day would hold.

That evening Samuri's paras asked him all sorts of questions, but his thoughts, questions, and feelings wouldn't come together into words. Today was like the promise of pleasant things to come; the chance to be friends and be loyal to the Township at the same time.

But Jewel hadn't paid attention. Didn't she care? Or didn't she understand? That was what he most wanted to talk about, but first he needed time alone to think.

Lying awake in the dark, he sorted through the events of the day. There was the huge Woods Shop itself, full of shelves, baskets, and tools of such a variety and abundance as he had never imagined. Then there was Gran Para Brody. After only one day, Samuri found himself drawn toward this unusual Director. He could barely sleep in his eagerness to learn more about the shop from him.

Lunch by an open fire, Samuri mused. *I'll never forget that. So bright. And we sat right in front of it.*

But why didn't Jewel try harder today?

He laid on his cot lost in thought. He wanted good things for Jewel, he wanted *this* for her, but could she do it?

I guess I don't just want this for Jewel, though, he admitted to himself, *I want it, too. It's perfect. We'll have time together, again. And I'll be able to help her stay out of trouble. If she'll try. We won't get an assignment like this again.*

When sleep slowed his thoughts, a faint whisper echoed through his mind: *You will always have help Samuri, always.*

"Uh, what?" he muttered, trying to wake up enough to think, but sleep came, and the whisper was forgotten.

11
into the dark woods

The next day Jewel, her typical, sleepy self, woke up to something *tap, tap, tapping* annoyingly near to her. Through blurry eyes she saw Para Madeline, leaning by her door, tapping impatiently on the wall.

"Well, nice of you to wake up, Jewel." Para Madeline threw the new green tunic and trousers on Jewel's cot, her sugary voice accusing her. "If you have to disgrace us by getting assigned to the Woods Shop, the least you could do is be loyal and on time. Tonight, Para Philip and I expect you to explain why you are there and what your tasks are!"

Jewel was still trying to pull her thoughts together when she reached the path near the trees. She didn't have any answers, and she didn't know what disgrace meant, though it didn't sound pleasant. Near the Woods Shop, she saw Gran Para Brody pointing to different areas of the sky while Samuri watched intently, nodding now and then in response.

Most of the morning was spent in the shop. Together with Gran Para Brody they gathered tools and gear like snippers, gloves, and buckets. Once everything was gathered, they laid it on a counter and followed Gran Para Brody outside.

"Sit here and I'll introduce ya to the *clearin',*" he said in a cheery voice, as he grabbed a stick and drew a large map in the dirt.

"Have ya been through the woods before?" he asked kindly, assuming they'd be hesitant, or possibly even shocked at the thought of it.

They both shook their heads, and Jewel blurted out, "Oh, no! It's not allowed. We don't even look at the woods." The lie came easily from much practice.

Gran Para Brody shook his head and frowned at the thought of that, though he already knew it was so. "Do ya think the two of ya be up to walkin' through the woods on yur own, or should I go with ya this first time?" Everything about Gran Para Brody invited an honest answer.

Jewel's eyes lit up. "I have wanted to go into the woods every day of my life." Her words were slow and breathy.

"Um-hmm," Samuri added, holding back a laugh, "I had to tell her 'no' hundreds of times."

Then, both youngs nodded and bowed, realizing what they had just done.

Gran Para Brody looked from one to the other and back. Not only had Samuri finally spoken up, but these two seemed to have history together. There was no way Brody was going to ask about that, though. It was better not to know some things.

He chuckled. These two were amusing. He'd fought against having help, but them . . . His eyes closed briefly, and the warmth of hope spread through his heart as he prayed silently.

Can this be just what we're needin'? The Young Jewel doesn't listen well, but surely, we can help her, can't we? And Samuri, aye, I'm thinkin' he'll take right to it.

"Alrighty, it be time," Gran Para Brody said, leading them back inside, and pointing to the shelves near the door. "Each of ya needs two buckets and a hat fur yurself. Find a bucket yur comfortable with n' can carry even if it be full. If ya find a handle with splinters, I'll fix it for ya ta take t'morrow."

Jewel gazed at a delicately carved wooden bucket hanging between the bunches of flowers above. Then she turned to choose two plain buckets and a small hat off of the shelves. She stacked her buckets together and repeated the name and use of each tool as Gran Para Brody dropped it into the top bucket.

When Gran Para finished, he added an interesting cloth packet to Samuri's bucket, saying, "Nothin' special for today, but it's filling."

"Oh," Jewel gasped. "I forgot to bring food again."

He shook his head, "No need ta waste yur time gettin' food ready every day. I can feed ya while yur doin' tasks fur me." His eyes twinkled and he added, "Or I should say . . . fur the Township, shouldn't I?"

With a quick little bob of his head, he nodded at them like he was correcting his mistake.

"Now, about creatures. They be hidin' everywhere so you're sure ta see 'em sometime. Ya need not worry if ya keep yur distance." Jewel's face glowed like a tiny with her first cookie, and Gran Para Brody's voice grew stern. "Even the small creatures can be dangerous—*if* ya get in their way—so leave 'em be. You can save m' dear Woods Shop a townshipful o' trouble by rememberin' that loyalty be our highest goal and safety be our greatest strength."

The way Gran Para Brody spoke gave deeper meaning to the Township's frustrating mottos.

"Samuri, I'll be countin' on ya to watch the sun. On yur way, loyal youngs."

With a serious nod from Samuri, Gran Para Brody turned and walked inside and straight to the hearth. He leaned his hands against the hearth with his full weight. "Ah, Lord, I'm thinkin' m' Rosie is a watchin' from your great cloud o' witnesses there. Tell her Brody is goin' ta be okay. I bow to ya, Lord. I am grateful. Incredibly grateful."

Jewel jittered with excitement as they walked away. "The woods," she whispered in awe, "We are . . . walking into the woods. Both of us." Jewel couldn't put it into words, but it didn't matter because she *knew* Samuri was feeling the exact same thing.

Actually though, Samuri, ten steps behind her, was only thinking about the map and enjoying the responsibility of being in charge of something. Hopefully, he wouldn't get distracted in some silliness with Jewel and forget what Gran Para Brody had said. Silently, he repeated each detail, especially about watching the sun journey across the clearing.

Um-hmm. I've got it. Every detail. No problem, he silently assured himself.

Where the path entered the woods, Jewel stopped. It still felt forbidden, like an *I-can't-wait* excitement bumping up against an *I'm-in-trouble* fear. Samuri watched and waited before coming next to her to wave her forward. He knew how much she had wanted this. She should be the one to go first. But she froze, peering into the shadowy path ahead.

"Hmm . . . whatcha doing Jewel?" he asked.

"Samuri?" she spoke hesitantly. "What if it's not everything I've thought it would be? What if I don't even like it?"

"What if it's everything and more?" Samuri replied.

Samuri glanced around to be sure no one was watching, took her free hand in his, and stepped into the woods beside her. It was like walking into one of her fanciful stories. A few steps, in she dropped his hand and walked ahead with her arms extended behind her, the gentle breeze flowing through her fingers. Jewel was awestruck at the scent surrounding them. The evergreens seemed to be breathing out their sharp, piney fragrance in welcome.

"Can you hear them breathing?" She was so full of wonder the hush in her voice sounded mysterious. "They're welcoming us."

Samuri laughed, nodded, and breathed in deeply himself. Yes, now that she'd said it, he could feel it too.

The first curve, about sixty meters in, turned enough to the south to block them from the view of the Township. From there it meandered another ninety meters before curving back to the south. Jewel continued on in silence other than her quiet gasps of "Ooo!" and "Oh!" until the evergreens gave way to tall woody trees with newly unfurling leaves.

"Uff, this pesky hat." Jewel used the hat ties to secure it to the bucket handle. Then, she pointed upward with delight. "Ri, look!" She slapped her hand over her mouth. Dare she call him by name, even out here?

The sunshine peeked through more with each step until they were standing at the end of the path drenched in the clearing's warm, full sunlight. The clearing's wild beauty captured them. Soft, new grass spread out before them, more fanciful than any story Jewel had imagined. Joyful smells of apple blossoms and fresh peppermint shook their senses awake. There was a burst of movement from a nearby bush as a playful group of wrens dashed into a bush on the hillside, singing spunky songs.

Jewel might have stood there spellbound all morning, but Samuri shook his head as if waking from a dream. He scanned the edges of the clearing on his right, slowly taking in every meter until he had come full circle.

"Samuri, what are you doing?" she asked curiously.

"The map," he said simply.

"The map?" She asked and shrugged her shoulders. "What about the map?"

Samuri stood still, one step off of the path, fitting the clearing into the details of Gran Para Brody's map.

"We have to know this stuff, Jewel," Samuri said with a hint of irritation in his voice. "It's, um . . . really important." He raised his eyebrows and rolled his eyes.

They exchanged a quarrelsome glance, which was unlike them and against the Laws for task crews, but who would know out here, anyway? Then, he put his hat on, and slugged her shoulder, making them both laugh.

"S-A-M-U-R-I! We're here!" Jewel exclaimed loudly, twirling with her hands stretched toward the sky. "How did we get here?"

"Hmm, how *did* we get here?" Ri asked curiously.

The quizzical expression on their faces gave way to laughter when they exclaimed together, "Because no one else wants to."

The humor of it faded as the reality of it struck them both. The Township would never reassign them if they were safe, pleasant, and loyal.

"Oh no . . ." Jewel gasped. "I don't remember anything Gran Para Brody said."

Samuri smiled calmly. It was clear in his mind, though he couldn't explain it. His eyes told Jewel everything.

"Samuri . . . the map—you remember it all, don't you?"

"Um–hmm, I thought through every detail while we walked."

"You! Are! Amazing!" Jewel beamed at him.

"Don't say that, Jewel." His voice was the closest to fear she had ever heard. "We're youngs now. Instead, we should only say 'Pleasantness to each, loyalty to the Township . . .'"

Her face clouded over with worry. For a moment she felt the eyes and ears of the Township pressing upon them, even here.

"Okay, I won't," she promised. "I guess I never thought about what that means."

Suddenly, two small creatures chased one another through the branches above them. They stopped to chatter as if scolding at the two youngs. "Stay out of our way swirly-tails!" Jewel shouted. "C'mon Samuri, let's get started!"

"Um–hmm. First . . . let me introduce ya to the clearin.'" Samuri's attempt to mimic Gran Para Brody's accent was weak, but the effect was like his impression of Town Master years ago. "Borderin' the clearin' ta the south, there be the apple trees."

"Remember how Gran Para Brody said we can start on the strawberries? They should be . . . there." Samuri pointed at the low, green patch across the clearing. Using hand rakes, they gently cleaned out the dead leaves, sneezing some at the musty, earthy smell, but delighted to discover dozens of berries, both red and green.

Samuri was pleased with Jewel. Sure, she had her distracted times, but she was okay when he reminded her to concentrate. Jewel didn't want to waste a moment of that first day any more than he did, and she didn't fuss about working in the dirt like most juniors did.

The day went fast. Samuri kept a close eye on the sun's steady movement across the sky toward the Township. *Funny, before today I never noticed how the sun changes throughout the day.*

Though it was tempting to stay longer, Samuri insisted they pack up on time. On the way back, Jewel lagged behind with a dazed look on her face. Samuri half expected her to stop and refuse to go any further, but then she ran to catch up with him.

"We can do this," she exclaimed, with sparkling eyes. "I know we can."

12
trust?

From the start, Samuri's habit was to be up and at the shop half-an-hourglass early most days. Jewel stumbled in a bit late, but bright as a Celebration Day. A strange joy welled up in the heart of the old shop director. He needed both of them.

The second day, they were equipped and headed for the door when Gran Para Brody called out, "Young Jewel, ya be needin' ta wear that hat today. I sees yur head is already a bit rosy from yesterday."

She nodded towards him respectfully and slipped the hat on as she went out.

"And ya be rememberin' ta watch the sun, Young Samuri." Gran Para Brody nodded upward. And they were on their way.

As soon as they entered the woods, Jewel slipped the hat off to gaze upward at the sunbeams glimmering on the evergreen boughs. Samuri chuckled to himself. Jewel belonged here, right where she'd always wanted to be.

When they reached the clearing, Samuri strapped the food pack to a tree branch.

"All right, let's get started," Jewel chirped, quickly hanging her hat on a branch nearby.

"Huh-uh." Samuri said firmly, but she rolled her eyes and walked off.

"Gran Para Brody said to," he protested.

"Seriously, do you do everything folks tell you to do?"

Her tone of voice stung him, but he still wanted her to understand.

"No, Jewel," he said, focusing his serious, but kind eyes on her. "Only folks I trust."

"Trust? What is trust? I don't know what you mean." Her voice softened, sorry but also confused.

Samuri realized *trust* might be a word his paras only used in the bungalow. Instead of answering, he made light of it, laughing, and heading across the clearing.

"All right, let's get started, *Young* Jewel," he called back in a teasing voice, hoping to distract her.

"Loyalty to the Township." She mimicked the Town Master with a sweeping bow, then put her hat on.

Today, their tasks were on opposites edges of the clearing. Jewel moved about on her knees, cleaning dead leaves and sticks out of the strawberry plants. Without thinking, she slipped the hat off and tossed it on top of a nearby bush. She concentrated so intently on her tasks she forgot about snacks until Samuri called to her.

He watched her coming, bareheaded. Why couldn't she do what she was told? And what should he do? Should he ask his paras? Or was that being a disloyal friend? On the other hand, Gran Para Brody was in charge, and he said to wear hats. So, they should, right?

They worked together the rest of the day, digging a mulch pit and filling it with piles of dead leaves. Nothing bothered Jewel, not even worms. Samuri liked that. Now, if only she would wear her hat.

When they returned to the shop, they found Gran Para Brody lost in fixing something. "Leave yur things there by the door," he said, waving a screwdriver their direction, "I'll clean 'em later and t'morrow we'll chat about yur day."

That evening Para Patrick said, "Well, tell us about the Woods Shop. You didn't say much last night."

Samuri's worry spilled out. "Umm . . . the tasks are pleasant, really pleasant. We spend a lot of time in the clearing—Jewel and I, that is. Did you know the Township assigned Jewel to the Woods Shop, too?"

"Well, that is a surprise," Patrick said. "No, we didn't. That is pleasant indeed."

"Um, yes, but . . ." He spoke hesitantly, looking down, searching for the right words.

"We're listening," Patrick said, "and what you say will stay between just us three. Won't it, Para Chloe?"

Para Chloe nodded.

Samuri looked into Para Patrick's trusting eyes and began slowly and carefully. "I worry . . . about Jewel failing. It's frustrating, too, because she doesn't listen. She forgets a lot. Sometimes she even ignores instructions on purpose. I don't know what to do. I don't want to be bossy . . . but I don't want her to lose this assignment. It's perfect for her."

"You know what?" Patrick said. "It will probably work its way out if you're pleasant and focus on your tasks and let Jewel be responsible for her own tasks. Maybe you're taking things too seriously. You can't be responsible for all of Jewel's tasks and mistakes."

"Loyalty . . ." Chloe said gently, " . . . to both Jewel and the Township."

Relief flooded over Samuri.

Para Patrick knuckled him on the shoulder, grabbed the big

candle holder, and headed to light the small candles by their cots.

Samuri slept easy that night.

Jewel had a terrible night.

She tossed and turned, unable to find a comfortable way to lie down. The top of her head hurt. The back of her head hurt. Her forehead and nose and even her temples hurt. Was this why the supervisors had insisted juniors wear the hats provided for them?

The next morning when Jewel shaved, she bit her lip so she wouldn't cry out. Oh, it hurt! Did Para Madeline have to watch? Jewel knew she must not complain. Para Madeline would use it against her if she did.

To Jewel's surprise, Madeline muttered quite defensively, "Well, at least they could give you a hat!"

Jewel blurted out the entire story, and Madeline sighed. "Put the cream on while I get something." Her para was gone and back in a second, holding an unusually thin yarn hat. "The Township requests these for paras with outside tasks. These keep their sun hats on when it's windy."

Madeline slid her hands into the delicate hat, stretching it to place it cautiously on Jewel's head. Jewel gasped, expecting a sharp pain.

"Ooo." Her gasp became a delighted whisper. "It's so soft."

"I make them especially soft and comfortable," Para Madeline said, gazing into space. "Hats were much too scratchy when I was a young."

Jewel stared at Para Madeline, trying to grasp this side of her. Then, she sprinted out the door while things were still pleasant.

Samuri heard the jingle of her door but did not turn around until he neared the shop.

"Greetings, Young Jewel." He liked to say it every morning. What a great trick. The Township had made her a young so she could work at the Woods Shop. "Hmm, your nose looks like it hurts." Concerned filled his voice. "And what's that on your head?"

"It's my . . ." She laughed, and held her hand daintily beside the hat, displaying it. ". . . hat-holder-on-er!"

"Great idea." He nodded with approval.

"And you don't get one." She laughed again and shot forward to reach the door first, but he beat her.

"Greetings, young ones! It's a glorious day. Grab yur buckets and off ya go." Gran Para Brody popped his r's in the funny way they liked so much. "Everything's ready for ya."

He scowled at the sight of Jewel's sunburned, red nose, but whisked them on their way without mentioning it.

It *was* a glorious day, like a dream in every way. Jewel kept the hat on and worked hard all day. They didn't talk much, but when they did it was like old times. Samuri was glad he hadn't pressured her yesterday.

Para Patrick was right, Samuri mused. *Things are working out!*

Jewel cherished the memory of that morning. What had gotten into Para Madeline? She'd been so kind and even taken Jewel's side, but Jewel knew better than to expect it again.

It's something, at least. Even worth this awful sunburn. Oh, and this soft, beautiful knit hat! She reached up to touch the side of her head. She would always remember this morning.

Each day of that first week held wonderful new experiences, but the last day was the best of all. That morning they schemed to beat Gran Para Brody to the greeting. They pushed the door open, stared straight at him, and burst out, "Greetings, Gran Para Brody!"

Pleasant lines radiated across his face like a sunrise. He laughed loudly, but it was about much more than their greeting.

"Well, the two of ya have done a mighty fine job with yur tasks this week." His eyes twinkled as he spoke. "Yur just what this old Woods Shop has been needin'. A-n-d I can't be havin' ya call me that long, old name, can I? Not with us workin' t'gether. So, ya can just be callin' me Brody!"

They cast worried looks at one another.

"Not ta worry. I'll keep remindin' ya 'til ya get it. Alrighty?"

Samuri and Jewel nodded hesitantly at first. Gran Para Brody was convincing, but that was against the Laws of Loyalty. Could he *do* that? They didn't want to be reassigned for calling a gran para by name. Soon enough, though, they were beaming despite their concern.

While Jewel cleaned tools under the waterspout outside Gran Para Brody explained the day's tasks to Samuri. She popped inside just as Gran Para Brody winked at Samuri. What? Breaking another Law.

Samuri slung a pack over his shoulder, grabbed his buckets, and gave Brody a thumbs up. The whole trip to the clearing, Jewel pondered what the wink could mean. The morning passed smoothly except for a brief rain. Sheltered under the trees, chatting, Jewel could tell Samuri was up to something, but what?

Midday, he grabbed the food pack, set off for the hill on the south side of the clearing, and motioned for her to follow.

"Hey, what are you doing? Where are we going?"

"Hmm? Should I tell you or . . . " His voice was playful.

Jewel ran to pass him, but his arms shot out abruptly.

"Hold on!" The seriousness in his voice could not hide his anticipation. "You have to give me space and let me lead. Because a-c-t-u-a-l-l-y, I don't know for sure where we're going, and I may have to back track."

"Ooo," she said enthusiastically, "like a surprise? Lead on."

Near the hillside, they spotted a barely visible, rock-strewn trail snaking its way up. Why hadn't she noticed it before? Each step felt off balance. Neither of them had walked uphill before. The scree of rocks and pebbles on the trail added to the difficulty, but they thrived on the challenge. A far away sound beckoned to them. It murmured like a slow rain pouring over the rooftop and trickling down the windowpanes to splash musically into the puddles below.

Glowing with wonder, eyebrows raised, she whispered, "What is it?"

He shrugged, but his eyes glowed. "Some sort of water source. A brook."

A water source? Jewel had never questioned where the water in the pumps came from. She walked behind him speechlessly, both of them imagining what sight could belong to such a sound as this.

The largest rock they had ever seen sat to the left of the trail. Samuri smiled proudly, nodded to it, and said, "A boulder." He felt taller and stronger introducing Jewel to each new sight.

Jewel trailed her fingers across the top of the boulder, lagging behind as she passed it. A flat path parallel to the hillside appeared and meandered into a patch of thick trees. Now it was impossible for her to watch where Samuri was going.

"Wait 'til you see *this*," he called out, and she followed the sound of his voice.

Near the last tree, the ground sloped down to a soft, grassy bank, and . . . the brook. She twirled twice, threw her bucket and her pack to the bottom, fell on the ground, and rolled down the slope.

"A brook," she said, sitting up and hugging herself. "A surprise from Gran Para Brody!"

The way Jewel acted, you would have thought Gran Para Brody had made the brook himself. Samuri was delighted to see her acting like a little again.

I wish you could see her, Gran Para Brody. But you knew, didn't you?

After their midday snack on the grass Jewel put her feet in the brook and shrieked. It was chilly and ticklish. She shrieked again when a cluster of luminous, winged creatures whirred past her ear to skim across the water and up the brook.

Samuri stood twirling his hat on his hand, taking in every

moment, and thinking. Then, he spoke slowly and reflectively. "Trust is a word my para says to me. She says it often. 'We trust you, Samuri, we trust you.'"

Jewel's expression was comical. Tilted head. Scrunched up eyes and nose. Searching and perplexed.

"Um . . ." How could he explain? "I think it means something like 'I know you care, and you'll do the best you can.' That's what trust is."

He paused while Jewel *tried* to piece it together. It seemed important to him. She shook her head, apologizing for not understanding.

"I know," he said. "Why did you follow me today? Did you feel like you had to? Were you worried?"

"No. Not at all."

"There it is. You trust me."

A shiver went up her spine. It was an uncomfortable thought, but Jewel had no idea why.

"Maybe it's a word they made up," Samuri added. "I don't know if other bungalows use that word, so please don't tell anyone. Okay, Jewel?"

"I won't," she said quietly, but firmly. "I give you my word of loyalty, I won't."

On their way back to the path down she started to race ahead of him, yelling, "I'll bet I can beat you."

"Stop!" Ri nearly shouted as he reached out and grabbed her arm.

The suddenness of it caught her off guard. An angry look crossed her face. Samuri feared she might let it ruin this amazing day.

Who does he think he is? I know where we're going, Jewel fumed, clenching her fists.

"Listen, Jewel. I should have explained." Then he tried to mimic Gran Para Brody. "'Young Samuri, be sure ya don't let the Young Jewel run down that hill today. It's not safe with them rocks.'"

This time his accent did not amuse her. The mad part of her wanted to be mean, but a new thought unfurled inside of her. She had wanted to run and race, but deep inside she knew Samuri would never stop her without a reason.

Is that trust?

The thought embarrassed her, so she threatened him in a teasing voice. "Oh . . . it's a good thing lunch by the brook was great, or you'd be in trouble."

Samuri laughed, relieved she was okay. The rest of the day was splendid.

That night, Jewel went to her cot early, blew out the candle, and lay quietly, trying to relive her moments by the brook.

"Brook . . . boulder . . ." She whispered them over and over, letting them bring back the sights and the sounds.

The new places stirred something in her. Something right. Something bigger than she had ever felt. Something she couldn't understand or explain. After a while, the thought of trust came to her again. Trust. Samuri said his paras trusted him. Did he trust them? It sounded like he did.

What about me? she wondered. *Does Ri trust me?*

Beyond that, she wasn't willing to think about it. Undefined ideas about trust swirled through her mind, until the memory of the murmuring brook pushed them aside and carried her to sleep.

13
like the wind

Oh, the things Brody knew! Drying herbs and pruning trees, the names of birds and the best times to harvest wild onions. He knew all the berries and mushrooms, which ones were delicious and which ones you could make you sick or even kill you. Samuri listened intently, soaking up everything Brody said and did. Jewel listened intently, too, but not much stuck with her.

Jewel often called on Samuri to repeat details. "What did Brody . . . call that . . . ask me to do with that?" Samuri was more patient now. He didn't understand, but he knew she was trying.

Day after day they worked, back and forth between the Woods Shop and the clearing. Samuri and Jewel began to recognize the names and types of flowers. Each variety of flower needed to be cut and tied into big bunches at the right stages of blooming. Sticks must be gathered for kindling for the next season of Brave Days. Smooth, perfectly-shaped stones were needed for warming stones. Best of all was making new strawberry plants. All you had to do was press this season's tendrils into the soil and soon they took root making a new plant grow. Who could have guessed?

During the summer, Gran Para Brody sorted and cleaned the

mushrooms, berries, and herbs that Samuri and Jewel brought. Fresh mint, rosemary, and other herbs were separated into bunches. A third of the fresh bunches were sent to the Exchange for daily orders. The rest were hung from the rafters to dry. All lavender and flowering plants were dried for teas and remedies.

Messengers specifically chosen for their sharp memory came daily with a list from the Exchange. Gran Para Brody always invited them in, but they preferred to stay by the door while he checked on the items they requested. Most messengers shifted nervously from foot to foot, trying to be pleasant, but hating the Woods Shop as much as the terrifying woods. Gran Para actually knew what was in stock, but he liked the messengers to have time near the woods. Samuri and Jewel had reawakened his hope that youngs and apprentices might discover the beauty of wild growing things. Two clerks came along when the messenger returned to the Woods Shop with the Exchange's final order. The clerks followed Gran Para Brody through the shop filling their empty baskets and bags while the messenger called out the list from the door.

On the busiest days, Brody kept Samuri and Jewel at the shop to clean, sort, and store the overwhelming amount of fresh produce while he filled orders. Daily sweeping and scrubbing became their tasks, too. At first, they had races scrubbing all the way from one end to the other. Jewel had enough experience to win for a few weeks. Then, Samuri, with his size advantage, began winning every time. No matter who won, they always finished in a heap of laughter, sweaty and red-faced.

Outside they sorted and stacked willow shoots for basket making and small sticks for kindling. Were they free of all dirt? Were the willow shoots stacked smooth and flat? And what about the nice stones they found? Those had to be cleaned and sanded for perfect smoothness before being sorted and stacked by size.

Eventually every corner of the Woods Shop, inside and out, was bursting with goods. Inside, bins of produce overflowed on the back counters, and bunches of drying plants hung from rafters everywhere. Outside, tidy stacks heaped with supplies were multiplying. Jewel and Samuri marveled at all the abundance, laughing deep, happy laughs together.

And to think they had helped make this happen!

Despite all Brody's tasks, he kept a close eye on his two youngs. He noticed when Jewel, generally cheerful and eager, grew moody and difficult midmorning. At midday snacks she stuffed herself with bites almost too big for her mouth, looking lost in the eating of it. Yet Jewel, who ate more at midday snacks than Samuri or Brody, was outright skinny.

One day it clicked with Brody. Maybe Jewel wasn't eating in the mornings at all. Brody tested the idea by inconspicuously offering extra snacks under the guise of experimenting with new recipes.

"Looky at my new concoction, you two," Brody baited them when they arrived in the mornings. "Would ya take a minute ta try it before ya start yur tasks? Let me know what ya think."

Samuri ate a couple of bites and gave his honest opinion. Jewel nearly breathed it in, forgetting to give her opinion, and never refusing seconds if Brody offered. The whole thing embarrassed Samuri, but Brody only smiled.

"Ya might as well be havin' a bit more," he encouraged. "Or do me a favor and take the rest with ya. All these berries and herbs makes me want ta cook, but I can't be eatin' it all m'self." And he held his sides, chuckling like it was a great joke.

Jewel followed Samuri's example each time he declined, but soon she was convinced Brody meant it, so she took whatever he offered.

Aye, look at her, Brody noted to himself. *She eats half now and carefully wraps the rest up for later.* Soon he started putting food out in the late afternoons as well.

Whether it was the food, Brody's cheerful strength, or being in the fresh air day after day, pleasantness gradually became more natural for Jewel. The tone of her skin grew to be as healthy as her bright eyes. Her baggy tunic and trousers began to fit rather than merely hanging on her. And she never got into trouble working with Brody or Samuri. Oh, she still got moody and a bit cross sometimes, but the way Brody and Samuri handled problems gave Jewel space to work it out. Time with Brody was better than with anyone she had ever known, except Samuri, of course. She wished she could work at the Woods Shop the rest of her life.

One day toward the end of the summer as Jewel and Samuri sat eating their end-of-the-week "feast" by the brook, she said, "I don't completely understand it, but I think I know what you mean about trusting Brody."

Samuri simply nodded. He was glad to hear her say it, but it brought up other thoughts he'd wanted to ask her.

"Um, I do trust Brody," Samuri said, "but I worry about how careless he is with the Laws.

"I think it's his points. You know. You used to tally Exchange points."

"Hmm." Samuri was still hesitant, unsure, "I never thought about it much."

"Me either, until the red flag. Then, I found out what a big deal it is. Paras get points for *their* tasks and for ours. We all need them for food, fuel, blankets, and even tunics. Brody has everything. He doesn't need points."

"So, when you got the red flag, you lost points?" Samuri asked skeptically.

Jewel told him how Para Madeline threatened her and grounded her from snacks and warming stones. Openly, she admitted lying to the official who questioned her. Samuri frowned. Other than hearing Para Madeline call Jewel a townshipful of trouble, Samuri had been blind to how different their lives were.

"Don't be mad." There was no shame in her voice. "I only did what I had to do." She was humble but sure. Only the softness in her eyes hinted at her deep need for him to understand.

A grin spread across his face. "Mad? At you? For that? No. Asking you not to look at the woods is like telling the wind to stop blowing in the treetops."

Jewel shut her eyes and smiled, considering the thought. *Asking me not to look at the woods is like telling the wind to stop blowing?*

The sun drifted behind a cloud, reminding Samuri to check its location. "We should head down. Do you want to pack the snack stuff or start on the pebbles?"

Jewel headed straight for her pack and the tiny pebbles she had laid to dry on the small sandy shore. Scooping them up, she let the sand sift through her nearly closed fingers, enjoying the soft earthiness.

"Do you think I could call you Ri while we're up here?" Jewel said lightly when he came to help her finish. "I'll be perfectly careful to call you your given name the rest of the time."

His nod was immediate and definite. He had missed her calling him Ri.

In the hush of the moment, a soft-looking creature, taller than Samuri, emerged from the woods on the other side of the brook. Four slender legs stepped forward one at a time testing for safety. The creature's deep brown eyes as it lowered its head to drink, stopped the youngs in their tracks. Samuri put a finger to his lips. Jewel followed him toward the nearest trees in noiseless, fluid motions. The creature, who had been watching them for weeks, did not stir.

Neither of them said much heading back. The creature was too much to put into words.

Then, Jewel's thoughts turned to the idea of living without the Township's help. Could *she* live at the Woods shop someday?

Ri was deep in thought comparing Brody and Jewel. Both were so alive, and both seemed unable to do what the Township insisted. Brody had gotten away with it easily, and Jewel had not.

A chill ran down his spine despite the hot sun on his back. Once again, he found himself questioning what loyalty really meant.

14
the secret of the bees

Brody sat in his corner so deep in thought he didn't hear them enter. White, semi-transparent material flowed down on all sides of the strange thing Brody held in his hand.

It might be a hat, but if it was, it was the strangest hat Jewel or Samuri had ever seen. Unlike the Township's typical willow or yarn hats, the crown and brim were a stiff tunic-like material. Attached to that was a thin material long enough to touch your shoulders.

"No. It just won't work!" Brody exclaimed firmly, turning toward them. "No! Brody cannot be sendin' two youngs ta do this no matter how loyal and safe they've been."

They were confused. Did Brody want one of them to wear his crazy invention? And what was it?

"I'll have ta be goin' m'self again," he muttered, shrugged his shoulders, and gave them an exasperated glance.

Hmm . . . Samuri tried to think what he could say.

But Jewel just blurted out, "Brody, what are you talking about? What is that? Please, don't be sad. We will help you with whatever it is."

"Um-hmm," Samuri agreed.

Brody looked directly at them and simply said, "There be the bees."

Then, as if *that* was a perfectly understandable explanation, he went silent, shaking his head at the odd contraption. Jewel and Samuri looked at each other blankly. What were bees?

"Ya know the tasty bread ya like so much? The bread I bring out ta cheer ya on dreary, gray days? What makes it so good?" he asked, still frustrated.

"Honey," Jewel said. They knew that. But what did the gooey sweetness of honey have to do with this?

"All right, all right, come with me." Brody beckoned to them. "Let's start at the beginning. I guess we've not yet talked about such stuff."

He led them to the counter where he had often taught them how to identify leaves, flowers, and berries. The drawers below the counter held dried specimens of all sorts. His stiff joints complained as he bent to sort through the bottom drawers. Jewel and Samuri leaned in hoping to see the drawers' secretive-looking boxes.

"Ah! Yes." Brody's voice was bright again. He cradled a box in one hand and secured its lid snugly with his other hand.

Jewel felt goosebumps prickle her skin as Brody gingerly removed the lid and laid it on the counter. Pausing a moment, he cast a mysterious glance at each of them. They felt his mingled trust and warning. This box held secrets to be kept.

"*Nobody* knows Brody has these, only us three. Understand? We can't tell nobody else." He spoke endearingly to them, and they nodded back with wholehearted sincerity.

Within the box lay the perfect length of soft material, folded protectively over its contents. Slowly Brody laid back the folds revealing six, dead, winged creatures of differing sizes.

Jewel smiled. "Oh. Are those 'bees'? I think we . . ."

Hearing Jewel call them bees shocked Brody back to his senses. "Jewel. Samuri. Ya must wipe the name *bees* out o' yur mind. I meant ta say buzzin' creatures. Alrighty? From now on these is just buzzin' creatures. Now go ahead, Missy."

"Oh. Okay, Brody. Anyway, I think we've seen them near the white flowers by the brook. Haven't we R . . ." Ri was the name on heart and her tongue, but her mind caught and corrected it. "Samuri?"

"Um-hmm. And you showed me a dead one on the ground, didn't you?" he added, bending to take a closer look.

Jewel wanted badly to touch one, but Brody was acting awfully protective.

The sunlight streamed through the window perfectly, allowing them to see the distinct markings on each bee. Brody explained the buzzin' creatures' individual features, differences, and purposes. The story of the day he discovered them came tumbling out. His eyes held a faraway look like he was living it all over again.

"Not a soul, not even Brody—" His voice was low and hushed. "—knew there was *bees* so near the Township. This was after the Township got rid o' the flowers and the apple trees."

"What?!" Jewel interrupted. "There were flowers in the Township?"

"Ah flowers, Jewel, more kinds o' flowers than you can imagine. Every bungalow had flower boxes filled to overflowing. Our first two town masters was crazy about flowers. And when ya walked down the path, ya knew the favorite of the folks in that bungalow just by the scents ya passed. Lemon verbena. Honeysuckle. Roses. Freesia." He smiled sadly, remembering his younger days in the Township.

"Hmm, who knew?" Samuri shook his head, letting out a slow sigh.

"I thought flowers couldn't grow here," Jewel said, her voice full of disbelief. "I-I don't understand. Why?"

Gran Para Brody looked at them tenderly, touched to be able to share his love for all things wild and beautiful with them. On he went, caught up in stories he had never intended to share.

"Well, missy, we took 'em all out. Ya see, some dreadful things had happened in our lovely Township. Ah, it was beautiful, until one man's pride and bitterness tricked him into using force to get his own selfish way. He and another man died. Then a kind of craziness happened and some foolish youngs set a fire . . . Folks was struck deep in their hearts with sadness n' anger, fear n' worry, too. Our leaders were weak, not loyal. They did nothin'.

"Folks was desperate' ta stop all that bad from happenin' again. That's when we realized who was the kindest, wisest, person we knew, and made him our first official town master. We asked him ta think for us, and he did his best to change what folks thought should be changed. But the fire had ruined his lungs and he didn't live long.

"The second town master . . . ah, she was wise and lovely, but she got bullied out of leadin'. The third town master got carried away with change. It was him who thought laws could solve every problem. But I be thinkin' he went too far with it."

A shiver, like waking up from a dream, ran through Brody's body. His hand flew to his mouth and regret shone from his eyes.

"Oh, m' disloyal soul!' Brody slapped his head so hard they heard the smack. "I got carried away. I shoulda never told ya all this. Can ya pretend ya never heard it? Brody's so sorry. Ya must not ever repeat it. Not ever."

The desire stirred in them to know more, but his pale face scared them. Samuri nodded. Jewel followed, nodding, too, but also biting her lip to squelch her tears and questions. The three of them paused, numb and unsure how to go on from there.

It was Samuri who spoke first, not even knowing what he was talking about, but saying it confidently just the same. "What's the plan?"

The spell of sadness that held them broke.

Brody's grabbed the sides of his legs. "So, my knees are weak, and my hip is stiff. There's no getting' m' legs up a ladder again."

"Um, what about me?" Samuri offered. "I *could* go with you and help."

Brody rubbed his hip and chuckled. Their faces were so serious it was funny. His failed attempt to climb the hillside two weeks ago was even funnier.

Jewel's face brightened. Brody knew that look and put up a hand to stop her. "Jewel, ya got ta let me figure this one out. It's not like the other tasks. Them buzzin' creatures can be dangerous, even deadly."

Brody's eyes narrowed as he calculated the potential risks. *That missy, I don't dare ta let her start. She could talk me into anything. What's best ta be done?*

Samuri could do it. But not alone, not this first time. And Jewel, well, she's a different story.

Life was better with Jewel around. Lively she was. Unfortunately, she was also sporadic, and easily distracted.

"Al-righty . . ." A hint of hope and excitement crept into Brody's voice. "If the two of ya promise to do *exactly* what I say." He shot them a stern look. "And! Ya *must* wear the hat, Samuri. Nobody gathers Brody's honey without a beekeepin' hat on! I'll never let the two of ya go again, if ya get yurselves stung up. Ya can be sure of it!"

Despite Brody's gruff voice, they knew he was as pleased as he was concerned. Within half of an hourglass, it was settled. As usual, Jewel missed some instructions in the excitement of it all, though she truly tried to listen. Samuri took in each detail, looking ahead in his mind's eye, preparing. After an early midday snack and a few stout reminders, they were loaded up and on their way.

15
the ladder incident

Samuri looked awkward carrying the bulky ladder toward the clearing, but Jewel didn't laugh this time. This was big. Brody was willing to trust them to do something he himself was uncertain about, and Jewel knew Ri took it even more seriously than she did. Their packs were heavier than usual, weighed down with equipment solely for this task. Jewel fit her buckets inside of Ri's bigger buckets and carried them all. It was easy with empty buckets, but she wondered how she would manage to bring four full buckets back. Honey was heavy.

"Ri, I don't know how I'm going to . . . "

That was all she said before Ri tossed his head, and said cheerfully, "Just wait. You'll see."

His eyes were laughing at her; his quietness earlier wasn't from worry, as she had supposed. It was the excitement of being trusted with such brave tasks.

She freed a few of her fingers to poke his arm, and said, "Bug" while running ahead clumsily, the buckets clanging like crazy.

"Not fair," he pretended to scold, but he was pleased.

Up the hillside they trekked, planting their feet firmly and carefully.

At the boulder Ri explained the next steps. "Okay, Jewel, take the food pouch out of your pack and hide it under the hollow on the far side of the boulder. Put everything else inside the two big buckets and strap them to your pack. I need your help with the ladder now."

She laughed when she was done. "Now who looks the most awkward?" she asked.

"Bug," Ri teased her, but this time there was no chase as they made their way up the steepest half of the hillside.

Shortly before cresting the top, the murmuring, magical, almost deafening hum of hundreds of buzzing creatures caused them to stop abruptly. Jewel's eyes shone with delight, but Ri attempted to shake the sound away. This sound wasn't like the mellow hum of the two or three buzzing creatures they'd heard by the brook on sunny days. This racket confused him. Could he think enough to remember Brody's instructions?

On the hilltop, barely past the edge, they laid the ladder down and unpacked Ri's pack. A berm lay ten meters ahead, concealing the bees another ten meters beyond it.

"Now, hand me the pine needles you brought," Ri instructed, pulling an earthen jar from his pack.

Jewel was amazed to discover Ri had been carrying that heavy jar, but she was even more amazed when he started a small, aggravatingly smoky fire inside of it. While the smoke built up, Ri put Brody's beekeeper jacket on and pulled the drawstring tight at his hips. Handing her the hat, he paused to assess the scene carefully and plan his approach.

Jewel looked closely at the jacket. *If it was smaller maybe I could gather honey, but it's too big even for Ri.*

The memory of Brody's insistent voice broke through her thoughts. "Missy, ya be lettin' Samuri do the honey harvesting. NO arguing!" He'd even scowled at her. She would not need to be reminded, not even by Ri.

Samuri bent, gathering the smoky jar in one arm. He tucked

the ladder under his other arm and led the way to the berm. Jewel followed close behind carrying the strange hat and the buckets. At the berm they stood trancelike, taking in their first sight of the cloud swarming unpredictably around the tree. Laying both ladder and jar on the ground, Ri asked Jewel to put the gloves and hat on him. She stole one more glance at the buzzing creatures, then tied the hat to the jacket as securely as she could. Once she had his gloves tucked snugly under the jacket sleeves, she handed him the ladder on one side and the smoky jar on the other. Threads of smoke stung their eyes and lungs, while the all-consuming sound dulled their senses.

"Ri how are you going to get the ladder under the tree with all that stuff?" she asked, but there was no answer.

Samuri surveyed the ground between there and the spot he had targeted to place the ladder. Jewel stood near the berm and watched, biting her lip. This was the part she had missed at the shop. The ladder was secured over Ri's left shoulder, with a bucket looped in the crook of his left arm, and his left hand holding the ladder against his hip. He held the smoky jar in his right hand as far away from his face as he could. Proceeding intentionally, he did his best to remember how the ground looked before he was wearing the hat. He placed each step carefully but firmly, and slowly moved forward. Now he was at the tree, with creatures buzzing curiously around him. He placed everything on the ground before settling the ladder beside the tree. Then he set the bucket on the shelf.

Only one step at a time, he repeated Brody's reminders to himself. *Safety is yur greatest strength. Loyalty is yur greatest goal, even with them buzzin' creatures. Be peaceful with 'em.*

Reaching up, he placed the jar strategically on a sturdy branch where its smoke wafted up into the hole of a huge hollow one. Before Jewel knew it, he was on the ladder, with creatures circling closely, exploring, covering him, but gradually growing sleepy. He hung the bucket over a branch, clumsily retrieved a scooper from his pocket, and reached into the cavity of the tree exactly like Brody had told him.

Jewel watched each of his movements intently. She noticed the slightest shift each time Ri moved. The ground under the ladder was uneven, but he was concentrating too hard to feel the slight tottering increase. Without even thinking, Jewel moved stealthily up to steady the ladder. Despite the smoke-induced calm of the bees, Ri panicked seeing her there.

Brody's warning replayed in his head. "Remember, them buzzin' creatures can sense calm. No fast movements. Those stings hurt like crazy. Too many stings and it'll make ya mighty sick."

Do I risk shouting over the noise and upsetting them?

No, he couldn't. He strained to see Jewel better but the netting, combined with the sunlight streaming through the leaves, made it impossible. The creatures hummed sleepily, seeming unconcerned about her presence.

The subdued murmur of the buzzing creatures and the slight whispers of the breeze were the only sounds. Each moment pressed against Ri, but he forced himself to use slow, calm motions, focusing only on his task. For Jewel, time stood still, and worry ceased. Awe tingled through her body, keeping rhythm with the sweet humming around her, while she held fast to the ladder.

When the small bucket was filled, Ri's anger at Jewel was replaced by a new concern. How could he get her back to the berm safely? Possibly his presence on the ladder would distract the creatures and allow her to retreat safely if she carried the smoky jar. Leaving the scooper in the thick honey, he pointed to the jar and whispered for Jewel to move slowly back to the other side of the berm. A few bees began to trail lazily after her, but soon lost interest in her calm demeanor and pine-green clothing.

Once she was safely beyond the berm, Ri shifted slightly, grabbed the bucket, and climbed down. On the second to last step, the ladder tottered, causing him to slip sideways. He pulled the bucket closer and steadied the ladder with his other hand as he stumbled to the ground. The swarm buzzed louder, circling tighter together for a moment. Ri paused and waited. When they were calm again, he stepped carefully away, leaving them behind.

At first, he had wanted to shout "What-were-you-thinking?" but at the berm he felt more relief than anger. What if the ladder *had* tipped before the smoke had calmed the bees? What if he had fallen and she had rushed in too fast?

"Here, let me help you get that hat off. Are we safe here? I'm glad you're okay." Her words tumbled out, but he heard her voice differently now.

He paused, staring at her while she untied the hat, pulled it off and set it aside. His anger and irritation gave way to admiration. She was brave! Seriously brave. And capable, not flighty and silly. Ri was sure he'd never see her quite the same again.

Midday snack by the brook gave them time to regroup. Ri sat motionless gazing at the trees, even while Jewel packed up. By the time they returned, Ri had a plan for the ladder.

Jewel stayed by the berm to watch. Gathering the honey took longer than expected. Ri filled a bucket at a time, slowly carrying them to the berm. None of the buckets were completely full, but they were heavy. Jewel covered each one exactly how Brody wanted. After Ri brought her the last one, he retrieved the ladder and laid it against the back of the berm. Then he hid two buckets under the nearby bushes.

"Oh, I see." Jewel laughed with relief. "We don't have to carry everything back today."

"Brody told us when we were getting ready, but it was a lot to remember," Ri said with a kind smile.

The way Ri remembered details and yet was so patient with her amazed Jewel. *What would I do if I was assigned to tasks without him?*

"Thanks, Ri! I'll try to listen better. Really, I will," she promised.

On the way back, they talked about the ladder incident. Ri told her about slipping when he came down. Ri said they needed to fix the ladder, so they must tell Brody, but Jewel still wasn't sure. They walked without talking, letting the breathing of the woods soothe them. Jewel held a medium sized bucket, enclosing it in her arms with her hands clasped together hugging it. The bucket was so heavy she had to step carefully to keep from losing her balance. She glanced down often, smiling at how perfectly she had secured the cloth over the top. Tight and not one wrinkle.

"To keep it clean n' purty, cuz I'll not be wantin' bugs and dust in our honey," Brody had told her. She was delighted to see how nice it looked.

So, she walked carefully, not able to see the lovely, honey-goldenness, but dreamily thinking about it.

"Okay. We can tell, but if he gets mad at me, you . . . "

"Hun-uh, I'm sure he won't be mad." Ri interrupted. "I'll explain about slipping off the ladder. He has to know. We have to brainstorm together how to fix it. And besides, you're doing your tasks so loyally, Jewel. I think Brody knows he can trust you."

Jewel was shocked. "Trusts *me?*" Her jaw dropped in disbelief, but a feeling as golden and warm as the honey itself filled her.

When she could speak again, Jewel's voice was urgent. "Let's hurry, Ri. Can we? Brody was pretty worried. It'd be nice to get back early, wouldn't it?"

The golden, warm feeling in Jewel radiated out to Ri as well. It was a wonder how much had changed.

"Um-hmm, very nice," he agreed, nodding.

How glad they were that they did. Brody was already sitting on the stump outside the shop watching even though they were back earlier than usual. He stood quickly and waved at them. Then, he walked to the path and took Jewel's bucket. Brody's eyes shone with pleasure when he paused like he was weighing the honey. Brody nodded to each of them, delight radiating out from dozens of smiling wrinkles. And though he insisted on carrying Jewel's bucket, he couldn't help but limp.

Inside the shop, they placed the buckets on a counter where it was easy to see. Brody praised Jewel for the tidy work covering each bucket and motioned for Samuri to take the cloth off. You

142

would have thought Brody had never seen honey from the way he stood gazing into its gooey, goldenness. As he breathed it in deeply, the expression on his face mirrored exactly what Jewel and Ri were feeling.

"Ah, my loyal youngs, ya done well, as well as I coulda done m'self."

The tender looks that passed between the three of them embarrassed Jewel. The urge to hug them both pulsed through her body, but she resisted it. She had never felt so . . . she had no idea what to call these best ever pleasant feelings.

Then, there were all sorts of questions to answer about the day, until Ri became especially serious and said, "Um, Brody?" and Jewel knew he was about to tell.

Brody knew something was up, too, and listened intently while Ri unraveled the story of the ladder incident. Jewel kept her eyes on Brody's face every second that Ri talked, not realizing she was barely breathing.

The instant Ri stopped, she burst out, "I didn't mean to Brody! I just-couldn't-help it."

She looked down preparing to be scolded.

"Young . . . Jewel . . . " Brody tried to talk, but he was overcome by emotion.

When she finally looked up, Brody's face was only tender and proud.

"Young Jewel, you are a wonder." Brody's voice held such respect. "So brave, so loyal. Did ya know that loyalty to the Township has ta begin with loyalty to each other? Do ya know, Jewel, I think ya did the exact thing Samuri or ol' Brody would a done if we'd been in yur place." He nodded with respect at Samuri. "I don't just think so," he went on. "I know it!"

"Um-hmm," Samuri agreed solemnly.

"Ya did it, my two youngs!" Brody spoke so loudly it startled them. "And if ya can do it this first time, the rest'll be easy."

Nothing more needed to be said.

That night, Samuri on his cot, and Jewel on hers, relived the marvels of the day and pondered what might be ahead. Cooler weather and shorter days were coming. What would the Brave Days be like at the Woods Shop? Would they go to the clearing at all? Would Brody have enough tasks to keep them there? Or would Apprentice Tuckit reassign Jewel? Could he? She had been mostly pleasant and loyal.

No, Gran Para Brody wouldn't let the apprentice, not now that they knew the secret of the bees. Plus, Gran Para Brody couldn't gather the honey. He needed them.

With the comfort of knowing, their tiredness carried them off into pleasant dreams of a life lived loyally, forever at the Woods Shop.

16
crunch

The sunlight slipped away earlier every day. The breeze felt fresher, not exactly cool, just different. Flowers shriveled up, each in their own timing, while the vast space of luscious, green grasses became dull and faded. Jewel felt sad, like she was fading, too. If only she could gather the clearing in her arms and save it from the death of the Brave Days.

"Ah, look at it pour," Brody said, holding the door as they rushed in sopping wet from the rain. "And it be good timin' cuz we got us lots o' talkin' ta do. Alrighty, let's get started. Who's makin' the tea and who's makin' a fire?" Brody asked cheerfully, instead of assigning the fire to Samuri, like usual.

"Oh, I want to build a fire," Jewel burst out quickly. "If you help me."

Brody placed a covered, flat earthenware stone near the empty hearth and settled into the closest chair. Samuri arranged mugs and herbs on the bench between their chairs and the hearth. In no time, Jewel's fire popped with sparks, and promising wisps of steam curled above the kettle.

"Once this storm passes, we'll be doin' tasks differently. Listen close . . . " Brody said energetically.

A huge basket beside his chair was filled with dried vegetables, bark, and pinecones. Brody placed each vegetable on the bench, one at a time, named it, and explained where it was found. Samuri recognized the onions, papery-looking potatoes, thin carrots, and sweet potatoes he'd worked with at the Exchange. Next came the pumpkins and squashes, which grew by the brook farther up the hillside. Brody talked on and on about all they must gather before the Brave Days. Jewel and Samuri shook their heads. How could there be so much yet to gather? How had Brody done all of this alone?

"Not alone." He explained with sparkling eyes and animated motions. "M' Rosie had always helped me some, but a few years ago the Township made m' Woods Shop her only assignment. M' Rosie, *she* was the best help. When she was gone, I had ta work daystart ta full dark." The light in his eyes dimmed and his shoulders slumped.

"Oh." He shook off his storytelling suddenly and returned to the tasks before them. "Don't worry about rememberin' all this. Tomorrow ya begin comin' at daystart and we'll share a tasty snack while I give ya the details of each day's tasks. I sent messengers ta tell Town Master Cree and yur paras."

Jewel was speechless, trying to take it all in. Brody nearly laughed watching how earnestly both she and Samuri bobbed their heads to assure him they were listening. The tangy aroma of Brody's sweet potato flatbread told them it was time for a break. Brody brought it to the bench and cut it into three huge chunks. Samuri poured bubbling hot tumblers of tea while Jewel drizzled thick ribbons of golden honey into the tumblers and over the sweetbread. Mmm . . . the sweetbread was melt-in-your-mouth delicious. The shop grew quiet except for the crackling fire and satisfied smacking sounds. They burst out laughing.

That afternoon they examined the specimens of bark, nutshells, and pine needles. Bark helped you to identify a tree. Nuts were tasty little snacks hidden in hard shells. Pine needles made nice teas, cleaning sprays, and powdered bug repellents when ground-up properly.

That's it. Jewel thought. *That's what I smelled when I used to rake, only mixed with something else.*

Brody insisted they memorize the names of those specimens, then he brought out a drawer with several varieties of leaves. "Trees with these broad flat leaves be called deciduous. Can ya see the similarities and how they're changin' now? Those leaves will fly away soon, but the needles of the evergreens . . ."

Jewel's face lit up with understanding, and she finished his sentence. ". . . stay green. Oh!"

"Start bringin' me leaves now and then so ya can learn the names. After all, how can ya be friends with a tree if ya don't know its name?" Brody winked at Jewel before he realized what he'd done. He stopped abruptly.

Once again, his thoughts had slipped out too easily with them. Now Jewel would ask him about friends and what could he say safely? But he need not worry this time. His wink had distracted Jewel from noticing the new word at all. He hurried on more seriously now.

"We'll also be matching nuts with their shells and their trees so you can find 'em easy. I promise ta teach ya all sorts of ways ta use 'em, too."

All this and more waited for them in the cold Brave Days ahead.

The next day Jewel rose early and beat Samuri onto the damp, earthy-smelling path. At the sound of Samuri's door closing, she pointed a bug-poke in his direction, as if to say, "See if you can catch this bug."

He nodded farewell to Para Patrick and sped up a bit leaving enough space behind Jewel to be Township-safe. It was invigorating to be out so early.

"Apple gatherin' starts now," Brody declared with a stout nod once they'd arrived. "But I warn ya, it's hard work even for a para. Pace yurselves. Be careful how much you carry, especially you,

Jewel."

Jewel's heart swelled. Brody truly cared about her. Still, it was maddening to be so small.

As if Brody had read her mind, he added, "M' Rosie was a head taller than Jewel, but she never did the heavy carryin'."

Am I like Brody's Rosie? She felt she would burst at the pleasantness of that thought.

Brody loaded Jewel with baskets, Samuri grabbed the ladder, and they were at the bottom of the first apple tree in no time. The ladder tottered on the odd, bumpy ground under that tree, and they moved on to the next tree.

Samuri motioned upward, explaining, "You pick, then hand me the full baskets."

Jewel scrambled up the ladder into the leafy branches, balancing one basket on the shelf, and hanging another basket from a short branch. Sunbeams and leaves alike tried to draw her into wild, fanciful stories.

"No daydreams today," she whispered to each rosy apple she picked. She would be focused and quick.

Samuri filled their packs with fallen apples while also keeping a careful watch on the ladder. After handing Ri the seventh basket, Jewel climbed down. They strapped their heavy packs on, grabbed a basket in each hand, and started back.

"Wait," Samuri said near the big curve. He chose the two biggest apples and offered one to Jewel. "One, two, three." *Crunch!* Their teeth sunk into big juicy bites. Samuri devoured his first apple and was halfway through his second apple before Jewel finished her first one.

Baskets of apples were so much heavier than buckets of fresh lavender or herbs. By the time they reached the empty shop, their strained muscles had begun to protest. Still, they unloaded apples out of their packs and onto the counter with caution. Next, they placed baskets along the edge of the counter so the other apples could not roll off. It was a relief to start back with light, empty packs and baskets.

"Young Jewel. Young Samuri. Wait," Apprentice Tuckit called out as he strode toward them. "Here." The apprentice handed them a large snack packet. "Gran Para Brody said to sit inside the shop for midday snack. It's muggy today and he can't have you overheating."

They nodded and turned to leave.

"Where are you going? Eat your midday snack now. He'll have more for you on the next trip. Remember, safety is our greatest strength. And sometimes your strength is your greatest safety."

Extra snacks were a loyal idea, because their third trip back, Jewel was shaky and starving. On their fourth and last trip of the day, Samuri suggested they leave the baskets at the shop and only fill their packs this time.

"Hmm." Samuri admitted. "I wanted to try climbing way up past the ladder to gather apples, but not today."

"Uff. Not today," Jewel agreed with a sigh, glad he had admitted it first. Suddenly she perked up, threw an apple at him, and announced, "Fresh, tree-picked apples."

They forgot their tired aching bodies for a moment. No one else had apples whenever they wanted. No one except Brody. It was worth the pain.

Or so they thought until the next day. Oh, how their muscles ached. They tried to hide it, but Brody already knew.

"Here be some salve," he greeted them, handing them pocket-sized wooden boxes. "Rub a wee bit on yur sore muscles every hour."

Jewel opened hers immediately and smelled a distinctly familiar scent. "Mmm. Peppermint. There's something else, too. Isn't there Brody?"

"Ya got a good nose for scents, Jewel. Rosemary be in it and the base be a thick hazelnut cream. Once ya start workin' with herbs, yur goin' ta learn fast. Now here's the plan. No apples t'day. T'day yur goin' up ta gather hazelnuts. That's the way we'll be doin' things. One day for gatherin' apples, then one day for gatherin' lighter goods."

Samuri laughed as he opened his tin and rubbed his neck with the powerfully scented ointment. Brody knew everything.

By the next stormy day three weeks later, the Woods Shop and the Exchange were overflowing. Jewel and Samuri burst into the shop anticipating a day of cheery fires and tasty snacks, but the shop was dim and cold.

Brody rushed to close and latch the door behind them. He immediately motioned for them to follow as he cut across the shop grabbing two large hourglasses on his way.

"No fire?" Jewel questioned, pleading for light and warmth.

"Aye, sorry missy." Brody spoke in a low, hushed voice. "It won't do ta have folks come in unannounced t'day."

Brody stopped in front of the large shelves to the left of the hearth. "Alrighty. Let's get started. I need ya ta move these shelves. Pull em out straight and even. We only have four hourglasses of time before messengers come."

Jewel looked like a cornered creature. Samuri doubted she'd last even one hourglass. He moved to do whatever they must do as quickly as possible. Jewel mimicked his actions and grabbed her side of the shelves. Though both of them pulled with all their might, only Samuri's side budged. He came to her side, and they shimmied it out together. They continued tackling it one side at a time until a massive rug appeared on the wall where the shelf had been.

"Perfect!" Brody exclaimed and slapped his hands together so loudly, it startled them. "Now the rug comes down."

In no time Samuri climbed the ladder, released the thin but heavy rug and was staring at the largest door they had ever seen. Jewel scurried to move the rug while Samuri put the ladder away.

Her eyes never left the heavy, intricately carved, metal handle of the door.

"Alrighty! Jewel, see if ya can turn that handle to the right until it clicks twice."

Jewel grasped the handle with both hands, leaned in, and pressed with all her might, anticipating a shimmering path beyond the door. The bulky handle resisted momentarily, groaned, and then gave way abruptly, throwing Jewel off balance. A gust of chilly air swept over her. Instead of the warm, fruit-lined path of her imagination, she faced the dark, gaping emptiness beyond the door.

"It be m' cellar." Brody quipped cheerfully. "Not ta worry. There be candles for ya on the left."

Brody edged past Jewel, unaware. "C'mon missy, light a candle. Wait 'til ya see this, Samuri. Not a minute ta waste," Brody chided.

Brody grabbed the only lantern on the narrow shelf, lit it and moved to the top of a deep staircase. Samuri lit a long, sturdy candle and rushed to Brody's side, ready for the unknown. The steep steps and Brody's knees required him to steady himself with his free hand. Jewel hung back, but Samuri followed Brody, lighting the candles along the side of the staircase as he went. Finally, Jewel set her jaw stubbornly, lit two candles, and followed.

The large dirt room below was glowing dimly by the time she reached them.

"Look missy," Brody said, "the best underground cellar ever. It's ta help the Township through the Brave Days." With animated gestures, he showed off each invention he'd crafted for the optimum storage of produce.

Then Brody climbed back up, one painful step at a time, instructing them which produce to take down. Samuri and Jewel carried apples, onions, squash, potatoes, and carrots to the edge of the landing. The next hour, Brody shouted out instructions while Samuri and Jewel went up and down with buckets and baskets.

Jewel flinched at each shout and every flicker of a candle. Samuri rushed to finish soon. At the sight of baskets full of carrots, Samuri suddenly knew what to do.

"Um, Jewel, can you do the carrots, so I don't have to?" Samuri sounded perturbed.

"It doesn't matter to me." Her voice was barely audible. "As long as we get this done fast."

Samuri moved a basket of carrots to the dirt-filled wooden bins and buried a carrot for her to see. Jewel knelt hesitantly and grabbed a handful of carrots. The moment her hand touched the dirt she began chatting.

"Sorry small carrots," her voice was kind, but matter-of-fact. "It's not pleasant being stuck underground, but loyalty is our highest goal; we have to do what we have to do."

With every mound of dirt, Jewel was more herself. When the carrots were all stored, she sprinted up and down the stairs twice as fast as before, and in no time, they had finished.

Once everything was back in order, Samuri asked, "Why do you hide it, Brody?"

"There be lots o' reasons. Folks get unpleasant and fearful. If folks *know* there's more, they want it, even if they have enough. But there's rarely enough anymore. So, Town Master asked me to keep it quiet, and I'm not sayin' another thing about it. My story is my story, and *this* I got ta keep ta m'self."

Jewel's troubled eyes questioned Samuri, but he only shrugged. He didn't know the answer this time but talking always helped. A day in the clearing was what Jewel needed most of all.

17
the perfect year

Snow, a rarity in the Township, came swirling and twirling outside the high window above Samuri's cot. There would be no trip to the clearing today. Instead, there would be freshly baked snacks and the promise of a leisurely day with his paras. And Jewel? Samuri imagined her curled up by her heat box eating fresh snacks and laughing with her paras. Maybe *this* was what Jewel needed.

The storm subsided the next morning. The two youngs tied cloths around the bottom of their trousers and waded through the snow to the Woods Shop. The warmth of the sun filled the shop inside and melted the snow outside. But Jewel never forgot the cellar.

The next day they were back in the clearing to finish gathering apples. Samuri cleaned, sorted, and packaged the apples that hadn't been stored. Brody worked to start Jewel on processing the herbs that were sufficiently dry. Rosemary, her favorite, came first. Herbs seemed to unlock Jewel's brain. Her hands followed Brody's details remembering whether to measure or crush the tiny leaves for medicinal teas and ointments. Jewel was surprised how much she enjoyed the Brave Days, except, of course, when she had to make a delivery. She would do *anything* rather than deliver orders or go into the cellar again.

"Here, Samuri, I'll take care of the lavender today," she would offer eagerly. "I can tie it perfectly careful, exactly like Brody likes it. I know it's such a tedious job for you."

Jewel was right, too. Samuri thrived on taking produce to the Exchange, herbs to the medics, dried grasses to basket weavers, or any order anywhere. At least until he made his first delivery to the Big Bungalow. The Young Daro, the one who had troubled Jewel, greeted Samuri at the door.

"What is this?" The stocky, self-important new door attendant searched through the order and scolded Samuri. "Can't you folks at the Woods Shop get anything right? Do I have to come to the Woods Shop myself?"

The next week, the Young Daro began sending messengers to the Woods Shop with time-sensitive orders two to three days a week. Samuri rushed to fill and deliver them within an hourglass, but each time Daro sent him away, shocked about some strange mistake. Once, Daro requested Town Master Cree come out to talk to Samuri.

"Greetings. You are the young from the Woods Shop, isn't that correct?" Town Master Cree's furrowed eyebrows held a peculiar displeasure. "My attendant tells me you often bring incomplete, incorrect orders. Do you deny it?"

Samuri paused to think. It was forbidden to accuse Town Master's messengers, or door attendants, but lying was forbidden as well.

Samuri bowed, first to Town Master Cree, and then to the Young Daro. "Loyalty is my highest goal. I'm unsure how such misunderstandings occur. I have attempted to do my best."

"Are you displeased with your tasks?" Town Master asked with an odd, calculating voice.

"My tasks give me opportunities to be pleasant to all, loyal to the Township, and to provide a safe, long life for us all. This is

154

my highest goal."

The Town Master's face lit up, obviously pleased. "Greet the Director of the Woods Shop for me." He nodded and returned to his office.

This time, Samuri could not shrug off Daro's swift, smug farewell, or anything about that incident. When Jewel was out of earshot, he explained the details to Brody quickly. Brody rolled his eyes, patted Samuri's shoulder, and told him not to worry. Samuri nodded, hiding his discouragement, and returned to his tasks, reluctantly.

Three days later, the young door attendant showed up at the Woods Shop bragging about a special request for Town Master. Unfortunately, Jewel was closest to the door, making it easy for the Young Daro to corner her. Jewel lifted her chin and greeted him with her best forced smile and her loudest, most business-like voice. Then she motioned to a counter across the shop and pushed past Daro to fill his *important* order.

Daro visited frequently for a while. If his list was short, Jewel filled it herself, gave Daro a business-like farewell, and went back to her tasks. If not, she politely promised to send it as soon as possible. Samuri was pleased to see Jewel handle Daro so well.

But one day, Daro slipped around the corner and into the door unnoticed. Samuri and Brody were involved with tasks at the edge of the woods, south of the shop. Jewel sat near the fire, deep in thought while crushing and mixing herbs. Without warning, Daro stood by Jewel's side snickering. Her pulse raced and her hands begged to curl into fists, but Jewel ignored it all and continued her task. Finally, Daro stepped in front of her, and narrowed his eyes, staring at her like a dangerous creature.

"Do you know what I am now?" Daro snarled. "I am Town Master's personal attendant, so you owe me even more than before."

Jewel's hands continued their mechanical grinding, but her mind went blanked.

"Jewel, do ya know where . . ." Gran Para Brody shouted from halfway across the yard.

The evil in Daro's eyes faded. He asked for one small tin of ointment, grabbed it from her, and slipped out the north door. Jewel's fear turned to anger. It was a ridiculous threat. She didn't owe him. Why did she let *him* make her feel so unsafe? Her feelings were unreasonable. Jewel determined to find a solution, a way of moving her tasks swiftly, without ever telling Samuri and Brody.

Then the coldest of the Brave Days hit, and Daro failed to come again. Cozy days in the shop were the best of times, especially for Brody, but also for Samuri and Jewel. Brody welcomed them into his own bungalow-like corner of the shop. His quaint wooden table to the right of the stone hearth was the best place to do tasks in the huge chilly building. Working. Laughing. Learning. Together. Samuri and Jewel were becoming more than helpers in Brody's heart. Did he risk letting them closer only to have *them* taken from him, too?

In the late-night hush, Brody listened. Understanding spread through his heart, like the firelight's warm glow shining across his face. Samuri and Jewel hadn't just been given to help, comfort and cheer *him*. They'd been given to him to keep *their* hearts alive in this stark, lifeless Township. Brody gasped at the realization. "Alrighty." He felt like the wind had been knocked out of him. "Show me how."

Stories seemed to be a part of it, but he'd already let too many stories out without thinking. Stories were tricky. He must tell the right stories, in the right tone, with the right words, and not get sidetracked by his emotions. Each night he listened for intentional, well-chosen stories to share the next day during the mindless tasks of deep cleaning and repairs. During the hourglass before lunch, they gathered around his table to learn new recipes.

"Snacks be about more than fillin' yur stomachs. Snacks should satisfy yur tastes, cheer yur heart, and strengthen yur body."

Of course, that led to lessons about mushrooms. Jewel and Samuri had not eaten a single mushroom without Brody's

156

permission. What did they still need to learn?

"Ah, mushrooms. Delicious, but potentially deadly. Tellin' ya isn't enough, Brody's got ta see ya really know yur mushrooms. Ya need lots o' experience. *No takin' risks.*"

Jewel squirmed. Her fear of failing flared up, but not for long. Each of Brody's lessons on seasonings, scrumptious recipes, and medical concoctions emboldened Jewel. She remembered flowers, herbs, and mushrooms better at Brody's table than out in the clearing. Tea blends were the first recipes Brody actually let them make. Those were the easiest of all because one cup of tea wasn't too much to throw away. Daily mugs of steaming tea were their training ground *and* their best moments of the day.

One dreary, overcast day, Samuri asked permission to make his own blend of tea. Brody nodded and watched Samuri sort through the dried herbs, considering his choices. Jewel pulled her knees up, wrapped her arms snugly around them, and watched from her chair by the bright, flickering fire. Toasty warm, listening to the sound of their voices, Jewel felt her favorite dreamy, golden feeling envelop her.

If only I could be assigned to the Woods' Shop all of my life, she thought. *That's what I want. To be here, doing this, with Brody and Ri forever. That is all I want.* She closed her eyes imagining it. *I'd never have trouble being pleasant and loyal again. I'm sure of it.*

Worried thoughts crept in close behind the warm thoughts, but Brody's laughter brought her back in time to see Samuri make a funny face. He tossed that cup of tea and tried again. Soon, Samuri brought a lovely little tray complete with mug, spoon, and a bit of honey, just for her. He hovered near her, explaining each detail of the blend he'd made.

Brody took it all in. *Aye, look at Jewel sittin' there as peaceful as a plum. We did it.* He wiped away a tear and sent up silent thanks. His part seemed small in proportion to the overwhelming joy she'd brought him. *A year ago, I never coulda imagined it.*

"Samuri, this is amazing. Teach me, too. Okay? Not today, though. Today I'm busy enjoying."

"Um-hmm!"

Such opposites they be, these two, Brody thought, *yet so good for each other.*

Samuri was practical, steady, and quiet. Always present in the moment, watching carefully. Always alert to help if Brody should need him, even when he was tinkering away at his own new idea. Brody protected that, giving Samuri plenty of freedom but staying close enough to lend a helping hand if the young should need it. Brody listened when Samuri talked, celebrating every idea he thought up for improvements and inventions. But it was Samuri's questions that meant the most. Brody hadn't met a young so humble, so teachable, so interested. At least not for many years.

That night Brody knelt by his cot for the first time in months. *What a pleasure it be havin' these two workin' beside me, Samuri listenin' and Jewel chatterin' away. It be like days long ago. I hope m' dear Rosie is watchin' from the great cloud o' witnesses.* He chuckled and wiped a tear away. *It looked like m' life would fade away lonely and without purpose, but it's not goin' ta be so. One thing, though, Lord . . . is it safe ta tell 'em about thee yet? I can't bear ta put 'em in danger nor ta have 'em takin' away.*

The Brave Days, which Samuri and Jewel feared would drag endlessly on, had their very own delight, rushing by happily and a little too quickly. Shortly before the cold winds loosened their grip, a bustle of unexpected activity ignited the shop. Few folks in the Township knew how much the Woods Shop did to prepare for Celebration Day. No one questioned where the gorgeous, handcrafted trays and tables came from each year. Most folks merely drank in that short splash of delight, so lacking in their plain lives.

The tables, now decades old, were stored in a tunnel off the main cellar. Town Master Cree had dragged them up himself the past four years to ensure the cellar remained hidden. Now, Samuri and Jewel did it quickly and carefully while Brody brought serving trays out from the lowest shelves around the shop.

"Did you and Rosie do all of this on your own?" Jewel burst out.

"Well, I cannot say all on our own. We had the best o' help," Brody said strangely, and moved to a corner away from Jewel's constant questions.

The story was about to spill out. This, Brody's first intentional story, must take what had been and weave it together with a loyalty that would sustain these youngs through the difficulties ahead. After midday snack, he brought out honey-baked hazelnuts he'd been saving for such an occasion. Then, he began. "The idea of tables an' trays was brought ta me." It had been Rosie and Nyah, but he did not say so. "Ya see, I was no craftsman, the woods and the clearing was m' life."

Brody went on to tell of the old gran para, Jasper, who taught him to cut, carve, and build with pine. His words painted a fascinating picture of the Brave Days he'd spent with Jasper before the Township's third Celebration Day. Brody avoided the parts about Edward's worries, and Town Master Creeander's failing health. Instead, he told of Jasper's knowing ways with both wood and folks.

"Bro-dy." He imitated Jasper's slow, kind, husky voice the best he could. "There's a way to say no to the folks you disagree with, and still be completely loyal."

Jewel gasped. She would like to learn that.

The shop became a flurry of purposeful cleaning, sanding, and oiling. Occasionally a table leg had to be repaired or rebuilt. "Ya know, it's not just anybody can do these kinda tasks," Brody insisted as he taught them. "Ya got ta have a certain eye for the wood, like it's alive. And a feel for the tools. A special touch. Of course, watchin' and listenin' helps, too." The gran para in

Brody's story came to mind, and the three of them exchanged a knowing glance.

Brody checked their work daily, nodding, making corrections, and praising their concentration and ever-improving skills. The result was pebble-smooth trays and tables. Finally, Samuri moved the last table near the north door with the others, and Jewel stacked the last smooth, shiny serving tray on the counter, wrapped in a clean cloth.

"Done," all three exclaimed in unison, beaming at one another.

The next two weeks they bustled about with last-minute tasks. The cooks for the celebration needed help chopping onions, grinding rosemary, and making hazelnut milk. The Exchange needed the Woods Shop to pick up their lists and return with their orders as soon as possible. Those lists required sneaking into the cellar from time to time. Jewel shuddered every trip down, both from her own claustrophobia and from the fear of someone discovering the cellar.

Two days before Celebration Day, Brody slapped his hands on his thighs and exclaimed, "Aye, now the torches. T'morrow when ya leave yur bungalows, tell yur paras that you'll stay here 'til full dark."

He saw Jewel and Samuri, glance at each other with mingled interest and doubt.

"Not ta worry, I'll be walkin' ya to yur bungalows m'self," Brody said firmly. "Bring yur warm things for goin' ta the clearing in the morning, and for bein' out after last snack. Don't forget! Tell your paras the Director of the Woods Shop has special tasks from the Town Master. There'll be no trouble about curfew. I'll send a messenger from the Big Bungalow with more information, but don't tell yur paras 'til yur leavin', then fly like the buzzin' creatures."

Brody seemed to have thought about every detail, so they shrugged away their concerns. Instead, they thought about how they would make torches. As they shut the door, they heard

Brody chuckling and talking to himself. Certainly, something special awaited them.

A terrible thought occurred to Jewel, something she had to tell Ri before they spaced themselves to walk back.

"Samuri, remember what Apprentice Tuckit told us the first day? What if they reassign us this year?"

"Hmm? *No*, Brody would tell us if there was still a chance of that." He laughed to make light of it, but Jewel wasn't convinced.

"Torch making tomorrow, over forty of them. Whew." Ri made a big deal of it, hoping to distract her. "Sounds like too much. Do you think Brody will let *us* light one?"

"Yes," she burst out with confidence. "Brody lets us do everything."

There was no reason to worry about being reassigned. Together with Gran Para Brody, they had pulled off the perfect year.

18
sparks

The next morning the side door was open when Jewel approached. Before she pulled on the east door, she heard voices speaking in hushed tones. One was Brody, and the other . . . hmm, where had she heard *that* voice? She waited for Ri. Maybe it was a messenger or a clerk and he'd recognize their voice.

Samuri was perplexed when Jewel motioned for him to be quiet, but then he heard the hushed voices, and he knew. It was Town Master Cree.

Maybe they shouldn't have come so early today; they had only wanted to please Brody. Then, without even knowing why, they slid to the corner of the building to hear better without being seen. They smiled. Surely Town Master Cree had come about the torches. That was it.

"Listen to *me*, Brody." Town Master spoke in the tone of a frustrated para speaking to an unreasonable tiny. Then he shifted to a more pleasant, convincing voice. "Surely two of the new apprentices will be better for these tasks. More mature. Stronger. I'll bring them by myself the day after Celebration Day. Or at least consider some older youngs."

Jewel's eyes popped wide open, and Samuri put his hand over her mouth. It would be just like Jewel to gasp and expose them. She nodded, pushed his hand away from her mouth and replaced it with her own hand.

A long silence followed. Jewel's temper rose. An overwhelming urge to run and yell at Town Master grabbed her. Instead, she paused. What was Ri thinking? Would he stop her? She peeked at him out of the corner of her eye. Concern shone from his eyes, yet he waited patiently—perfectly still—eyebrows arched, eyes alert, listening for Brody's reply.

A different sort of thought came to her as she watched him. Trust. What had Samuri told her about trust? Wasn't it that trust meant you knew someone cared and would always do their best for you?

Am I afraid that Brody will send us away, she asked herself, *or am I just afraid Town Master won't give Brody any choice?*

Jewel fixed her eyes on Ri's face and waited, trying her hardest to give trust a chance.

Finally, Brody's voice broke through the silence, stern and unwavering, like a spark bringing hope in great darkness. "Cree, I'll not be givin' up these two youngs!" Gran Para Brody wasn't budging.

More silence followed, as Town Master searched for a new angle to get his way. Why hadn't he brought Apprentice Tuckit along? Tuckit always found the right thing to say. On the other hand, Apprentice Tuckit had been the one who convinced him to try Samuri and Jewel in the first place.

After another long pause, Brody's voice broke the silence. "I'll not . . ." he insisted loudly.

Then, his voice, though still exasperated, came more softly. "I'll not be given' them up, Cree. Ya said I needed help, so I put up with two years of dull apprentices, comin' and goin', always bein' more work than help. This year I gave it one more try, but only ta be loyal to ya, Cree. Yur Apprentice Tuckit is a loyal one. I like 'im. Because yur Tuckit was so sure about these two little sprouts, I let 'em into m' very own dear Woods Shop. Tuckit was right. These two are more help than four or five others could ever be. *They* are my choice. There's no changin' m' mind this time, Cree."

Samuri tugged on Jewel to follow him to the far end of the shop, but before they turned to leave Town Master spoke again. "All right, Brody. I did say you could decide this time, but it was an unwise move. I should've stayed within the Laws. Exceptions always cause trouble. So, reconsider it."

Brody remained silent. He sensed Cree had more on his mind than the Laws, but it was almost time for Jewel and Samuri to come, so he must speak now. The things he must say were not for their ears. Brody stepped closer to Town Master Cree and put his hand on Cree's shoulder. Cree flinched for a moment.

"Cree, I've kept m' promise," Brody said softly. The compassion in his voice was tangible. "I've done the best I can, just like I told ya I would. And ya know what it's cost me. Still, ya have m' word of loyalty that I'll keep with it as long as this here body lets me."

Only Brody saw Cree's picture-perfect smile slide right off his face and tumble over his sagging shoulders, revealing the tiredness he hid from all others. Without speaking, he gazed appreciatively into Brody's eyes and nodded before he turned toward the door.

"Oh, and Town Master," Brody said kindly, with much respect, "t'day be the day for makin' torches. M' helpers need ta be here late. Can ya please send Apprentice Tuckit with a message for their paras? Paras like ta be sure their Town Master knows and that it's a loyal assignment."

Town Master Cree's stunning smile returned, and he drew himself up straight and tall as he stepped out toward the Big Bungalow.

A few minutes later, Jewel and Samuri rambled in nonchalantly to find Brody bustling about flustered and upset. He merely nodded and began explaining what they'd need to gather for torch making. When they popped in with their first load of grasses, Brody was more settled. Each trip they took replaced Town Master's unpleasant words with anticipation. After all, they were being *allowed* to break curfew. The three of them would watch the sun set and light a torch at full dark. And best of all, Brody would not let them be reassigned.

Midafternoon they returned to help Brody build torches. The last of the torches was finished in time for them to grab last snack together and sit outside watching the sun set.

"Sorry ta disappoint ya, but there'll be no celebratin' for us, tomorrow." Brody sounded matter-of-fact, but he avoided their eyes, unable to bear the disappointment he might find there. "Nope. Ya see, we need ta be right here in case a torch burns out or a table breaks."

"Yes, Brody, yes. We'll be right here." They chorused wholeheartedly their eyes riveted on the apricot sky fading into dusk.

"Please be givin' your paras my apologies t'morrow, an' greet 'em for me with pleasantness ta each an' loyalty ta the Township."

Jewel pushed the thought aside. Yes, she would be loyal to Brody and tell her paras, as much as they would let her. That wouldn't go well, but tonight all she cared about was this, this time, this place, this first Celebration Day together.

The stars were coming out in the moonless sky overhead when Brody let Samuri light the first torch. Jewel leaned against the shop gazing at the night sky, basking in the glow of the torchlight. This . . . was worth whatever it took.

On Celebration Day, Samuri felt giddy. There'd be no searching for Jewel in the crowd this year. Together with Brody, they would celebrate their own little feast, with their own recipes, and chat by firelight about their perfect year.

"Ya know," Brody explained, "Town Master always insists ol' Brody stay inside and keep the doors open in case a messenger be needin' somethin'."

Sure enough, they cleaned up and halfway through their first cup of steaming tea, a loud voice called nervously from outside the door.

"Greetings. Send two torches. Loyalty."

The messenger hurried off without knowing whether he'd been heard. While Jewel looked out at the candlelit silhouette rushing away, Samuri grabbed two of the extra torches and was gone in a flash. Moments later he ducked back into the shop as quickly as he'd left. Brody was puzzled. Why hadn't the Young Samuri lingered at the Square?

Samuri stretched, invigorated by his quick trip, and asked, "Did I miss anything?"

Brody laughed the deepest, happiest laugh they had heard yet, grabbed something from his pocket and threw it into the fire. "Here's somethin' for ya, Samuri."

A boisterous pop startled them. Sparks of brilliant colors exploded in the hearth. Tiny fountains of color sprung to life from the depths of the flames, starting at the back, then spreading dangerously close to the front, but no one moved. Brody blew out the last lantern, leaving the shop dark except for the hearth and the colored shadows dancing at the edges of the room.

"Ooo . . ." Jewel stood, turned slowly, and took in every dreamy, flickering shadow, before settling back to gaze intently into the flames.

"Breathe, missy! Yur scarin' ol' Brody." Brody begged, fearing she might pass out any minute.

Brody sighed a deep, contented sigh. There was no doubt in his mind now. Jewel and Samuri hadn't missed a thing. No, this was where they wanted to be. His way was becoming their way.

For three years now he'd suffered, alone in everything, mourning Rosie's death, mourning the loss of Dupree and

Maggie. No one could replace *them*. But Samuri and Jewel, these two were making his life bearable, even hopeful.

His only worry now was Cree.

19
spiral

A chill hung in the morning air, but Jewel and Ri knew the day would be perfect by full sun. Plus, they had the new scarves Brody had made them. "A gift," he had said, "for Celebration Day."

A gift. Jewel mused. The words comforted her mind like the brilliant colors touched her heart. She had never had a gift.

"But ya must only wear 'em during tasks," Brody had insisted. "Cuz, I made 'em m'self, only for you, and I don't want 'em ta be gettin' lost!"

The moment Jewel entered the shop, she wrapped the nubby scarf around her neck. On their walk through the pines, she lifted a fold of the scarf, rubbing its silky softness against her cheek. Brody's hands seemed increasingly stiff lately. Was it from the hours he'd spent making their scarves?

"Ri! Do you think these are a kind of scarf of remembrance made specially for our first year here."

Samuri nodded, pleased, but said nothing.

"Or . . . ? Oh, no." Jewel looked and sounded like she might cry. "What if Town Master reassigns us? What if the scarves are Brody's farewell? Is it because of all the trouble I was in before?

Should I go tell Town Master I've changed? Do you think—"

"Jewel!" Samuri interrupted. "No, you shouldn't. I mean, I don't know why, but I talked with my paras and they—"

"What?! You told your paras about Brody and Town Master?"

"Um-hmm, I did," he answered, perfectly confident with his decision. "Para Patrick is a great listener. He understands. He said we can't always know why things are the way they are, and sometimes it's actually better if we don't know."

It was nearly impossible for Jewel to listen in her panicked state. Samuri had insisted *she* keep all sorts of things from her paras—not that she had ever minded—but now he was telling his paras this?

"What if they report Gran Para Brody to the officials?"

"Listen, Jewel." Samuri's voice became low and serious. "I didn't tell them about the way Brody *talked* to Town Master Cree."

Jewel sighed with relief. "It made me feel mixed-up, Samuri. Kind of afraid, but kind of safe, too."

"Exactly!" Samuri was really going now. "And that's why I think we can stop worrying. Town Master *let* Brody talk to him that way. Brody even called him Cree. Whew! I don't understand it, but Town Master let Brody get away with it."

Jewel concentrated on taking slow and intentional steps, her eyes lowered to the path, her head throbbing with the weight of these new thoughts and worries. Samuri waited for her where the path met the clearing, sunbeams flooding over him. One glance and Jewel rushed past him, dropping her buckets and tools to twirl about wildly.

"I - will - be - loyal - the - rest - of - my - life!" she vowed to the unfurling pale green leaves and to the birds bickering in the swaying treetops.

A delicious spring breeze swirled out of nowhere and she shouted victoriously, "This is ours. They gave this *to us!*"

"And we both know why." Samuri sounded serious but pleasant, like a kind para steering their junior away from trouble. "Bugs and dirt and creatures. C'mon." He tossed one of her buckets near her feet and locked eyes with her. Yes, they knew.

A nod between them made an unspoken pact—a vow to do all they could to stay here. And so, Samuri and Jewel began their first day of this second year with increased vigor.

In the middle of pruning bushes, Samuri stood up and shouted over to Jewel, "You've really got it this year."

She straightened up and waved at him, smiling warmly, then went back to pulling weeds and smoothing out the ground around the strawberry plants. His encouragement meant more to her than ever before. Lately, her bungalow was nothing but accusations, demands, and threats from the time she came in until she managed to fall asleep. *How can the Township put up with such a troublemaker? Why can't you be like other youngs? What do you do when you're not at the Celebration ceremonies?* Instead of waiting for an answer, Para Madeline simply insisted Town Master Cree would get even with Jewel sooner or later.

Each night Jewel curled into a ball and squeezed her small bundle of clothes against her ear to block out as much as she could.

Night after night Para Madeline demanded that Para Philip do something about it. At first, he only asked her why it mattered. Folks didn't know Jewel was their young or that she was assigned to the Woods Shop. And folks all looked the same in the crowd anyway. Para Madeline never answered. Para Philip wondered if she missed Jewel or if she just wanted to be in control. Whatever it was, he figured he'd better figure it out before he went crazy.

Jewel dressed silently, shaved quickly, and slipped out unnoticed each morning. That was some small comfort. On her walk to the Woods Shop, she pretended she was sweeping everything behind her and stepping into a fresh story. A story where she belonged all the time. A life where the Woods Shop and the clearing were her bungalow. Where the peace and beauty of her stories became reality.

One night, the tone of Para Philip's voice sent shivers up

Jewel's spine. "I'm done with this Madeline. Here are your choices. I will have Jewel sent to the dorms tomorrow; she's always in her room, anyway. Or you will *stop* the crazy talk. If Jewel goes to the dorms, her Exchange points go with her. The Township will *not* allow her to return."

Oh, how Para Madeline whined and moaned, insisting she cared about Jewel, not the silly Exchange points. She swayed over and slid Jewel's door open to gaze at her adoringly. Jewel watched Para Philip from the corner of her eye as he stomped close to Para Madeline and stared at her with piercing, cold eyes.

"Fine. She stays. But . . . one more comment, only one, and she's gone. For good."

An hour later, Para Madeline was mumbling cheerfully about new knitting patterns as if nothing had happened, but life in their bungalow was never the same after that.

Jewel never mentioned the trouble with her paras to Samuri or Brody, but Brody saw it and heard it in her forced cheerfulness and short temper.

"Young Jewel, can ya go out and stir up some of that there clay for patchin' holes?"

She practically danced out the door, always glad when Brody asked her for extra help.

"Samuri . . ." Brody called, motioning him to the back of the shop. "Does our missy say anythin' to ya about her bungalow?"

Samuri thought for a minute, but nothing stood out in his mind. Honestly, his mind was stuck on how to fix the axe he'd broken that morning. "Huh-un."

"Do ya ever hear her paras chattin' in the evenings? Maybe even chattin' a bit too loud?"

Samuri shook his head. Why would Brody ask such odd

questions? The only difference Samuri had noticed in Jewel was her pleasant, loyal attitude toward tasks. Still, Brody watched her closely.

As if that wasn't enough, the Young Daro showed up on the path again. Multiple mornings they spotted him on their way to the Woods Shop and some days on their way back as well. Samuri made Jewel lead so he could see her and reach her quickly. Samuri got his greeting to Daro out first. That gave them the advantage.

Jewel nodded politely but kept her eyes to the ground and passed by quickly. Samuri quickened his pace, reaching the other young shortly after Jewel had passed him. Even that was enough to tie her stomach in knots. They simply could *not* risk being accused of trouble, especially after the conversation between Town Master Cree and Brody.

Everything seemed to go wrong after that.

The early blueberry harvest was near, and Brody assigned Jewel the complete responsibility for it this year.

"Ri, you will never guess . . ." Jewel shouted when he came in. She stopped abruptly and slapped her hand over her mouth.

Brody laughed, and burst out, "Aha, now Brody gets ta keep one of yur secrets. And not ta worry. Brody be a mighty loyal secret keeper. The two of ya know that, yes?"

Jewel, rescued by Brody's kind reply, fought the urge to throw her arms around him in a gripping hug. Instead, she bug-poked Ri, who laughed with the same joy she felt.

"So. What's the great announcement?" Ri asked, heartily.

"It's a secret . . . for later." Jewel teased, closing her eyes, and shaking her head playfully.

Just before the clearing Jewel burst out. "Brody put me in charge of the blueberry harvest. Me! I'm going to check them first thing every day."

There were at least twenty-five bushes, filled mostly with dark green, unripe berries. Mixed among them were some larger, light green berries and then a smattering of ripening ones with a blush of blue. Jewel knew from last year she must only pick berries that were plump and deep blue with a light grayish dusting on the surface. The first day she only came away with one bucketful, and it took her almost until midday snack to pick them. It was as if her hands had forgotten. The berries ripened through the week and soon Jewel's hands picked so swiftly Ri had to help carry the buckets back.

Toward the end of the harvest Jewel spotted a furry brown tail in a nearby tree. "I see you swirly-tail." She called up and *swish*—the creature effortlessly skittered away. Jewel followed, as she often did, keeping Brody's rules for safe distances with creatures.

There, practically in her path, was a new bush of plump, ripe blueberries just waiting to be picked. It was seriously the most beautiful blueberry bush of all. She filled her pockets and was about to toss a handful in her mouth when she saw a startling sight. Two tiny, black swirly-tails swayed between the trees, following a black swirly-tail twice their size. Why hadn't Brody told her about these soft, graceful swirly tails? She clutched her handful of berries and rushed to share them with Ri.

"Look! I discovered a bigger, fuller blueberry bush, and . . ." She held out a handful for him to examine.

"Those?" Ri interrupted skeptically, before she could tell him about the black swirly tails. "Um, I don't think so. See the smooth ends? The end of a blueberry has a small bumpy trim."

Uff. Jewel folded her arms across her chest and glared at him. Ri thought he knew everything.

"Okay. What color were the stems?" Ri pushed back, not arguing, but not giving in either.

"Stalks, Ri. They're called stalks," she said pridefully, sure that he was wrong this time.

"Okay then, stalks," he said, shrugging. "Listen, Jewel." Anger rose in his voice. "Brody said some berries can trick you. A handful can make folks sick and sometimes even kill you. So, check the *stalks*. If they're bright pink, those are the berries he warned us about. Now, I'm going to get the food pack and eat.

Come if you want."

Pink? She faintly remembered Brody saying that. The anger drained out of her. Ri had never talked to her that way. And she deserved it. What if she had eaten that handful? She usually did. What if they had both eaten them? Her hands trembled as she walked back, grabbed a spade from her pack, and dug a deep hole far from the clearing.

When the berries were safely covered under layers of stones and dirt, she returned, poured water on her cloth napkin, and scrubbed her hands thoroughly.

"Do you think it's safe for me to eat?" she asked quietly.

He nodded and handed her his empty napkin for her food. "I thought you weren't coming." His voice was still strained.

"I buried them, deep, because . . . you were right. And you're right that I didn't listen like I should have." Jewel's voice was brave, but her eyes were sad.

"Um . . . okay." Ri conceded, slowly. "Well, you do listen better now than at the beginning. At least most of the time."

The silence was deafening while Jewel ate. Both of them were wrestling with the same thoughts. What if they had eaten those berries? And what of Brody's consistent reminders that safety was their greatest strength and loyalty their highest goal? He didn't mean it the stifling way the Township did. The reality of it was frightening.

Later, back at the shop, Jewel willingly told Brody about the poison berries. Brody's face grew pale. He bit his lip and shook his head, too upset to even scold her. No one spoke and Brody sensed the tension as thick as rain clouds hanging between the two youngs.

Hopefully that'll be mendin' itself soon, Brody thought as he watched them leave.

Then, Jewel spiraled like never before. Ri was confused. Jewel had handled the berry incident honestly and bravely, but now she was a wreck. Before this, she'd stuffed her unpleasantness, never letting Ri know the pain she felt inside. He had cheered her in dark times, again and again, without ever knowing it. This time, there was no cheering Jewel up.

"Who cares about tasks? Who cares about loyalty?" she muttered continually. "I'll get in trouble eventually and Town Master Cree will send me away, and . . ." Her voice wavered back and forth between blowing up and giving up.

On and on she went, avoiding tasks with Ri, only finding relief when she did her favorite tasks alone. At the shop she was pale and quiet, smiling at Brody with half-hearted smiles, trying to hide her feelings.

At first Ri tried his typical distractions—shiny rocks, crazy races, and bug pokes—but that made her more irritable. Finally, Ri blocked Jewel out and focused on his own tasks. By the next week, her tantrum was over, but the darkness was still a cloud around her. Now Ri came face to face with his own tug-of-war.

"What was I thinking all these years? Me, keeping Jewel safe? Because she obviously doesn't want me to. Or maybe she can't even see it. Either way, I'd rather do tasks with someone other than unpleasant, unsafe Jewel." It was just too much for him. She was too much.

In the evenings he held his feelings in, unwilling to hear Para Patrick's advice this time.

On the fourth day, while Ri cut wood outside, Jewel quietly called for Brody's attention.

He grabbed the bag of lavender he was sorting and moved closer.

"Brody, has a she-para ever been the Director of the Woods

Shop?" Her voice was strained and secretive but determined.

A faraway look came across his face. "Well, Young Jewel," he answered pleasantly, "yes and no. What be ya thinkin?"

"I'd like to work here. All of my life. Here, and in the clearing. I could do it. I know I could. I'm determined to concentrate better. And Brody?" Her voice, though still determined, was barely above a whisper, not willing for Ri to hear her most private feelings. "Brody, I don't think I could ever be bungalowed."

A look of surprise passed over Brody's face, but he kept listening.

"You see, I'm not good with folks. I'm not pleasant with anyone. Not all the time. Not like the Township wants." A tear slipped down her cheek.

Brody's eyes and voice mourned with her. "Well, missy, those be some interestin' thoughts, but don't be worrin' yurself with 'em. Ya have plenty o' time ahead for figurin' it out."

"Okay, but we'll talk again later, right?" She spoke like she had when she was a tiny, insisting more than asking.

He tipped his sunhat, in agreement. "For sure, missy, anytime." The warmth and cheer of his voice reassured Jewel. Her secrets were safe with Brody.

20
help!

Thwack. Thwack. Thwack. Ri was chopping away with the fixed axe by the time Brody and Jewel came out, ready for the day.

"Glorious . . . I mean, pleasant day," Brody corrected himself cheerfully, "for yur end-of-the-week snack, my youngs. I tucked it away in Jewel's pack this time."

Jewel rubbed her hands together and chirped. "Mmm. Let's go." The cloud seemed to have lifted.

The entire walk they were lost in thought. Jewel was relieved to have pleasant thoughts again. Ri was wishing he was more pleasant and loyal like Brody, not like the forced Township way of most folks.

My paras are like that, too, Ri thought. *They're always ready with the right words. Why is that so hard for me? Why don't I have the words to help Jewel?*

He missed the days of being Jewel's hero just by helping her chase bugs.

On the dark part of the path, under the thickest canopy of trees, Jewel confided in Ri. "I need help! Something inside me is all wrong." Her hand moved to her stomach, the bucket swinging awkwardly against her.

A sincere searching had replaced her gloom and anger. Ri could tell, but his lingering frustration wasn't willing to let her off so easily. Now was his chance to tell Jewel to get over herself and try harder!

He opened his mouth to speak, but what came out shocked him. "Be brave and be true, Jewel. You have many things to do in your life, but you will always have help! Always."

The words were strong, but sweet, too, overflowing from deep within him. Something about them was familiar but he had no idea why. He only knew those words were loyal, like something Brody or his paras might say.

Jewel felt it too. A gasp of deep breath filled her lungs. The words had a powerful effect, opening her heart to a new understanding of what was true about herself, her life, and the choices before her.

I am stronger than all the thoughts that have been shouting in my head. I can be pleasant, even more pleasant than the Township way. And Samuri . . . he's been loyal to me over and over. I won't make him put up with my craziness anymore. I don't have to, and I won't.

The wind, always beautiful to her, stirred unexpectedly in the treetops, leaving her with the feeling that help was indeed on the way. She smiled, nodded to Ri, and walked on as if he could read her thoughts.

Ri entered the woods to gather mushrooms, pausing now and then to ask Jewel's opinion of questionable ones. Jewel glanced up into the treetops, took another deep breath, then stooped down to start gathering. Ri knew now things would be okay.

After two buckets were full, they left them near an apple tree and wandered along the edge of the clearing, gathering rosemary. When they had filled the bags of rosemary, Jewel and Samuri decided to head to the brook early. Just before they reached the path up, a patch of stones caught Ri's attention. Why hadn't he seen these before?

178

"Hmm, those would be perfect for the smaller warming stones. Should we gather some now, and leave our packs here while we go to the brook?"

There was no answer. Jewel stood motionless, gazing at the stones.

"Catch it . . ." Jewel whispered, forcefully. "Oh, Ri, catch it."

He looked down in time to see a brilliantly colored bug scamper between two of the stones.

Dropping to his knees Ri tossed the stones aside. The bug stared up at them, waiting, as if it *wanted* them to catch it. But when Samuri reached for the bug, it scampered under the next stone. Jewel dropped to her knees on Ri's left side, picked up the next stone, and found herself staring at a small triangle of material peeking out of the dirt.

"Hmm . . . " Ri's voice and face were puzzled.

"What is it?" Jewel asked, looking back and forth between the dirt and Ri.

A curious shiver of anticipation and caution rippled through each of their bodies as Jewel reached to tug at the material. Whatever it was, it looked like it had once been completely buried, hidden under both dirt and stones. Had rain, or digging creatures, exposed that bit of a corner? Or what? Jewel grabbed a sharp stone and began digging.

"C-a-r-e-f-u-l-l-y," Ri urged her.

For no explainable reason, Ri felt convinced this mysterious object was significant. He shook his head to push the odd feeling away and grabbed a sharp stone to join Jewel. How long had this been buried? Who had buried it so securely, and why?

The corner was made of stiff material similar to the small backpacks and oiled satchels Brody used for rainy days and sharp tools. A small bundle appeared when they brushed away the dirt from digging. They both reached to grab it at the same time, but the dirt on the far corner wouldn't give way.

"Some bug, huh?" Ri's eyes were wide with the adventure of it. He motioned for Jewel to have the final tug.

She pulled, and Ri scraped a little more soil away. The next tug sent Jewel sprawling on her back, gripping the bundle and its torn strap as dirt flew everywhere. She held it out for Ri, wiped off her face, and spit the dirt out of her mouth.

"Come on. Open it. Hurry!" she pressed, but Ri took time to lay the bundle on the grass and brush it off.

It was like their backpacks, only smaller, made of thicker material, with more straps for closure. Ri guessed it to be about thirty centimeters wide and fifty long. It was impossible to tell whether the dusty brown color was its real color or the result of years buried in the soil.

"Hmm, someone was taking great care to protect whatever's in this," Ri mused. He stopped to prepare himself, and then pulled.

Something was squeezed inside the pack, wrapped in tightly woven cloth. Inside of the soft cloth lay a rich, hazelnut-colored satchel of thin, yet durable material. The flap on the front was sealed with an ornately engraved metal buckle. Jewel's eyes met Ri's. Simultaneously, they scanned the clearing and what they could see of the path. No one must see this, at least not until they knew what it was.

Ri removed his pack briskly, replaced the satchel in its wrapping, and handed everything to Jewel. "Put them in my pack and start up to the brook."

She was confused. What about the pack she was already wearing? But, this time she didn't hesitate or question him. Jewel acted quickly, put his pack on awkwardly over hers, and started up. Ri replaced the dirt and the rocks as if nothing had changed. Then, he rushed up the scree path to catch her.

"Lunch as usual?" His voice was calm, but his eyes were alive with dozens of questions.

At the brook Ri motioned for Jewel to put snacks out, then wandered into the woods. He came back obviously pleased to have accomplished what he set out to do, but Jewel was clueless. The satchel laid safely beside her while they shoved their midday snacks in their mouths. They shook their snack cloths free of crumbs and laid them side by side in the grass, clean sides up.

Jewel unbuckled the pack and held it upside down over the snack cloths. The satchel slid out. Next, she laid the satchel across her lap, reaching in carefully, until she touched something soft and dry. But what? Her fingers grasped loose pieces of material and pulled them out. For a moment she sat breathless, letting them rest in her hands before offering them to Ri.

Ri was more puzzled than impressed. He sorted through four or five of the thin, rectangular pieces, placing them one at a time on the cloths. Then he piled the rest of the sheets on them and thought. They were similar to the Exchange's tally sheets for tracking points and purchases. Only these sheets were made of lighter, thinner, more delicate-looking material. And the markings?

A spellbound *"Ooo!"* escaped Jewel's lips.

These markings were not the blunt, straight markings the Exchange used. These markings, of varied sizes and shapes, practically fluttered across the sheet, line after line, filling each sheet with its own unique beauty.

Ri raised his eyebrows and glanced at the satchel in Jewel's lap. Again, they exchanged a puzzled look, and Jewel handed the satchel to Ri, who probed deeper, hitting something stiff. He handed the thin pile of board-like squares to Jewel and reached in one last time, searching every corner, but finding nothing more.

The quizzical squares mystified Jewel. When she picked up the top one, it stuck to a pile of sheets containing a few large markings and whimsical pictures. The board above and below those sheets bound them together.

"Ooo . . ." Jewel whispered, reaching out to touch a drawing, lightly tracing its shape with her finger. The only drawing she'd seen before was the rough map of the clearing that Brody had drawn in the dirt for them.

Ri watched and waited, giving Jewel a few moments of wonder before he scooped up all of the sheets. He returned them to the satchel, put the satchel in its pack, and walked away.

"What? Why are you . . . ?" Jewel exclaimed, but Ri was halfway to the trees with the newfound treasure. She followed him, demanding an explanation.

"Come with me, Jewel. We're going to hide them for now," Ri said.

"But, but I," she tried to protest.

He stopped and smiled at her patiently, but said, "Think Jewel. We have tasks to get done. We can't draw any attention to this. Nobody can know! Do you see?"

But she didn't see.

"Brody." Jewel said sweetly, confident of her solution. "We can take them to him because we trust him. Right, Ri?"

Ri shook his head and kept walking until he came to a large evergreen behind a broken-looking boulder. There he laid the tightly-covered treasure in the hole he had dug earlier, spread soft dirt over it, and covered it with a flat rock. Together they sprinkled pine needles and small rocks over the dirt. No one would have guessed it was there.

"Um, I want more time with it, Jewel. We don't even know what it is. We don't know who hid it, and . . ."

Jewel gasped. "Do you think somebody hid it to get us in trouble?" He watched her hands ball into fists, only this time it wasn't in anger, but in fear.

"Jewel, everything's okay," he reassured her. "Maybe someone long ago buried it. Maybe no one knows. But something in me says those sheets are forbidden. So, no matter what, safety is our greatest strength." The strong, kind way Ri said it put Jewel at peace again.

"Forbidden." Jewel mumbled cautiously. Her furrowed eyebrows spoke of her inner struggle. Thought after thought flooded her mind. Finally, she asked the only question that mattered for now. "When can we look again?"

"At the end of next week when we come up for midday snacks."

Her shoulders slumped forward, and she started to pout.

"We want to keep our Woods Shop tasks . . . *and* figure this out, right?" he asked.

The truest, most sincere smile lit up her face. Jewel flexed both arms, then poked him hard.

"Bug!" she exclaimed and dashed back to the brook ahead of him.

Midweek, Ri awoke on his cot questioning whether he had made the right decision. Pouring rain and howling winds dashed against the high window. *So much for this week's trip to the brook.*

Surprisingly, Jewel welcomed the waiting that week. Sure, being shut in brought out her fidgety side, but she kept every impatient, awkward question to herself.

The wonder of their discovery chased the typical evening sadness and boredom away from her cot. The first night, she pieced it all together.

Exactly what did Ri say?

"Be brave . . ." She understood that. "And be true." *True* sounded a bit like trust. Was it? "You will always have help."

Yes, that was what he had said, but somehow it was more than that. New strength had risen up in her when Ri spoke. And what about the bug? Were they imagining it or had the bug waited for them to pursue it?

"Here I go again," she scolded herself, "always thinking up some silly thing. The bug has nothing to do with the satchel!"

But as soon as she said it, she felt an unexplainable nudge. The bug, Ri's words, the pictures, and the markings *were* each a special *help*. A warm, safe feeling filled her room, not the Township kind of safe, but safe the way Brody meant it. Even waiting for sleep to come was pleasant when you felt safe. Even with a bundle of clothes over her ear blocking out the noisy wind and rain. She had no doubt the weather would clear, and they would go to the brook.

The last night doubts tormented Ri from every side. What if the downpour soaked through to the satchel? Had he made the right decision? Or should they tell Brody?

"You will have help. You will always have help," someone called to him in the dark. He squinted at his doorway expecting to see Para Chloe, but blinding darkness blocked his gaze. A voice he did not recognize continued to reassure him, and his eyes grew heavy.

Jewel woke unusually early, looked up expectantly, and saw the sun beaming through her window in all its glory and strength. She wrapped her arms around herself, squeezed tight and slid quietly to the floor.

The words carried her out the door, feeling like the brook bubbling down the hillside. "Be brave and be true. You will *always* have help. You *will* always have help."

21
decoding

Waiting for midday snack took every ounce of self-control they had. The moment they reached the brook, Ri dumped his pack on the ground and headed to unearth the bundle. Jewel laughed and began to lay their midday snacks out. She had watched Ri nervously shifting his jaw back and forth all morning, worried about the satchel, but *she* had no doubts. The satchel was safe; she knew it was.

"Look at this, Jewel," he called to her before he reached their snack spot. "It's perfect, not a bit wet."

She laughed. "Good job hiding the bug."

He barely heard her. Shoving a blueberry bar in his mouth, he rushed to open the pack and then the satchel. Next, he handed Jewel the loose sheet on the top and picked up the next one for himself.

"Um-hmm. They seem to repeat. I didn't notice it that first day, but I thought about it every night and it just came to me." Ri's hands trembled slightly with anticipation.

"I don't get it." Jewel said, still preoccupied with the feel of the material. What could it be?

"Look here. This first mark is round, see?" Ri sounded delighted. "It's like *your* mouth when you're really surprised." He laughed. "And look how many times it's on this sheet."

"Oh. It is!" Jewel gasped in astonishment, her mouth gaping open unconsciously exactly like Ri had described.

He touched several points on the material, then said, "Check yours."

Her eyes scanned her sheet, and she nodded. Then Ri pointed out the consistent spaces between the small groups of markings. Yes, she had those, too.

"Ri, compare my sheet to yours. Do you think they're the same?"

"Hmm." He looked and sounded puzzled as he spoke. "No. They're not the same but look."

Jewel leaned in, focusing intently as he pointed out several groups of markings.

"See how these markings are put together the same way on both sheets? The only difference is they're grouped in different orders at different places."

They pulled out four more sheets, each taking two to compare.

"Ri, it's the same with these! The order's different, but many of the same markings are grouped together."

Some birds began squabbling in the treetops, reminding the youngs of their tasks. "Let's take a sheet with us this week," Jewel exclaimed.

Ri shook his head. "Huh-un. I just don't want to risk it . . . at least not yet."

She started to argue but realized how odd it was for Ri to be cautious and secretive. Maybe he had his reasons. She handed the sheets back to him and gave him her goofy, all-is-well smile.

"You hide the satchel. I'll pack up and fill our drinking jars."

His eyes acknowledged her gratefully, relieved not to have to explain something he himself didn't even understand.

Jewel was glad to have an afternoon of favorite tasks before her. It helped keep her mind off of the strange markings. Instead of talking on the walk back, they focused on remembering the look of the markings and the spaces. They would have to wait a whole week to look again! How many times could they see the markings before cold weather kept them away from the brook? Could they discover the meaning of the markings before that? *Should* they risk asking Brody? Question after question wandered through their minds, but the answers would have to wait.

At the beginning of the next week, Ri exclaimed, "I have an idea. What if we find a place to hide the satchel near the clearing?"

Jewel stopped what she was doing, tilted her face to the sky, and pursed her lips, thinking hard.

"That way," he explained, "we can look at it every day."

"Yes!" She agreed quickly, but then questioned it. "Is that safe? I mean, is it safe to have it in the clearing with us?"

Every day they talked through it over midday snack, considering the logical pros and cons of scheme after scheme.

"I've got it," Ri finally said. "We'll hide the satchel on the far end of the clearing. At lunch, you can sit facing the Township path, and I can sit blocking our food. That way, if someone does come, you can see them and signal me. I'll have time to put the satchel and our snack cloths in my pack before they reach us. Only you can't gasp or make a face. Okay?"

"This is silly," Jewel said, shaking her head. "No one comes to the clearing."

In the end, though, she agreed to it. They would act normal, but they would also be perfectly careful.

By the end of the week, they were ready to bring the satchel down. The long-legged creature drinking by the brook, the buzzing bees, and the whirring-winged creatures went unnoticed. Each step of Ri's plan went smoothly, and by the end of the day, the satchel had a new hiding place. The anticipation and secrecy delighted Jewel, but Ri was just relieved to have the satchel safe and easy to reach.

In the days that followed, they found a new rhythm. Rushing

to eat gave them time to study the markings every day. Jewel grew bored with the meaningless groups of markings and brought out a set of the bound sheets. The first sheet displayed a charming group of simple everyday items—apples, a bug, a cot, leaves—in a circle surrounding the markings "A B C's". These were hand drawn with a realistic, yet jovial representation of each item. The back of that sheet held two larger drawings. A red apple sat at the top with the large markings 'Aa' beside it and the smaller markings 'apple' directly below it. Jewel smiled at the drawing of a bug on the second half of that page and the different markings beside it. 'Bb'.

Who would have put a bug on this? And why? As she puzzled and puzzled, she remembered lying awake in bed pondering Ri's words that she would always have help. Quietly her thoughts reached out, searching. *Are you there? Whatever you are, are you still there? Life has been more pleasant, but we need help figuring this out. If you're there, will you help us again?*

Nothing came to her before she put the sheets away, but she wasn't worried. The flowers and the fruits of the clearing were teaching her that all pleasant growing takes time.

Ri was still busy scanning the markings for similarities when Jewel reminded him to pack up.

"Hmm," Ri said without looking up, "we won't be back tomorrow. I wish I had more time."

"Don't worry, hand me your pack and I'll do this," she chirped, savoring the anticipation of the help that would soon come to her. While she packed up, Ri took a few more minutes with the markings.

When they returned to the clearing two days later, Jewel ate her snack bars too fast to taste them and pulled the bound sheets out before Ri finished eating. She hovered over the markings beside the first three pictures, "apple, bug, cot". Hadn't she seen the markings "a" and "t" together on the loose sheets?

Where are you? Jewel grabbed the bound sheets and flipped to the end to find "Tt" beside the picture of a tree.

"Tree," she said followed by the *t* sound. Then without even trying she put the sounds together. "apple . . . *a.* tree . . . *t. a . . . t,* at."

"Ri, look at this!" She burst out and scooted over to show him the pictures of the apple, the tree, and their markings. Then she grabbed the sheet he was holding and scanned the first few lines. Plunking her finger right under a set of *a* and *t* she proclaimed, "At!"

"At?" Ri said hesitantly.

"Yes, Ri 'at'. Like *at* the Woods Shop, or *at* midday snack."

Now Jewel knew. This was the secret to it all.

"The markings are sounds that go together to make the words we say. Match the markings to their sounds and use a group of markings to make a word.

"How did you . . . " Ri started to ask, but she interrupted him.

"It's the help thing you said at the very beginning of this, remember? You said I would have help from . . . somewhere. Or someone. But let's *talk* later." Jewel exclaimed and scooped up the pictured sheets.

After that, things came together quickly. Jewel was a natural at matching sounds to markings, so she did that part. Ri, on the other hand, was a genius at putting the sounds of the markings together on the sheets without pictures.

The day before the next rest day, Ri announced, "I'm folding this sheet and taking it with me, Jewel."

"What?" Her voice quavered with concern. "To your bungalow? I . . . think . . . we should tell Brody and keep it at the shop."

"No, to my bungalow. That will give me the most time with it," Ri said firmly, tucking it inside the top of his trousers and folding it tightly over the waistband.

The next day of tasks, they met shortly before the shop door. Ri rolled his eyes at her and shook his head a couple of times.

"Oh no," Jewel gasped. "Did your paras find it?"

"No, but I have a lot to tell you. Later though, not now. Maybe at midday snack."

Though Brody noticed a difference in Ri, he felt it was best not to ask, not yet. He'd wait to see how things seemed after a day of tasks and fresh air.

This time, at midday snack, it was Ri who barely ate. "Hmm. So, I made some big guesses and figured out a lot," he began. "You were right, Jewel. The markings are messages, but there's more. Listen to this! Remember about having help and what you told me?"

Jewel nodded, wide-eyed, silent, and waiting.

"Follow my finger under these words and listen. 'Call . . . to . . . me . . . and I . . . will . . . answer you . . . and . . . tell you . . . great . . . and . . . unsearchable . . . things . . . you . . . do not know.'"

Jewel's jaw dropped, and she sat there speechlessly staring at those words.

Ri waited, letting it sink in, until she could speak. "Really? The markings say that?"

He decoded them for her again several times, touching under each word as he said it. Now there was more than the warm, safe feeling she had grown to recognize. Now, there was a rush of excitement like torches lighting up the night sky, sparks flying everywhere, the promise of remarkable things yet to come. She wrapped her arms around herself and sat there dazed by the wonder of it while Ri packed the snack cloths.

Words. Words you could see. Words saved to remember later, or to give to someone else. Amazing words. Words sent to them simply because she had asked. She closed her eyes, pulling those thoughts close, tucking them into her memory.

Ri continued decoding as often as he could safely. Actually, he couldn't seem to stop. Some of the words were difficult, like the words *great*, *know*, and *unsearchable*, but he kept at each one until he was sure. Still, no matter what new words and sayings he figured out, those first words remained his favorites. He read them so often he could say them without looking at them.

190

Call to me and I will answer you and tell you great and unsearchable things you do not know.

Jewel loved the idea of the words, but once she had figured out the drawings and sounds, she was never interested in decoding. Of course, she was excited to hear every new word Ri showed her, but what meant the most to her was that something, or someone, was with them, helping them each step of the way.

22
voice in the night

Who knew life could be so . . . so . . . pleasant? Samuri and Jewel had been rescued in so many ways. Tasks together. Brody. The clearing. The satchel and its words.

Some nights, unwelcome feelings still crept in, threatening Jewel. The pain of her paras excluding her. Her fears of getting into trouble. The overwhelming anger and failure that had once nearly driven her to insanity. Now, she rarely needed to make up stories to push those feelings aside, she was living her own fanciful story.

The hardest part for both Jewel and Samuri, in all that good, was the motto, "Loyalty to the Township". It was hard to even think about it—harder still to recite it. Why were they determined to keep their discovery a secret even from Brody? And what about Town Master Cree? He would want to know, they were sure of that, but they never said so. What kind of trouble would they be in if someone found out?

Well, they *hadn't* told, and they *wouldn't*. Maybe not telling Brody was actually protecting him.

Shorter days and harvest tasks demanded Ri put the markings aside. Harvest was his favorite time of year. This year every detail of his tasks came naturally for him, so he recited the satchel's words to Jewel while they picked apples and carried honey slowly down the hill.

"Call to me . . ." was his favorite so he usually started with it.

"Now mine." Jewel would press him if he paused too long.

"The wind blows wherever it pleases . . ." Ri always stopped there to wink at her.

Usually he finished the whole saying, but occasionally she interrupted. "'You hear its sound, but you cannot tell where it comes from, or where it's going.' Like me, right?"

"Like you when you're not chattering," he'd tease her. "Now, what do you want to hear next?"

Some days Jewel asked for the words about being hidden in a shadow or the tree planted by a stream. Most days she was content to let Ri weave the words together however he chose.

Now their biggest concern was the Brave Days ahead. It would start with a stormy day here and there, and then stretch into weeks of staying in the shop. Ri's time with the words would stop, and it would be entirely too risky to recite them to Jewel. At first, they were confident of finding a solution. That summer, anything had seemed possible. But the perfect idea never came. So, they treated each day as if it was their last day outside.

Each night, as Ri lay on his cot waiting to fall asleep, he would say the words to himself. *Call to me and I will answer you and tell you great and unsearchable things you do not know.*

What was it about those words? Why did they resound so deeply inside of him?

Ri saw now that in a sense, Jewel's moody spell had led to

this. It was then he'd spoken unexpectedly, "You will always have help." *That* was the beginning, the words about help. The same day they had discovered the satchel.

Ri wondered if there were more sheets filled with words somewhere. *And who made the markings. Who buried that satchel? Does anyone know? Does Brody know?*

The strength and beauty of the satchel's words demanded his attention, at times hitting him forcefully, at times comforting him. He didn't tell Jewel. He didn't even know how to explain it. Then, one night the desire in his heart grew so strong that a silent plea rose up relentlessly in his mind.

Who are you? Who . . . are you?

The next morning, he awoke blank from a deeper sleep than usual. Suddenly he sprang to his feet and tossed the blanket carelessly over his cot. He rushed to get ready. *This* he must tell Jewel!

That morning, Brody was sitting outside watching the clouds when they arrived. "If the storm rolls in," he said standing up and scanning the sky, "ya need ta be comin' back straight away! First, it'd be mighty nice if ya can get more o' them hazelnuts an' a bucket o' late sweet potatoes. Get as much done as ya can. Might be awhile 'til ya can go again."

He raised his eyebrows and looked intently at them. They knew that look.

Ri gathered tools impatiently. *Please,* he thought, *we need this last day.*

Jewel chatted away about toasty fires and the new recipes of the coming Brave Days. Brody hurried her along, helping her get ready, despite the fierce pain his hip felt with the coming storm.

Again, Ri pleaded silently, *Please, just enough time to tell her.*

He threw on his pack, gathered both his and Jewel's buckets, and waited at the door. Jewel followed, flashing her cheeriest smile at Brody to assure him she had listened.

Jewel continued to chat away about all sorts of things as they walked. What would the weather do? How many more hazelnuts could they find before the weather changed? She wasn't expecting an answer, though. After they passed the clearing and crested the hill, it hit her. Ri had not made one single sound, not even his typical 'um-hmm'.

At her first glance toward Ri, she gasped, "What?" He was gazing at her with the oddest look on his face.

"Hmm. Well, it was the dark of night, and I was sleeping when he woke me."

"Wait. What was the dark of the night? Who woke you?"

"Jewel, please listen." Everything in Ri seemed to be begging her, but especially his earnest voice, and his intense, pale blue eyes. "It's hard for me to explain; hard for me to tell you this."

Fear tugged at Jewel. What could be hard for Ri to tell her? She'd always thought their talking was what kept them sane and strong. Talking together pushed their foolish ideas and fears away. Her eyes scrunched shut and she drew her breath in slowly before attempting to sound calmer than she felt.

"I'm listening," she said in a very matter-of-fact, yet welcoming voice.

Ri pointed east at the trees ahead of them and said, "We have a lot to do. Let's get to the trees and work while we talk."

The old, sturdy hazelnut trees were strong enough to hold Jewel's small frame. So, she shimmied up into the branches to twist off the clusters that had not yet fallen. Ri waited below to catch them in a basket.

Clearing his throat nervously, he began again. "It was the dark of night when a voice woke me. I sat up, puzzled. 'Para Patrick?' I asked, but there was no reply. So, I laid back down, but on my other side. You see, I thought maybe I'd heard the wind and imagined in my sleep that it was a voice. I had almost forgotten by the time I settled in with my face away from the outside wall. Then I heard it again. I mean I heard *him* again."

Ri paused mysteriously, forgetting the basket he held. Jewel wrapped her arms around a branch, laid her cheek against it, and waited.

"It didn't sound like Para Patrick, but who else could it be?"

Jewel knew Ri wasn't one to rush. She closed her eyes to concentrate, peeking now and then to reassure him she was interested. On the third peek, she saw that Ri had closed his eyes, as if he was living it all over again. His face was peaceful, though searching, too. Jewel closed her eyes, again, hoping she could understand what he was about to tell her.

"Like I said, who else could it be? But, paras are forbidden to speak to us in the night unless it's an emergency, right? Well, I got off my cot . . ."

Jewel giggled inside. Ri leaving his cot in the night? Sure, she'd done it before, but it was different with Ri.

"I walked carefully to my door, heel, toe, silently each step. There was no light shining under my door, so I slid it open. It's odd, Jewel, all these years supervisors told us not to leave our cots 'til morning light. I expected to feel awful, but it wasn't a big deal. The only thing bothering me was . . . I didn't *want* it to be Para Patrick's voice."

His voice took on an air of mystery. "Still, I walked slowly down the hall and stood across from their door. Para Patrick's breathing sounded slow and deep and steady. I could even hear Para Chloe's quiet breath with funny sounds in between. I don't know how long I stood there just waiting. Waiting even though I didn't know what I was waiting for. I felt mixed. The sound of them sleeping was so peaceful, but the thought of them discovering me by their door was disturbing." He opened his eyes, needing to know she understood. "I've always done what my paras said and trusted they had a reason, because I *never* want to disappoint them, Jewel. *Never*. That's why we *have* to keep the satchel a secret between the two of us."

Jewel slid out of the tree, and leaned against its short trunk, impatient to hear the rest. "Ri. Tell me what happened."

Ri moved to sit beneath the hazelnut tree beside hers. "Um, okay. So, I walked quietly back, slid my door shut, and lowered myself onto the cot. The voice spoke again. 'Samuri, it's me.'"

Ri looked at Jewel for what seemed like forever, searching her face, deciding whether or not to continue.

"I'm listening." She said earnestly, nodding.

"*That's* what I said, Jewel!" The excitement in Ri's voice gave her goosebumps. "I said *I* was listening. Then he said, 'I know, Samuri. You *are* listening. You're listening with all of your heart, and I'm with you.' I heard it deep inside, but it was as clear as if I'd heard it with my ears."

Ri stopped to take a deep breath.

"And guess what Jewel? Suddenly everything felt right inside of me, like when I was a tiny. Everything! Then, somehow a soft breeze stirred in my room, and I got so sleepy I couldn't keep my eyes open. That's all I remembered when I woke up."

Jewel was stirred too, not by a voice, but because something unexplainable was drawing her. She didn't want to move. She didn't want to speak. She wanted to keep this . . . whatever this was, in her memory forever.

Samuri's eyes were fixed upward, searching the sky. When he finally glanced at her, the peace of knowing was all over his face. He *knew* this was real. And he was pretty sure Jewel knew too. The moment was so intense Ri felt awkward. He stood and scanned the nearby trees for hazelnut clusters.

"Hey, Samuri. I'm glad you told me," Jewel said lightheartedly, and poked his arm before she grabbed her basket and climbed up again.

Ri winked at her, not just once, but first with one eye and then the other. It was the funniest thing and the perfect way to go on from there.

Before they ate lunch that day, the wind shifted, and the air became unbearably cold. One quick swoop and they dashed away with packs and baskets full of hazelnut clusters. Their teeth were chattering by the time they reached the bottom of the hill. Why hadn't they brought their heavy tunics or a hat?

The run back to the shop was exhilarating. The wind whipped their tunics, and sloshy bits of rain pelted their heads. They cut through the woods and burst into the shop sopping wet, shivering, and laughing. Ah, Brody had a blazing fire waiting to warm them. What a luxury! This was real heat, not the puny heat of their small, metal heat boxes. They sat a meter away from the flames, drying out and sipping big mugs of Brody's newest concoction. The Brave Days had begun.

Whenever there was a break in the cold, Brody sent them off in search of overlooked rosemary, apples, or onions. One day a messenger from the Exchange arrived begging for more warming stones, so they bundled up and wrapped Brody's scarves snugly up to their chins. Together, Ri and Jewel found fifty of the smoothest stones, brushed them off and brought them back. By the end of the day, they were exhausted from rushing back and forth carrying heavy bags and packs. It was worth it, though. The very word *stones* brought comforting memories to mind, almost as if they could feel the warmth of their own stone tucked securely under their chilly toes on a blustery night. Plus, the memories of their silly games, that first bug, and most of all the satchel. Memories shared only by Jewel and Ri.

On one of those days away from the shop, Jewel said, "Ri, we need to figure out something to call . . . whoever it is. It's so awkward not having a name. I don't think it would matter what, just something."

"I think it would matter," Ri answered firmly. "Names are important. Each step has been there at the right time. Right? So, waiting for a name is part of it. Let's just wait."

"But we could ask, couldn't we?" she pushed back, truly convinced she should.

At first her eyes were reflective, then they grew bright, and she rushed on, "Remember those first words you figured out?

'Call to me and I will answer . . .' Why don't you ask the voice?" She held her hands out palms up as if to say *this makes perfect sense.*

"Oh, Ri. Why didn't we think of this sooner? Ask him. So, we can stop calling him *he* and *him* and *the voice* and *whoever.*"

Ri sat silently, considering it. Jewel held her breath, trying to give Ri time to say something, but she couldn't wait.

"Surely, he has a name!" she burst out. "He cared enough to talk to you once. I think he wants to talk to you again. Ask him!"

Behind Ri's serious face, he was smiling, struck with Jewel's spunky confidence. Many times, she had been merely impulsive, but not this time. She was right this time and Ri was glad he wasn't alone in this, even if she was annoying sometimes.

"Um-hmm, we could." He paused, and double-winked, "I think we should."

His eyes turned upward to the sky, and her eyes followed as he simply said, "We want to call you by your name. So, let us know, okay?"

Ri felt awkward saying it. Silence. The breeze stirred in the treetops bringing out the fragrant smell of the nearby pines. More silence. Jewel waited with closed eyes sure *she* would be the one to hear this time.

After a gust of wind and a short pause Ri spoke confidently. "Faithful One. His name is Faithful One."

A third time he repeated it, though quietly and slowly this time, treasuring it. "Faithful One."

"Faith . . . full?" Jewel asked. "What is *faith?* I've never heard that word before. Have you?"

"Huh-uh, I haven't." Ri shook his head, smiled, and looked her straight in the eyes. "But that's what I heard, and the minute I heard it, I understood it. It's like what he said at the very start about always being here to help us. Always."

Jewel scrunched up her nose in frustration. A tinge of jealousy rose up in her heart. Deep inside, something told her 'Faithful One' was the perfect name, but she felt left out. Why had Ri heard the voice the first time? Why had Ri heard now, instead of her? Asking was her idea, not his.

Instead of her usual sparky response Jewel flatly said, "Okay, that's great. We'll call him Faithful One." In the rush of the discovery, Ri didn't notice.

What a pleasant time Ri had with his paras that night. He felt so alive hearing Faithful One's voice again! He wanted that for his paras too, but he would never tell them without asking Jewel first. The minute he laid on his cot, a strong, serene sleep overtook him.

That same night Jewel went quietly, unnoticed, to her room again. Laying in the dark, she pressed her hands against her forehead trying to block out her jealousy and feelings of inadequacy. Did it really matter that she hadn't heard?

"Faithful One . . . " she whispered.

It was lovely, even just saying it, and her sad feelings melted away. After all, she and Ri were . . . she wished again, for the hundredth time, that she had a word for what Ri was to her. A good crew? Yes, they were definitely that, and more, weren't they? He wouldn't have thought to ask if she hadn't. Then they still wouldn't know.

"Thank you, Faithful One," she said unexpectedly. "Thank you."

Those were Brody's words, special words like Para Chloe's word *trust,* words other folks didn't use. Jewel hugged herself, holding on tightly to peacefulness, determined not to let a single jealous thought back in.

23
best and worst?

Before they knew it, their second Celebration Day at the Woods Shop was approaching. They bustled about with Brody, preparing with as much excitement as if they themselves had invented the idea of the Celebration Day. They worked their hardest, together, to make this Celebration Day the best ever for the Township. Still, their favorite part was being a crew.

This time, Jewel and Ri knew Brody would prepare special gifts and snacks for them. How surprised he would be to discover they had gifts for him, too. Ri had found the perfect broken branch by the clearing, stripped the bark off, and sanded it into the smoothest, most handsome walking stick ever. A hollow log near the first curve made the perfect hiding place for it.

Jewel snuck yarn scraps from Para Madeline's task room and made up her own way of knotting and weaving them together. Late each night she wove one wide strip. She slept with that strip around her middle, stuffed it under her cot during her morning tasks, and then wrapped it around her middle again before she walked to the Woods Shop. It was tricky, all the hiding she had to do, but Ri always covered for her at the shop. The final result was a soft, small blanket, for the chilly nights Brody sat outside watching the sun set.

The night of that second Celebration Day together was a wonder through and through. Brody heartily celebrated the beginning of this new year with Ri, now a fifteen, and Jewel, now a fourteen. It was as if they'd always known one another. After they finished their own scrumptious feast, Jewel and Ri brought Brody his gifts. Brody practically burst with pride, holding each gift up in the firelight, chuckling and going on and on about their creativity and workmanship.

Then Brody gathered them up in a big hug, which was embarrassing *and* forbidden, yet perfect. Samuri and Jewel knew what the Township would think, but they brushed those troublesome thoughts far away. Hadn't Brody said folk's loyalty to each other was as important as loyalty to the Township? They still questioned that, but not enough to change a thing.

They watched Gran Para Brody sitting by the fire, wonderstruck, running his hand slowly over the softness of the blanket and the strength of the wood. Jewel giggled to herself. She couldn't help wondering if he'd sleep holding them, just like she had slept clutching her soft scraps of yarn so long ago.

They stayed, as they had been told, waiting for Apprentice Tuckit to get them after the festivities.

"Pleasantness to each and loyalty to the Township!" he exclaimed heartily, his face beaming.

Apprentice Tuckit was already the most pleasant leader of the entire Township, but they'd never seen him quite like this before. His face shone with a dream-come-true look. He fixed his eyes on Samuri and Jewel with something near to amazement and appreciation.

"I'll escort the Young Samuri and the Young Jewel to their bungalows," he announced. Then, turning his gaze toward Brody, he bowed low with deep respect, and said, "The best of evenings to you, Gran Para Brody."

Ri and Jewel exchanged glances with raised eyebrows. What

had just happened?

They nodded farewell to Brody, gathered their things, and strolled out into the crisp air. All of the other Township folks were snug in their bungalows, leaving the path silent and empty. Samuri and Jewel followed, listening with great satisfaction as Tuckit shared a moment-by-moment replay of that perfect Celebration Day. Not one torch had burnt out. The honey harvest had yielded enough for a second round of cookies. And Apprentice Tuckit was pleased how much easier serving was with the four newly-crafted trays they had made during the Brave Days. He talked to them like cherished friends, and that was another wonder.

Apprentice Tuckit, strong and tall, stood in the torchlight nodding farewell to them as they turned down the private paths to their own bungalows. If anyone was loyal to the Township, it was Tuckit. And somehow *their* energetic, creative work had touched his heart. They would remember this night forever.

The next morning the two youngs gathered tools and snacks briskly, not wanting to miss a moment of the first full day of their third year in the clearing. Brody stood, leaning on his walking stick, Jewel's blanket draped over his shoulders, gazing after them as they whisked down the path.

Shaking his head in disbelief, he murmured, "Ah, look how they've grown, thank ye. It's for sure they came at just the right time. For sure yur givin' back to me a bit o' what was lost." Brody lingered, with his eyes closed, comforted by the sun's heat on his tired old body.

At the clearing Ri watched Jewel flutter about from plant to plant as if she were waking them up, welcoming them into the warmth of the coming weeks. He laughed at how much she seemed like her little self of long ago. Half an hourglass later she focused intensely on cleaning and digging in the strawberry beds and carrying buckets of dead leaves and grasses to the mulch pits. Brody had agreed to let her build two new pits this year. Samuri glanced over at her from time to time, laughing to himself, pleased. What a change from her first year.

Their attention during midday snacks turned to the second bundle of attached sheets. The markings and combinations were mostly the same as the other sheets, but lighter, smaller, and less exact.

"See this." Ri opened the bundle and read. "The wind blows wherever it pleases."

"What? *My* words are in the bundle?"

"Um-hmm. Three times on the first ten sheets. And this word . . . I think it's *para*. It's not on any of the loose sheets. The other bundled sheets show the sounds of the markings, but this bundle . . ."

Ri waited to be sure she was following. She nodded, starry-eyed with anticipation, but completely focused.

"This second bundle is kind of like a daily report. Only it sounds more like a story being told. This word, *meadow*, seems to describe the clearing, after a walk back from the brook."

Jewel's mouth dropped open, and she sat there speechless. The wonder of finding someone's personal thoughts about the wind and the meadow made Jewel feel like those sheets belonged to her. Or that the words were written about her or for her. This feeling was both unsettling and thrilling. She still wasn't interested in figuring it out herself, but she did want Ri to tell her every new detail. The more time Ri spent with the second bundle the more *he* thought of it as Jewel's bundle, too.

This year they settled into their routines like apprentices assigned to their lifelong tasks. Of course, they still had silly moments, but never when it would compromise their tasks or their safety. Late afternoons, they reported to Brody, eager to share the day's accomplishments and bursting with new ways to do tasks.

"You two!" Admiration beamed from Brody's voice. "Why, the two of ya have more ideas n' wisdom than I thought up in all m' years put t'gether."

Woods Shop tasks together were marvelous, a way Samuri and

Jewel could be loyal to the Township, but also to each other and Brody. The only thing they withheld from Brody were their conversations about Faithful One, and Faithful One's odd nudges toward new ideas and improvements.

That summer was the best yet, the fastest one, too. Before they knew it, the harvests were gathered, and they had settled into the cozy routines of their third Brave Days with Brody. It felt like the only life they had ever known. Preparations for the coming Celebration Day went as smooth as the sands of an hourglass slipping effortlessly away. The evening of their third Celebration Day Feast around Brody's hearth, gray clouds blew in from the north.

"Whew, it's a damp wind. Greetings." Apprentice Tuckit burst in the side door, grabbed Samuri, and pulled him outside.

Brody and Jewel heard Apprentice Tuckit ask Samuri about extra torches, and then the door closed.

Apprentice Tuckit's cheer faded. "Listen, I'd hoped to talk with you, but a lot is going on." He lowered his voice and leaned closer to Samuri. "Stay by Jewel's side tonight and keep your eyes and ears open. I'll explain in the morning. Come straight to the porch of the Big Bungalow at daystart. Here's my leadership band in case anyone stops you."

In a rush, they came back in, and the wind banged the door shut behind them.

Apprentice Tuckit bowed to Gran Para Brody, like always. "Can your youngs come with me? If it rains, I'll need help with torches and escorting folks because two of our apprentices are missing."

Apprentice Tuckit was clearly irritated by such disloyalty, especially on a Celebration Day.

Without warning, the wind yanked the door open and spit one of the missing apprentices in. He stumbled, caught his balance, bowed deeply, and acknowledged Gran Para Brody and Apprentice Tuckit. The apprentice hoped to appease them with loyalty, but his guilty face gave him away. Wherever he had been, he shouldn't have been there. Apprentice Tuckit put his hand out to stop the other apprentice from speaking.

"I don't want to hear it." He addressed the apprentice sternly. "I'll take you to report to the Secretary when your tasks are finished." Tuckit needed time to calm himself.

He handed the apprentice two unlit torches and pushed him out the door.

"Samuri, I'll be occupied all night. You have the permission of the Township to escort Jewel . . ." He paused then continued in a more serious tone. " . . . *straight* to her bungalow. Finish your feast and take her. I want her in when her paras get back. Then you're to come straight back. If it rains and we need more help, I'll send for you."

"Pleasantness to each and loyalty to the Township, Apprentice Tuckit!" Jewel and Samuri chorused sincerely.

On the way to her bungalow, Jewel asked, "Does this year feel different to you, Ri? 'Cause, it does to me. We're older. There's no doubt Apprentice Tuckit and Brody trust us. Even being short and being sent home first doesn't bother me." She scrunched up her nose and tilted her head to gaze into the dark. "Uff. I'm sure *I* don't want to carry a fiery torch with a group of skittish township folks on my heels."

"Um-hmm, different." Ri agreed but walked silently ahead with the blazing torch, scanning the dark, alert to suspicious movements.

Mmm, no crowd tonight, Jewel pondered. *If only we could walk farther in the darkness and torchlight.* And for once, Ri was thinking the same thing, and more.

Ri felt desperate to talk to Jewel alone. He couldn't sort his thoughts out lately. What would it hurt if he and Jewel sat by the woods to talk for a few moments? Jewel could still be in before her paras came. No one would know.

For good? Or for now? Faithful One spoke the words with concern and kindness.

Faithful One had been saying that a lot lately and it wasn't just words, it was the feeling Faithful One was nudging him away from some unwise decision. So, Ri walked right up Jewel's bungalow step, and opened the door with his free hand.

Time stood still as Jewel paused in the torchlit doorway wishing she could make the night last longer. But what if something went wrong?

It's not worth the risk. I want this day to end perfectly. Jewel pulled her shoulders up expressively, smiled at Ri, and walked in. The urge to pull Jewel outside overwhelmed Ri but he *forced* himself to shut the door quickly.

Jewel lit a candle by the door, hugged herself, and twirled twice. Slowly, as if in a dream, she floated to her cot, blew out the candle and was sleeping snugly when her paras returned.

Two hours later, Samuri paused on his way past Jewel's dark bungalow, trying to recapture the joy sparkling in Jewel's eyes earlier. So heartwarming. So aggravating. They had switched places. Jewel was the pleasant, loyal, safe one now, but life felt difficult and dark to Ri.

He opened his door quietly, hoping not to disturb his paras' sleep, but there they were. The small, high gathering room windows had large snack cloths tacked over them. Para Chloe and Para Patrick sat waiting in the flickering candle flame. Three empty wooden tumblers and a stone kettle of sweet, frothy milk were laid out on a lovely snack cloth, awaiting Samuri's return. The cheer of it lifted Samuri's worries. It had been dozens of weeks since they'd done this.

"Years are going by swiftly, Samuri." Para Patrick's face and his voice were strained, unnatural. "Para Chloe and I can hardly believe you'll be an apprentice next year. We're so pleased with you."

Something was up. Samuri sensed it. His muscles tensed and his stomach churned, too tired to take on another challenge.

"I know you're pleased with me." The weariness in Samuri's voice was evident. "Whatever it is, just say it."

Like a balloon that had been poked, all of Para Patrick's trying rushed out of him. "All right, we need to talk about your apprenticeship. There are . . . um . . . some things we want you to hear from us first. To start with, has the Director of the Woods Shop talked with you about becoming an apprentice?"

"He'd like me to stay on." Samuri's voice was puzzled. Should he tell Para Patrick he wanted to be the next Woods Shop Director? "What are you getting at?"

Para Patrick set his lips, nodded at Para Chloe, turned to Samuri, and spoke plainly. "The Celebration Day that youngs become a seventeen and begin their apprenticeship . . . they see their paras for the last time. Any contact after that is forbidden."

Samuri's jaw dropped. His forehead wrinkled; his eyes strained with disbelief.

Para Chloe attempted to make it sound brave and purposeful. "Life in the dorms is important preparation for you to become a para and begin your own bungalow." But tears shone in her eyes as she stammered to get the next words out. "We've had . . . the best of years together and . . . every moment was worth it." Para Chloe sniffled but raised her chin in a pleasant, dignified manner. "You . . . you will go on to do the same with your own para and tiny."

Samuri pushed Para Patrick away, put his hand up to say, "no more," and strode to let himself out the weaving room door into the vast darkness.

"Wait. Samuri," Chloe begged. "We have to tell you about—"

Para Patrick put his hand on her shoulder. "It must not be time. Pray. Just pray."

Then he stole into Chloe's weaving room and hovered in the dark, squinting to see Samuri. "Be brave and be true. You will always have help, Samuri. Always." The words, barely audible, echoed out of the brokenness of Patrick's heart into the hush of Chloe's task room. Would there ever be the right time?

"*You* have to help him now. We've done the best we could."

24
strange happenings

Samuri had never been one to have dreams, pleasant or unpleasant, but that night he could barely sleep because of them. First, an indistinguishable shadow crept through the dark, snatched Jewel out of Samuri's torchlight, and carried her away. That scene was replaced by the sight of Samuri standing outside of bungalow seventy-six like a stranger, pounding on the door while his paras huddled inside crying. A loud, lifeless voice demanded, "The apprentice from bungalow seventy-six must report to the dorms."

Samuri ignored it, stubbornly forcing the door open, only to be met by dozens of the Township Officials. The Officials flooded out, bound him, and jostled him along carried sideways in their arms. The acrid smell of smoldering wood burned his nostrils. His sight was limited but he glimpsed giant torches near the Woods Shop engulfing it in flames. Bits and pieces of the dream repeated themselves throughout the night.

The first thin ribbon of light was touching the sky when Samuri was finally able to force himself awake. He dressed in a hurry, relieved to escape his tortuous sleep. If only he could pull himself together before he reached the Big Bungalow.

"Pleasantness. I knew I could depend on you," Apprentice Tuckit greeted him with a low, guarded voice. He handed Samuri two daystart snacks and motioned to the Square, changing to a loud, purposeful voice, like he wanted folks to hear him. "Let's walk while we assess today's cleanup."

Samuri was puzzled. He had never helped with cleanup at the Square. What did Apprentice Tuckit want? The two walked side by side, Apprentice Tuckit pointing here and there, giving the illusion they were formulating a plan.

"I'm pleased how loyal Jewel has been at the Shop," Tuckit spoke in hushed tones. "She's hasn't been in trouble, not once. Young Samuri, are you aware of a young from the bungalow by the Loyalty Park?"

Daro came to mind immediately. Samuri felt exposed. Embarrassed. He dropped his eyes to the ground to hide the surprise he felt. Was Tuckit trying to trick him?

Do I lie, Faithful One? Or do I admit I know Daro?

Samuri kept his voice even and steady. "I'm not sure what you mean, Apprentice Tuckit."

"Well, the secretary at the Task Office says the young from that bungalow was in two of the four reports about Jewel causing trouble. Did Jewel mention anything to you?"

"Um . . ." Samuri stalled. The Laws of Loyalty clearly forbid telling others about your task crew, but Apprentice Tuckit's voice sounded concerned, not accusing.

"Listen, we don't have much time." Tuckit sounded aggravated. He turned back to face the Big Bungalow. "I want you watching the path by bungalow seventy when Jewel walks to the Woods Shop. Now that I've observed Daro—that's the young's name— I'm concerned . . ."

Another apprentice approached on the path bordering the Square. "Pleasantness," Apprentice Tuckit called to her. "Do you have everything you need for today?" Then he quickened his pace, avoiding others on the path, and snapped his fingers to command eye contact with Samuri.

"Walk a bit further with me. We'll talk more later. For now, all I can say is the Township reassigned the Young Daro today, and he might take it hard." Apprentice Tuckit raised his eyebrows and locked eyes with Samuri, silently asking if Samuri was with him.

Samuri's mind was flooded with questions he wanted to ask Apprentice Tuckit and stories he wanted to tell him. Instead, Samuri nodded slightly and turned to go. Just then, a messenger from the Big Bungalow called out and rushed down the steps toward them. Simultaneously, Daro appeared on the northwest path heading toward the Big Bungalow.

Apprentice Tuckit nodded for Samuri to go anyway, but the messenger called out. "Stop, young! This is for both of you."

"Stay a moment. I'll get you out of this," Apprentice Tuckit assured him.

"Town Master Cree has summoned you to meet the Township's new baker." The messenger was pleased with this important but simple assignment. "The baker wants your opinions about new Celebration Day recipes, both of you."

Apprentice Tuckit bowed to her. "This young has a time-sensitive task. I'll reschedule with the baker. We have the year before us to consult about recipes. Loyalty."

The messenger waved one of Town Master Cree's bright scarves in her hands, a sign of the authority given to her. Her eyes sparkled as she motioned for them to go first, enjoying her power as Town Master's new attendant.

When they reached the porch, the Young Daro surged out of the door. His square jaw was set hard. He cast a shadowy glare in their direction. No smirky smile today. When the messenger led them through the door, they both looked back in time to see Daro enter the Exchange. He was reassigned, and he was inside. *Jewel should be safe for now*, Samuri thought.

The new baker had a dozen *thrilling* ideas to share with them. Town Master Cree walked through a few times, nodding with approval. Why must he insist upon this today? It took Apprentice

212

Tuckit half of an hourglass before he was able to send Samuri on his way without suspicion.

Now that Samuri was free to find Jewel, his mind went wild. Thoughts from the night before came crashing in. What would it have been like to sit in the dark with Jewel and get everything off his mind? Celebration Day did feel different this year. Becoming a sixteen meant he'd be an apprentice in one year. Could he bear never seeing his paras again? He shuddered and pushed that thought away. Would he be allowed to continue tasks at the Woods Shop?

Of course, I will. What am I thinking? Jewel and I could run the Woods Shop ourselves with a little help from Brody.

What about Brody? The thought startled Ri. Brody seemed powerful when they first came to the Woods Shop. Now he used the walking stick most days and not just because Ri had made it for him. What if Town Master assigned a different director for the Woods Shop? What would life be without Brody? No, Ri could not think of that either.

*I **have** to talk to Jewel!*

Could he talk about this without upsetting Jewel? Or would she spiral into discouragement?

Talking to her in the dark last night would have been so much easier. At least Daro was assigned to the strict Director of the Exchange now. Samuri would try to talk to Jewel today.

The main paths were a blur of green and gray tunics, as paras and youngs headed to their tasks. Beyond them he saw only empty paths between bungalow seventy and the Yards Shop. In his mind's eye he imagined Jewel rushing to the shop early that morning, waiting for him, and dancing about in her eagerness to get to the meadow.

When he passed his bungalow, Para Chloe's loose drying lines caught his attention begging to be repaired. *I will, I will, but it can wait until after tasks today.*

Thoughts of life without his paras weighed upon him as he turned toward the Woods Shop. He looked back at his bungalow hoping Para Chloe would come out for just a second. What he saw sent chills up his spine.

A stout, broad-shouldered figure with a somewhat flat head was emerging from the path in the woods, wearing the white trousers and tunic of the Big Bungalow. The left leg of the trousers and the sleeve of the tunic were torn and bloody. Samuri knew it was Daro at first sight. Sweat dripped down Daro's reddened face. His square jaw jutted out angrily. A pale blue bag like the one Jewel used for gathering flowers hung limply from his shoulder. Daro pushed forward, his body heaving and panting, his entire attention fixed in the direction of the Big Bungalow.

Samuri froze. Daro must not catch Samuri watching him. The second Daro was out of sight Samuri took off running. He *had* to see Jewel.

25
the chase

The gentle, pale light of daystart filtered through Jewel's window just as Samuri and Apprentice Tuckit began their walk. Her eyelashes fluttered drowsily unable to awaken until last night's memories flashed through her mind. It was early, but now she was wide awake. Maybe she could beat Samuri to the shop for once. She giggled. What a fun way to start their fourth year at the Woods Shop.

"Greetings, Brody." Her voice sang out like a melody when she entered the shop.

"Ah, missy, yur here right early. A pleasant start to the year."

"What should I do until Ri comes?"

"Aye he was up late. I wasn't expectin' the two of ya for a while. Come help me get some tea n' snacks t'gether."

Soon the steam of the kettle carried the earthy aroma of burning wood through the shop, and Jewel sighed contentedly. Brody asked for her help with a new recipe and then sent her to gather tools for cleaning the strawberry beds. Still Ri didn't come.

"Oh, this silly ol' brain o' mine. Last night Ri said somethin' about an early meetin' with Apprentice Tuckit, but 'twas pretty late n' I forgot. He'll be here as quick as a wink." Brody winked at her. "But how would ya like ta surprise him and be waitin' in the clearin'?" Here he winked again.

Jewel stared at him blankly, unsure if she had heard him right, but he nodded and stood there beaming, motioning toward the door. She straightened her shoulders in an attempt to appear taller and older than she was.

"Of course," she said in the most matter-of-fact voice possible. "I'll go and get started right away." She hoped she didn't sound as eager and bubbly as she felt.

Brody tinkered around a bit after she left, chuckling to himself. What a pleasant way to start the year. He was standing calmly in the doorway, soaking up the morning sun, leaning on his walking stick when Ri came into view.

"Jew-el!" Ri called toward the doorway as he covered the last few meters.

He squeezed sideways past Brody, nearly knocking him over. "Where's Jewel?"

Brody tilted his head, confused. What was Ri all up in a huff about? Brody shook off a frown, perked up, and answered Ri honestly. "'Bout now she be cleanin' strawberry beds."

Ri's head dropped into the palm of his hand, as if in pain. "Why? Why is she *there*? She never–leaves–without–me. You've never let her go without me."

Brody's story tumbled out followed by Ri's brief description of the morning. Ri talked while he stuffed his pack with warm snacks and fresh water. Brody threw in some washing cloths in case Jewel was hurt.

"I be comin' with ya, Ri." Brody's voice was decisive, but he stumbled and almost fell reaching for a pack without using his

216

walking stick.

"Brody, I need you here," Ri half pleaded, half insisted, "in case anyone comes."

Brody nodded. Ri was right, but Brody closed his eyes just the same, his head pounding with the pain of it all. When he opened them, Ri was gone.

"God be with ya!" he cried out, but Ri, who would not have understood anyway, did not hear.

Jewel had left less than half an hourglass earlier. In her excitement to go on her own, she had failed to see Daro walking east on the path across from her. Near the fork where the paths merged, a movement from the corner of her eye caught Jewel's attention. Her heart raced at the sight of him, but she forced herself not to run. It would be just like Daro to startle her into a run, and then report her. There was no one else in sight, and he was coming toward her at a pace forbidden by the Township. Yes, she was sure of it. *Thud. Thud.* The sound of his footsteps slapping the path grew louder.

Stay calm. Stay pleasant. I'll reach the woods before him, she assured herself. *There's no way he'll follow me there. And if he reports me for not greeting him, I can say I didn't see him.*

Where the two paths merged, she saw a flash of motion and bolted down the path. She couldn't help it. The sound of his feet grew louder as she approached the first curve. Daro was running, too, following her into the woods.

He called out to her, and his voice was closer than she expected. "You owe me! You know you do. Don't think you can outrun me. You can't."

His voice, more than being merely unpleasant, held a stranger threat than she had heard before. A half of a meter before the first curve she dashed off the path straight into the pines, thinking this would throw him off. He was winded now, puffing heavily, but determined in his pursuit of her. There was nothing to do but run the fastest and smartest she could, concentrating only on the placement of each step. Her right shoe fell off, but she pushed on without it.

A branch cracked behind her and she heard his body smash to the ground. An angry shout demanded that she come back. Daro might be hurt, but all Jewel felt was relief. A loud groan reached her ears, followed by the sound of small sticks snapping under the weight of his heavy feet as he pursued her.

Daro wiped his sweaty face against his sleeve and blood trickled onto his bare arm where the sleeve had ripped. His mouth curved into a delighted, evil smirk, and he stopped to shout at her.

"Ha! I've got you now. Wait until I tell them *this*. You can *try* to tell them your story, but they've never listened to *you*, have they?"

Daro found Jewel's shoe on his way back to the path. A cruel grin spread across his face. He rubbed the toe of her shoe against the blood on his arm. Here was the evidence! The she-young from the Woods Shop had detained him, pushed him down and kicked him until his shins bled, and for no reason.

"Pleasantness. What a perfect story," Daro gloated. "You'll listen to me after this, she-young. You'll see."

A creature chattered at Daro from across the path and he froze. He must get out of the woods or face certain harm. He stuffed the shoe into the bag as he fled, or so he thought.

Daro's muffled shouts reached Jewel, but she was too intent on escaping to pay attention.

Could he still catch me? Oh, I can't let him catch me.

She wasn't sure why she was just sure. So, she ran until she became unaware of anything but the rhythm of her running. Jewel ran on for several minutes, without thinking. Her arms and legs pumped powerfully. Her eyes adjusted to the dimness from the canopy above. The pines grew increasingly closer together, slowing her pace, seeming to block her way in every direction. Here the floor of the woods was thickly carpeted with pine needles, so she removed her left shoe and both of her socks and tucked them into the pocket of her pack. Running went more slowly now that she must dart right and left, avoiding rocks and branches. An invisible presence pressed against her as if trying to stop her, and she waved her right arm randomly in front of her, fighting it off.

"Leave me alone. I *know* where I'm going!" she shouted in a quavering voice.

Whispers of *the meadow* pressed against her again and again.

The meadow? I know! I'm headed to the meadow!

Jewel ran on, clinging to the comfort and power of her own strength.

The meadow. The meadow.

"Why shouldn't I run to the meadow?" she yelled through the trees with what breath she had left.

Sunlight? the voice asked more gently.

Sunlight! That was it. Where was the sunlight that came with the nearness of the meadow?

Suddenly aware of the dimness, she peered into the distance ahead. A fallen log blocking the way escaped her notice until the last second. Stopping as abruptly as she could, she fell to her knees and gasped, thinking what might have happened. Heart pounding, shallow breaths overtaking her, she stood and bent with her hands on her knees. Then she straightened up abruptly, threw her head back, and stretched as tall as she could, her lungs gulping for air, her mind crying out to understand.

The strong scent of pine filled her lungs and she realized, *I'm not headed for the meadow at all. Am I? What happened?*

In her mind, she tried to trace the path she had taken. At the curve, she had veered away from the path. She hadn't given it any thought; she'd merely assumed she would come out near the hillside. Wiping the sweat off her head she faced what was obvious now. In her desperate attempt to escape, Jewel had become absorbed with running and had failed to adjust her direction.

"It's not a problem. I've got this," she said confidently, palms outward toward the trees, as if calming them instead of herself.

A dozen memories rose in her heart like proofs she could do hard things well. Loyal memories. The time she rushed forward at the bee tree to help Ri. Her loyalty to complete tasks in Brody's dark, foreboding cellar, when everything in her screamed against it. Her fearlessness to pick apples high in the treetops where Ri was too heavy to go. The weeks after the red flag when she'd bit her lip raw, determined to do her tasks perfectly careful and make it to Ri's thirteenth Celebration Day. The cloudy day she dove into the brook like a wild creature to rescue four windblown sheets of markings.

Oh, the brook.

If only she were at the brook, now. Jewel was painfully thirsty, but their water and snacks were in Ri's pack. She'd only brought tools in her pack and a bag for early strawberries. Where had she dropped the bag? Maybe Ri would find it on the path. Did he know she was missing yet?

A breeze picked up, stirring the treetops with the scent of the coming rain, but she barely noticed. The fact was she was alone and lost, hungry and thirsty, and growing cold in her sweaty tunic and trousers.

A plan. The first thing Brody did when trouble faced him was to make a plan. She would put her fear aside and figure out a plan.

Yes, I can figure out where the clearing is now that I'm thinking about it. Simple. Then I head that direction, and I'll be there in no time. I can cover a lot of ground quickly.

But what direction had she gone and how far? She pushed the question away, extended her right arm directly behind her and her left arm in the direction the clearing must be. Then she set out directly between the two.

Nothing changed for minutes. Each step continued to look the same, and the log was nowhere in sight. A cramp in her side joined the pain of her parched throat and empty stomach.

"Only tinys and littles cry," She mumbled bravely. "Not me. I'd rather die than cry. I'm not just Township-loyal, I'm Woods-Shop-brave." Oh! That cheered her for a moment. Woods-Shop-brave. Brody and Ri would like that.

Standing as tall as she could, with her shoulders back and her face set in determination, she clenched her fists and tried to shout, "I Can Do This!" But her words fell to the ground weak and wobbly. A sickening feeling, the feeling she hated the most, overtook her already shaky body.

Abandoned. Her worst fear. The fear that no one would come for her. The lie that no one cared.

You can't trust them, not any of them, a cruel inner voice warned her. *Not Samuri. Not Gran Para Brody. And most of all, not even Faithful One. You will be left out here to die. Unless of course the Young Daro is still following your trail. Who knows what he'll do if he finds you alone and too tired to run?*

Jewel sank to the ground, tears sliding down her blotchy cheeks. She was too spent from the run to think clearly. Too spent to fight the lies. The scent of pine mingled with the mist of the light rain, beading up on the surrounding branches and tree trunks. The thought of rain threw her into a panic. Why had Brody sent her off alone this morning? Where *were* Brody and Ri? Why hadn't they found her yet? It had been hours.

And Faithful One? There was no proof he actually existed. What if he was only a fanciful story made up in their minds during a tough week? She couldn't deny that help had come time and again, but how could she trust something she couldn't even see? If he was here, why didn't he do something now? What if he left her here to die? Anger rose inside her. What had she ever done to be treated like this? She fell to her knees and beat the ground, shouting until her voice grew hoarse. Then she curled up in a ball and wrapped her arms around herself to keep warm.

With her eyes scrunched shut, she found herself asking Faithful One over and over, "Why? Why? Why?"

A picture appeared in her mind. More pictures followed, appearing as clearly as if they were happening at that moment. She ceased to notice the drizzle as she watched herself, just a tiny, forced to stay on her cot alone, hungry, for hours and days. Sometimes wailing. Sometimes shouting mean things. Sometimes exhausted from sobbing. But always alone. She saw Para Madeline time after time looking at her mockingly, refusing to listen to anything she said. She saw Para Philip disappearing from the room any time Madeline burst into accusations against her. And last of all, she relived how tenderly Para Philip had treated her the morning of her questioning, only to grow cold toward her in the days that followed.

Jewel sobbed as waves of betrayal and unworthiness pounded over her, suffocating, and drowning her until she was numb. She lay there unable to think, unable to feel, until the waves of a nameless emotion took her by surprise. *Love.* This wave washed away the pain, reassuring and comforting her, filling her lungs with breath again. Waves of trust followed, until suddenly she understood.

Trusting had been too disappointing. Trusting hurt. Her paras hadn't given her much reason to trust. So, her heart had

222

refused to trust anyone. It was too great of a risk. And today when that awful young chased her, she hadn't even thought of Faithful One. Instead, she had tried, and failed, to find the way on her own. Picture after picture of the kindness and respect Brody and Samuri had shown her flooded her mind. Faithful One had given them to her, hadn't he? Now she was crying again, but the anger and fear were gone. Tears of hope tumbled gently down her cheeks, warm and healing. She rolled painfully over to her knees. There it was. The feeling was unmistakable.

"Faithful One," she whispered, stretching her arms toward the sky like a trusting, beloved tiny.

She lost all sense of her surroundings, swept up in the awe of Faithful One's unexplainable nearness.

"I can trust *you*." Words spoken in awe, mingled with the overwhelmed, silly giggling of someone receiving a gift that was too great to be believable. "I trust you. Oh, Faithful One, I trust you."

The misty rain turned into a downpour, and then, as if Faithful One was moving her arms and legs for her, she found herself up and walking. Why or where, she did not know. Around tree after tree, she pursued an unknown goal, shivering in the chilly rain. In thirty meters, she saw the largest fallen pine she had ever seen. It lay uprooted, its fall blocked by a smaller, fallen pine beneath it, creating a perfect cave-like shelter. Bending low she slid in. Oh, the warmth rising from the ground. And it was dry.

Too good to be true, she thought. *Faithful One it **is** you.*

Dropping to the ground she prepared to smooth a place to sleep, but the same invisible presence that had pressured her to stop running earlier now hovered uncomfortably between Jewel and the ground.

"Please, oh please," she began to beg, but she knew now, she must trust no matter how impossible it seemed. As she bent to slide out from under the shelter of the pine, a picture of a crackling fire filled her mind.

She moaned. "I can't. Oh, Faithful One, I just can't. This

shelter is perfect." She tried to bargain with him. "I just need to sleep. Then I'll be better."

For a moment longer she paused, attempting to ignore the inner tug, but it was relentless.

"O-kay, it never pays to ignore you. Uff! I can barely move. A fire? Really? Okay. I'll try."

Plenty of sticks and small parts of broken branches lay sheltered near the cave-like fallen pines. She gathered enough for a good start and was about to throw it inside, but her eyes were drawn to a particular spot—near the entrance of the tree-cave, yet far enough away to keep the smoke out.

Normally she would have laughed with joy at how ridiculously perfect it was, but all she could offer was a weak, "Okay. But how?"

"My pack. Of course. Let there be a string. There just has to be."

Searching through her pack, she came across her water tumbler and placed it on top of a low branch to catch the rain. In moments she had a fair-sized pile of twigs and dried pine needles. With her makeshift bow drill positioned smack in the middle of the starter pile, she began wheedling it back and forth as she'd seen Samuri do.

Pft . . . pft . . . poof. The seemingly tiny sparks caught on the dry twigs and flared up into small flames. Jewel blew gently, adding kindling until there were enough flames to add small broken branches.

"No sleeping. No laying down," she warned herself aloud, until she had a nice blaze going and a pile of broken branches stacked close by.

Tugging a handful of soft, wet moss loose from the top of the fallen log, she slid in and settled herself on the floor of the tree-cave, washing her sore, blood-stained feet. She hung her shoe, socks, tunic, and trousers on a branch nearby, hoping they'd be dry when she woke. Finally, Jewel laid on the soft, warm ground, smiling sleepily at the familiar musky smell of pine needles and burning wood. Tiny sparks fizzed and sputtered away from the fire's dreamy glow. "Mmm . . . I'm so thirsty. She pushed herself up reluctantly, grabbed her tumbler off of the outside branch and guzzled it dry. Then she ducked back in and stretched out to sleep, warm despite her thin, damp underclothes.

"I trust you, Faithful One," she whispered, smiling at the sweetness of knowing she did. "I do, really. I . . ." Her words faded into the song of the crackling fire and the silent strength of the tree-cave holding her safe and snug.

26
call to me

"What were ya thinking, Brody?" Brody hammered himself. He stormed about in the shop, biting his nails and watching the rain clouds. "'Twas me that sent her. Why! Why??!"

He paced back and forth, forgetting to tend the fire until the rain picked up and a chill settled over the shop. Then he flopped onto a chair near the fire and prayed. Prayed hard like the driving rain battering against the roof. Prayed angrily like he had after Maggie disappeared. Prayed, remembering the day Dupree was taken from them. And then, like the night when his Rosie had died, and he had no more words inside him to pray. So, he just sat, one minute with his eyes lifted up, the next gazing numbly into the fire.

Ri took Brody's advice and entered the woods east of the shop. He went four more meters east before turning north toward the path and running as swiftly as he could. He figured his green tunic would disguise him well enough. Near the path, he turned east, staying hidden in the trees until he scrambled clumsily over a large fallen log in his path. There, stuck to a broken branch was a scrap of white, bloody material from the Young Daro's tunic as attendant at the Big Bungalow.

"Jewel?!" Samuri called into the woods, but the woods were silent.

Where are you, Jewel? This is crazy. Why am I so worried? There's no scraps of torn green material. You're fine.

Samuri knew he needed to calm himself and work through all the possibilities. Daro didn't have Jewel, Ri knew that much. Had she run into the woods to escape him? It looked like it, but she knew better than to go too far. Surely Jewel would have doubled back and headed to the meadow.

Ri didn't run far before he tripped and almost fell over Jewel's bloodstained shoe. It had slipped right out of Daro's hands when the swirly-tailed creature frightened him. But Ri felt it was a sign that Jewel *had* run for the meadow.

Pictures of Jewel flooded his mind. Jewel, his lifelong neighbor, co-worker, storyteller, troublemaker, woods wanderer, and most important of all, friend. Jewel, the one whose moods and lack of focus had made him angrier and crazier than anything else in his life, other than the Township. Jewel, weaving fanciful stories about places and folks fully alive, free from fear and ridiculous laws. Jewel, always caring about him, listening to him, keeping secrets, and doing her best to understand him, even though they were so different. And now, after last night, Jewel, a fifteen who seemed to be even more to him, though he wasn't sure what.

At the meadow, he squinted across the fresh grasses hoping for a glimpse of her straw hat leaning over the strawberry beds. Nothing. She wasn't by the mulch pits either. He called her name loudly and waited.

Where would she go? To the brook? No one but Brody and me would know to look for her there.

Then time stopped and Ri's mind went completely blank.

Call to me and I will answer you and tell you great and unsearchable things you do not know.

The voice was so clear Ri turned to look in each direction, half-expecting to see him.

"Faithful One?"

Listen.

The meadow was still but how could Ri be expected to listen in the midst of his raging thoughts? Raindrops pelted his face, dulling his vision. He slipped his pack off, pulled his straw hat out and ran to take cover under his favorite apple trees.

In sheer determination Ri whispered, "I'm listening," and his mind became unexpectedly calm and clear.

An intense thought shot through his mind. Faithful One wanted to help Jewel even more than he did. His jaw dropped. It was Faithful One who had drawn Jewel outside that first day so they could meet. And the strange, protective feelings he'd felt for her from the start—were those from Faithful One, too?

"Okay. Show me."

Ri leaned his head back, situated his pack over his legs to keep them dry, and waited anxiously but with anticipation.

Eventually he thought to ask, "The brook?" A clear picture came to him of rain splatting the surface of the brook and beading up on the grass near the beach. But no Jewel. "Huh-uh. Not the brook."

"The Woods Shop? No, not there either."

Then he shouldered his pack and ran for the log where he'd seen the bloody scrap of material today. "Show me, Faithful One," he called out. "Show me."

At the log, he walked in a small, circular pattern scouring the ground for clues, but found nothing. He paused and listened, as much for a sign of Jewel as for Faithful One, then expanded the area of his search.

"Did she go back to the shop after all?" Pause. "No? Okay, then where?"

Though Ri didn't notice, the rain had stopped. He backtracked in case he'd missed a clue. There it was, the small but deep footprint filled with rain, where Jewel landed so hard it knocked her shoe off. Shortly beyond that he found the trail of smashed sticks made by Daro's short, zigzagging pursuit of Jewel. After

228

that, the trees grew thicker every few meters, and Jewel's bare feet were too light to leave noticeable prints. He retraced his steps to the log and found glorious sunlight breaking through the clouds. The pines near the path shimmered with thousands of trembling, sundrenched raindrops. He had never seen it quite like this.

Jewel? Where are you?

Deep in the pines, Jewel, warm and rested, woke to the sight of tiny sunbeams peeking through the dense canopy of evergreens.

In the secret place of your presence, you hide them from the intrigues of men; you keep them safe from accusing tongues.

The words sifted from her mind into her heart. When Ri first recited that to her months ago, they hadn't known what the words *presence*, *intrigue*, or *men* meant. She still didn't, but in this moment, she understood the meaning of the words combined.

"Oh, Faithful One! You did. You hid me in this . . . this tree-cave."

Jewel rolled over and pulled herself up onto her knees, holding her hands out before her in trust and awe. Even here, completely vulnerable in the elements and the unknown, she knew she was safe.

"In the secret place of your presence, you kept me safe, Faithful One."

Jewel longed to linger in this fanciful place, but Ri and Brody were surely missing her by now. She gathered her things and stirred wet dirt into the coals of the fire. Now that the clouds had broken up, the sun's position would be her gauge back to the path. Not that she'd come out in the same place, but she could at least find the path.

"Thank you," she whispered in awe, pausing simply to breathe in the fullness of Faithful One's help and nearness. "Don't ever let me forget. Okay?"

At first, she walked away slowly, taking in the bird songs in the treetops and stopping often to glance back. Despite her sore feet she eventually set a better pace, marking the way in case she became disoriented and had to find her way back to the tree-cave. The trees gradually grew farther apart. It wouldn't be much longer. Should she go to the meadow or the shop? The course she was taking should bring her out a bit east of the first curve.

A sharp stick cut her right foot, and she cried out.

"Jewel!" Ri shouted, running in the direction of her voice. "Jewel, is that you?"

Within six meters he saw her and ran the rest of the distance to sweep her up in his arms and hug her. Laughing, she threw her arms around him and hugged him back. A minute passed and then two, but still Ri did not let go.

Jewel wiggled away from him awkwardly. "Hey, be careful of my foot. It's cut. And I'm so hungry. Did you bring anything?"

"Um-hmm. I have your shoe, too." He swept her up pack and all, like a para carrying a tiny. Then he plunked her down on the log and dug in his pack for the snacks.

"I can still walk, you know." Her voice was more perplexed than scolding. It was kind of fun to be carried, but awkward.

Ri took it wrong. He felt confused.

Jewel sat on the log munching away, beautifully quiet and content, but Ri felt heaviness pressing on him from every direction. He wanted to hold her again, but he knew he shouldn't.

*Yes, Faithful One, for good, not just for now. I **want** what's best for Jewel, even if I sure don't feel like it.*

"Ri." Her voice was the sweetest mixture of being star-struck and having a newfound maturity. "He spoke to me." Jewel's eyes sparkled. Samuri would understand her joy. "Faithful One spoke to *me*."

That broke the spell. One tiny tear actually spilled over Ri's eyelashes. He paused a long while before speaking. "Jewel, I think he's been speaking to you in lots of ways. But I get it. It's really

230

something isn't it? His voice always makes me feel . . . so alive. I wish we could tell . . ."

Their eyes locked intensely, and they burst out in unison, "Oh no, Brody's waiting!"

Ri grabbed his pack and led Jewel slowly west, a few meters away from the path, in the same way he had come. They spoke little, saving the story of their day for a better time. Jewel was limping by the time they turned south toward the shop.

Inside the shop, Brody was applying salve where he had bitten his fingernails until they bled. Unlike Ri, Brody did not hug Jewel when the two youngs burst through the door. His face, his shoulders, his voice all seemed older and weighed down with fear and concern. Brody placed his hands on Jewel's shoulders and held her at arm's length, looking at her as if trying to see through her. Was she okay? Dare he ask? Had the other young hurt her? Was she mad at Brody for sending her alone?

But words were unnecessary, Jewel's peaceful face assured him all was well. There were no silent questions pleading in her eyes, no disappointment tugging upon worried eyebrows, no fears lurking in her heart. There was only Jewel, his dear Jewel, shining like a sunbeam that had escaped to earth.

"Alrighty. Ri, the kettle's on the fire. Make up some soothing tea quickly. There be no time ta hear stories."

Brody lifted Jewel up next to the salve on the counter and proceeded to clean and bandage the cuts on her feet.

"Young Samuri, ya need ta report promptly to the Director of Tasks. Tell him the designated she-messenger can come. I requested her; she's a pleasant, strong one. She'll escort our missy ta bungalow seventy. Then, t'morrow she'll come for Jewel after daystart snacks and escort her ta meet with Town Master Cree himself."

Anger flared up in Samuri's face. His voice was testy and demanding. "No! *I'm* going straight to the Big Bungalow and insist Town Master Cree and the Director of Tasks take actions against Daro. It stops now!"

"Samuri . . . Oh Samuri. Ya see, I can't let ya do that." Brody said mournfully, taking Jewel's hand and leading her toward the fire. "Alrighty. We best sit n' talk while we finish our tea or Ri will be gettin' us all in trouble."

Samuri couldn't believe what he was hearing. "But you've always told us loyalty to the Township starts with loyalty to each other." His eyes were large with disbelief, his voice angry and determined, but he followed them.

They scooched their chairs especially close together, warmed by the glowing fire, as Brody laid out a plan for them. Brody believed Town Master Cree himself needed to see and hear Jewel. The messenger who came earlier had slipped and told Brody the other young's story was difficult to believe. Brody was sure Town Master would favor Jewel if he saw her small stature and frank ways.

Ri nodded. It was a valid point. And this intense anger was a rare feeling for him. His temper might cause *more* trouble. It was too great of a risk. He rose to leave but Jewel grabbed his arm.

"Oh! I need to tell you both one thing," Jewel insisted. Brody couldn't stand to say no.

"I found a tree to rest under during the rain, and before I knew it, I was asleep and dreaming. First, I walked out of my bungalow and stepped onto the path. Sharp, deadly, red flags began to fall out of the sky straight towards me. I froze, but before the flags hit me a huge, powerful, white bird swooped toward me and covered me with its wings. It hovered close enough for me to feel its soft feathers touch my face."

Her hands flew to her mouth, remembering and feeling it all over again. Her bright, luminous eyes gazed at them as if reflecting the softness of the creature's touch. "I can't explain the pleasantness that poured over me. Not one flag could touch me, either. Not one. And . . . I know everything is going to work out."

It was as simple as that for her. Ri took one long look at the two of them, nodded, and left for the Big Bungalow with renewed resolve.

Of the three of them that night, only Jewel rested peacefully. She laid on her cot recounting each detail about Faithful One, and of course about the tree-cave. Oh, how she wanted to remember today forever. Well, except for Daro chasing her. Goosebumps overtook her entire body at the mere thought of it.

In the secret place of your presence, you hide them . . .

Jewel breathed deeply and curled up to sleep, warmed by Faithful One's help this day. Faithful One had led her and kept her safe. Faithful One had spoken to her and held onto her through the pain of her raging feelings. She would trust him, no matter what was ahead, no matter how hard it was.

27
freedom

*As **Jewel shaved*** her head, memories of the tree-cave and her new-found freedom turned her heart toward Faithful One. *How can I feel so perfectly safe and pleasant after yesterday? Thank you.*

I'm not even going to think about what I should say. Not to Para Madeline, not to Town Master Cree, not to anyone. I'm going to trust you.

Did her paras know about yesterday? What story had Daro told the Director of Tasks, or whoever he'd reported to? There was no way of knowing. She laughed awkwardly, concerned but also curious to see how Faithful One would help her today.

Para Madeline stayed in her task room like usual. She would check Jewel's cot later and think nothing of finding it empty. The air was still as Jewel waited on the doorstep, devouring the extra snacks Brody had stuffed in her pockets yesterday. Drab clouds covered the sky, dreary and gray, but today she didn't mind.

"Call to me and I will answer . . ." she recited under her breath, enjoying the familiarity of the words. "The wind blows wherever it pleases. You hear its sound . . ." She wished for the sound of the breeze but there was none.

In the stillness it was easy to hear Ri's para open her task room door. It must be her washing day. Jewel smiled. A creaky noise like the opening of the shop's old ladder drifted through the air. Pleasant sounds. A hopeful start to a questionable day.

Jewel heard Para Chloe talking. "Oh, this loose line. I always forget to ask Para Patrick and Samuri to fix it. I guess I'll fix it myself before it dumps my clean wash on the dirt."

Suddenly there was a clatter, a loud shriek, and a dull thud, followed by terrified wailing. Jewel sprang up, forgetting her sore feet. She rushed to the drying line and found Para Chloe sprawled face down in the dirt with her twisted wrists trapped beneath her. Jewel gasped. The panic of unexpected situations and unfamiliar folks seized Jewel. She must shake it off. Ri's para needed her.

Para Chloe attempted to move, and her heartbreaking cry brought Jewel to her knees beside her. But what was she supposed to do?

Kneel by her face. Jewel's panic eased up at the sound of Faithful One's calm, quiet voice. *Put your arms under her. Lift her gently and slide your knees forward until her face is on your lap.*

Allowing herself to think only of that and nothing more, Jewel knelt near the bungalow and lifted Para Chloe's shoulders. She poured her full strength and attention into protecting Chloe from jolts or twisting motions. The para shrieked again, then began partially sobbing, partially gasping, as she tried to breathe through the pain. Jewel needed to lift her further forward, but how?

Ri was on his way to the clearing when he heard Para Chloe's second shriek. He turned, saw Jewel kneeling on the ground, and shot straight across the paths.

"Oh Ri, I'm so glad you came. Can you slide her up on my

lap more?"

"Para Chloe, I'm here." Samuri's voice was tender and comforting. He pulled her until the weight of her shoulders rested upon Jewel's knees and her face was in Jewel's lap.

Then Samuri laid his face against hers for a brief moment. "Para Chloe, listen." She nodded her head slightly and whimpered. "I have to go for more help, but I'll be back as fast as I can." Then he was off.

Jewel knew nothing about comforting or caring for injured folks, and for a moment she wished she wasn't there. She closed her eyes and listened again. Instead of a voice, there was peace, and the question of what Para Chloe's face felt like covered in dirt. Tenderly she wiped the dirt off, taking care not to wipe any into Para Chloe's eyes or mouth. The para sighed and relaxed for a moment before the pain hit her, again.

Help her. Oh, help her. I know you can, Jewel cried out silently.

Then Jewel began to speak, comforting Para Chloe, distracting her from the horrid pain. "Samuri will be back soon. He runs like the wind. He'll find help *and* send for your other para. Don't worry, Para Chloe. Be brave. Help is coming."

It was surprising how easily the words came once Jewel started. And she trusted every word she said, because she, too, had found help when she desperately needed it.

An hourglass seemed to go by before Ri returned. He was panting and sweaty, pulling the partially finished wagon he and Brody had been making for harvests. It was padded with Gran Para Brody's best blankets, to soften the bumps. Para Patrick, who was running from the other end of the Township, nearly collided with the messenger who was coming for Jewel. The messenger was startled. Township folks did *not* run. What was going on? The closer he came to the woods, the more it concerned her. Should she go back and report him?

Seconds later, Apprentice Dupree passed the messenger swiftly but gracefully.

"Pleasantness, loyal messenger." Dupree's slow, confident voice calmed and encouraged the messenger. The bright yellow medic bag over Apprentice Dupree's shoulder caught the messenger's attention. At the site of the bag overflowing with ointments and bandages and thin boards, the messenger stopped, and bowed.

Apprentice Dupree took charge fearlessly in the yard of bungalow seventy-six. "Don't try to lift her. Not yet. I need one of you to help me splint her wrists. The other two of you must kneel beside her to comfort her and keep her from moving."

Para Chloe *wanted* to be brave. She tried to muffle her screams as the splints were put into place, but the pain was too great. The nearby messenger froze, turned away at the far corner of bungalow seventy, and covered her ears until the screaming became quiet crying.

"Breathe as deeply as you can." Dupree's voice was confident and soothing. "It must hurt miserably, but as odd as it seems, breathing will help."

Together the four of them lifted Para Chloe and settled her in the wagon as gently as they could. Jewel followed the other three to the edge of bungalow seventy-six as they wheeled Para Chloe away. And there stood the messenger, watching the wagon pass.

"Pleasantness to each." The frightened messenger forced the words out hesitantly. "Are you the young from bungalow seventy?"

"Loyalty. Yes, it's me." Jewel's voice was trembling. "It would not be loyal for me to appear before Town Master Cree this way. I request a moment to clean up."

Jewel walked casually to a pine, pulled off a thin branch, and swept the dirt off of her trousers and her hands. The messenger gasped sharply and bowed low to compose herself. What else would she see this day?

When she straightened up her voice was urgent but not unpleasant. "Town Master Cree is *waiting*."

The entryway of the Big Bungalow was unlike anything Jewel had seen before, with lovely pale walls and smooth, shiny wooden floors. The gathering room beyond it was filled with large carved candlesticks and fine furniture she had no names for. The messenger moved to stand between Jewel and the gathering room, blocking her view and motioning her to the open door on the right.

"You were delayed?" Town Master Cree's raised eyebrows invited Jewel's explanation.

He seemed different, serious and aloof, sitting behind a shiny wooden desk, barely smiling. Jewel bowed slowly and gracefully, meeting his gaze calmly when she stood straight. Inside she was shaking with concern for Ri's para, but Faithful One's nearness calmed her.

"It isn't my story to tell, but I'm sure there will be a report."

He nodded, then held her gaze. He was surprised by her size. She was at least a head shorter than the Young Daro and probably half his weight. Did he really expect Town Master Cree to believe this petite young had dragged him into the woods?

Jewel couldn't read the expression on Town Master Cree's face. Was he mad? Did he feel she had been disloyal? Or was he testing her?

"You speak with loyalty. We'll focus on the matters more personally related to you. Is this yours?" He reached into a drawer of the desk and held up her blue carry bag.

Though it was a frustrating conversation, Jewel stayed relatively calm, pausing before answers, listening for Faithful One's thoughts. Yes, she had seen the young Daro. Had she called for him to come into the woods with her? No. Had she pushed him against a fallen log? She shook her head, but the accusation made her stomach knot-up. Town Master Cree continued, impressed by the attentive yet unflinching way Jewel dealt with each of his questions. She was not the typical Township young. Where might they assign her now?

"Are you hurt? Cuts? Bruises?" He noticed the blood spots on her clothes, but they looked fresh. "Slide your sleeves up."

She showed him her arms and shook her head. No, she wasn't hurt. Should she tell him about her feet and her run through the woods? Before she could decide, he stood up, rang the small bell on his desk, and the messenger returned.

The messenger, who was also Town Master's replacement for the Young Daro, had regained her composure. She was eager to prove herself, though this morning had been challenging.

"Take the young from bungalow seventy to the back room of the Complex." Town Master Cree smiled his kindest, most genuine smile at the messenger. He wanted his bungalow crew to know he valued them for their outstanding loyalty. And much was required of her this day—tasks near the woods, and now guarding this odd young.

"First, stop at the freshening room by the front office, then proceed to the last room of the west wing. Stay with her until Apprentice Dupree arrives. Wait in silence and utmost pleasantness."

The outer door of the Complex was similar to Brody's cellar door. Jewel wondered what secrets it protected. The messenger knocked three sharp knocks and they were admitted into an entry office lit with large lanterns rather than candles. The long hallway that stretched beyond the office and the freshening room was lit only by the office lights that shone dimly through the windows on the left. The office doors on the right had no windows. Then, as if the lack of light wasn't hard enough for Jewel, the muffled sound of Para Philip's voice came to her as she neared office number four. She fixed her eyes on the floor and followed the messenger cautiously past Para Philip's office. Other muffled voices and sounds came and went along the hall.

"Here we are," the messenger announced, opening the door at the end of the hall. Then she moved aside making room for Jewel to enter the room first. "Oh, no chairs. I could have grabbed some." Then a different sort of look clouded the messenger's face. There were no chairs for a reason. This was a holding room for troublemakers.

Neither of them spoke. Should they sit or stand? It was uncomfortable for both of them. There was no hourglass in this bare, dreary room, just monotonous, unmeasured time. Jewel, tired and sore from the day before, finally lowered herself to the floor. The messenger relaxed, leaned against the door, and stared at the lights down the hall. An absurd idea occurred to her. Was she here to stop this calm she-young from escaping? Or was she here to *protect* this young?

They were both beginning to nod off when a nearby door opened and shut, and they heard a refined she-voice announce, "I'll be back directly."

Apprentice Dupree appeared, dismissed the messenger, and stepped in the room. There was a candle holder in her left hand, and she extended the other hand to help Jewel stand.

"I only have a few moments. Here is what you need to know." Apprentice Dupree's voice was serious, almost harsh, despite the gentleness in her honey golden eyes. She expected Jewel's full attention. "The details of your situation weren't given to me, only the options. The outcome of what lies ahead for you depends on your willingness to be loyal and pleasant. Listen carefully. I'll explain, then you have a quarter of an hourglass to sort your thoughts and give your answer."

Apprentice Dupree had been sent without knowing a thing. Jewel nodded earnestly, her smile gentle and respectful. Dupree found that Jewel's unguarded expressions touched her like she had not been touched in years. This young had a spark like Brody and Rosie; Dupree must fight against its power, or it would rip her emptiness open and strip away her protective independence.

A startled cry from the next room rescued Dupree from her thoughts. "Option One," the apprentice hurried. "You can be assigned to this room during tasks every day. You'll be alone without any interactions. Even your midday snack will be placed in the room before you arrive. The yellow flag on your paras' bungalow will remain up until Town Master Cree deems it best for all involved to reassign you. Option Two. You can agree to take whatever task is available, but no details will be given unless you choose this."

A loud moan came from the same direction as the cry. Apprentice Dupree handed Jewel her candle and turned to go.

"Young Jewel, a choice can be . . ." Apprentice Dupree turned back, wanting to say *a gift* but it would be meaningless to a Township young. " . . . it can be a pleasantness if you don't make it about yourself and the unpleasant things folks have done to you." Then she pulled the door shut behind her.

The stale, closed-in smell of the room overwhelmed Jewel's senses. She had the urge to blow out the candle just to smell its earthy smoke, but that meant a pitch-black room.

"Faithful One." Her whisper was more of a turning than a question. "You are my secret place. I'm safe in you. Yes?" Suddenly the image of the tree-cave's cozy fire sprung up in the candle's flickering flame.

Jewel slid down into the nearest corner, liking the feeling of the walls holding her, and placed the candle slightly in front of her. Another moan echoed nearby, and she winced. It must be Para Chloe. Or was it Daro? Was he here, too? Her heart pounded hard against her chest, and she held her head in her hands upon her knees, fighting the fear and anger rising inside her.

No, not anymore. I don't have to be afraid. Faithful One is with me. Besides, that voice is too high to be Daro.

"Think . . ." she whispered with determination, stretching her arms forward, bent at the elbow, palms facing out, fingers extended.

Curling her fingers into her palms she began a list, like Brody had taught her. What were the pluses of being assigned here? In this room she was protected from folks getting her into more trouble. That was big. One finger went up on her left hand. She waited, then went on to the right hand. One finger for sparing Para Philip the disgrace of a yellow flag. One for keeping her points at the Exchange. She gasped. Without her points Para Madeline would surely send her to the dorms and she would never see Ri again. She added two fingers for that and thought for a minute. The craziness of being in this room settled it. The choice was pretty obvious.

Or was it? Her mind went wild. What if they assigned her to tasks with Daro? Would the Township go that far to teach them pleasantness? Could she survive it if they did?

"Oh, Faithful One, what should I do?"

Dupree's words came back to her, almost as if Faithful One was saying them himself. *A choice can be a pleasantness if you don't make it about yourself and the unpleasant things folks have done to you.*

And remember, Jewel, I will always be with you to help you.

Her cold, aching muscles began to cramp, still sore from the day before. Jewel pushed herself up and stood in the center of the room, shuffling in place, candlestick in hand, face tilted upward, lost in Faithful One's nearness. That was how Apprentice Dupree found her.

"Oh. Greetings." Jewel chirped, unaware of the apprentice's curious expression. "I've made my choice." The fact that the Township had *given* her a choice struck her with its full weight. "I'm pleased to be loyal in whatever task the Township has for me."

Where had those bold, loyal, pleasant words come from?

"Follow me." Apprentice Dupree's voice remained matter-of-fact, but a softness, or was it relief, shone in her eyes. "Para Chloe is in that room. I've given her as much as I can to dull the pain. Her hands and wrists are too swollen to perform surgery today. After the surgery, though, she will need a personal attendant. I requested you because of your skillful loyalty at the accident. That is your new assignment."

Jewel sucked in a deep breath. Her mouth became perfectly baby-bird-round, and she went pale, but only for a moment. Then Jewel stood as straight and tall as she could and nodded.

The apprentice placed her hand lightly on Jewel's shoulder, smiling for the first time since Jewel had met her. And suddenly this apprentice seemed strangely familiar. Brody's face flitted through Jewel's mind, but her mind was busy with too many other questions to let this one sink in.

"Town Master Cree's messenger will escort you to your bungalow. Be ready for me between midday snack and last snack. I'll come and take you to bungalow seventy-six to begin preparations for your new assignment."

28
an odd turn of events

Lingering strips of shadow and sunshine mingled together on the paths. Apprentice Dupree assigned the night medics their tasks and walked out into the apricot dusk. The earthy smell that rose from the warm path, and the cool, fresh air revived her, but not quite enough to shake off Para Chloe's pain-wracked moans. This was the worst injury Dupree had ever dealt with, much worse than the burned apprentice she'd helped Rosie treat on their last night together.

Momma. She almost sobbed at the mere thought of the word. *I need you. I miss you so bad it hurts.* She felt like a little again, but she set her face, composed and full of dignity, toward the east. The last few paras on the path glimpsed her dark, purple armband in the fading light and bowed to her. A medic. There were few medics left and folks were grateful to have them.

I know what you would say, Rosie, but I don't do that anymore. I want to, but I can't. You have to understand. Prayers seem . . . I simply can't, not alone. Forgive me.

Jewel's paras were arguing. Para Madeline wanted Para Philip to send Jewel to the dorms. It was unsafe to have *her* in their bungalow now that *she* was attending the para next door.

Para Philip snapped. He forgot a medic was coming for Jewel and began to yell. "Do you doubt the Township's decision, Para? And did you forget? When *she* goes, her points go with her. Permanently." Jewel's paras hadn't called her by name since their last fight over points.

Ting-a-ling. Jewel popped up, gingerly slid her feet into her shoes, bowed slightly, and was on her way to the door. Para Philip blocked her and turned to answer the door himself. He bowed low to Apprentice Dupree, expecting some small talk or at least an explanation, but Dupree had heard their yelling. She had attended to others like this, and she despised their weak, selfish way of living.

"Leave the latch unlocked." Her voice was aloof and full of authority. "I'll ensure the Young Jewel locks it behind herself, when we return."

Para Philip winced. Had this important medic heard him in his worst moment? He was sure to lose his position now. But more than that, his heart quaked at the thought of this medic returning to the Complex alone, in the dark. Not only was it unsafe, but it was disloyal according to his understanding of the Laws of Loyalty. It was also disloyal to interfere with a medic on Township business. Para Philip stifled his urge to offer to escort her.

Ting-a-ling. Para Patrick and Samuri sprang to the door, suddenly wide awake. Apprentice Dupree's face was still composed, but her eyes and her voice greeted them softly. What a surprise when the medic stepped in, revealing Jewel in the dark behind her. The

Young Jewel bowed properly, as if meeting them for the first time. Para Patrick bowed in return, mostly to regain his composure and wipe the grin off of his face. Whatever was going on, it was a welcome turn of events. Samuri stood speechless, staring at them awkwardly, forgetting to bow.

That was the strangest night their bungalow had ever experienced. Apprentice Dupree updated them on Para Chloe's condition and explained the specific tasks the two of them must do.

In parting, Dupree said, "If the cold packs and the rosemary salve work tonight, I will do surgery on her wrists tomorrow after midday snacks. There are no promises, but she is safe with me. I began my medic tasks as a ten with the most loyal medic of all time. I am skilled. I will do my best. Leave your latch unlocked during the day. I need to send medical supplies and a new cot."

Apprentice Dupree bowed low. "I give you my word of loyalty that I relate to your concern." Jewel bowed, too, kept her eyes to the floor, and followed her out.

Samuri and his para locked eyes. *What just happened?*, their raised eyebrows asked. Was the medic going to sleep on the cot? Why had Jewel accompanied her?

In the gray calm before daystart, Para Philip pushed an extra snack across the counter to Jewel. The two of them ate in silence as they walked to the Complex. Jewel followed ten steps behind her para as prescribed by the Laws. After they reached office number four and Para Philip closed the door behind him, Jewel took her first real breath that day.

Jewel was relieved to do tasks beside Apprentice Dupree rather than sit alone in the dark, musty room down the hall. While Para Chloe slept, Dupree quietly modeled how to make the tinctures, ointments, and syrups for this patient. The smells of honey, rosemary, garlic, and lemon lightened the strangeness of the Complex. Soon Para Chloe awoke. Jewel watched each detail as Apprentice Dupree iced the para's wrists, massaged the tension out of her feet and legs, and applied the specific remedies needed to keep pain and infection away.

Once the pain was dulled, Para Chloe slept again, but only briefly. Now, the apprentice observed as Jewel went through the protocol of icing and massaging. Ice was new to Jewel. Her fingers tingled for half of an hourglass after she had scooped and tenderly packed the ice around Para Chloe's wrists. Jewel wrapped her hands in a warmed cloth, rubbing them together briskly before massaging the para's feet.

In the rare moments when Para Chloe slept soundly, Apprentice Dupree insisted Jewel make tinctures, ointments, and syrups from memory, repeating the ingredients, and how to use them. The medic must know Jewel could administer them perfectly even under the pressure of attending to Para Chloe on her own. The heartbreak they felt in the face of Para Chloe's crushing pain was lessened by sharing it together. Apprentice Dupree had longed to know the wonder of that shared feeling again.

After midday snack, a tall, hulk of an apprentice accompanied Jewel back to bungalow seventy-six with a new cot and two carry bags of supplies. He slouched down on the doorstep, more bored than afraid, waiting for her. That gave Jewel the freedom to set the bungalow up exactly as Dupree had instructed her. She need not rush or worry because of some timid apprentice who was frightened by the woods.

Apprentice Dupree was waiting in the hall drumming her fingers together when they returned. "Safety and pleasantness, you're back," the medic sighed. "I need to operate. Now! And I need you to assist me, Young Jewel. I want you to. I haven't found anyone yet who understands this like you do. You don't have to watch, simply listen carefully, and anticipate when to hand me specific tools and remedies."

Jewel went pale, but grabbed the sterile medic gown Apprentice

Dupree handed her. After dressing, they sanitized their hands and began. Para Chloe's moans and shrieks no longer intimidated Jewel when she began to focus on the surgery. She marveled at Apprentice Dupree's deft movements with knives and setting the broken bones. Medic Dupree was sheer compassion melded with authority, just as Jewel's bees were sweetness melded with danger. An awe-filled peace overflowed in Jewel's heart.

Back at the bungalow Samuri and Para Patrick sat eating last snack, hoping with every bite to hear an update. What was taking *so* long? Sleep overtook them when they leaned on the gathering room wall to wait, shoulder to shoulder, head against head.

Just as Dupree put her tools down and turned to Jewel, a sliver of the crescent moon peeked out from the cloud-dappled sky. "We did it." Her voice was strangely both somber and elated.

The dull, hulk of an apprentice hovered at the end of the hall, ready to escort Jewel, while another apprentice sat with Para Chloe. As Apprentice Dupree and Jewel washed up, Dupree noticed Jewel standing funny and insisted on attending to Jewel's cuts.

"I could stay." Jewel tried to hide her eagerness behind a matter-of-fact tone of voice. "It would be better for my foot. And we could take turns sleeping."

"No, Jewel, though I'm glad you're willing. This will be your last night in bungalow seventy for several weeks. Get as much rest as you can. After tonight you will stay beside Para Chloe day and night. You alone will attend to her needs until I'm certain it is no longer necessary."

Apprentice Dupree's confident gaze met the Young Jewel's wide-eyed shock. Jewel bowed in reply, too surprised to ask a single question. Then Apprentice Dupree addressed the apprentice who waited in the hall. "Be sure you take her by bungalow seventy-six, first."

She looked back at Jewel. "Young Jewel, tell them it went well, and I wish I could let them see her. Give them my word of loyalty that I will stay by her side until she is back with them.

Hopefully, we'll have her there around last snack tomorrow. As for you, sleep in as long as you can. *I mean it.*"

Jewel giggled, partly from exhausted silliness, and partly from the ridiculous notion that sleeping in could be a loyalty. The huge apprentice led her noiselessly into the night by lantern light.

At bungalow seventy-six, he jingled the bell, greeted Para Patrick blankly and stood back for Jewel to enter. "Greetings," Jewel said. "I have news from Apprentice Dupree." Jewel kept her head down as she spoke. One look at Ri and the whole story would rush out.

Instead, Jewel spoke only of the necessary details. The surgery had gone well. Apprentice Dupree planned to bring Para Chloe to their bungalow tomorrow near last snack. And Para Chloe would not be alone at any time; Apprentice Dupree had given her word of loyalty to stay by their para's side. Jewel flashed them a quick pleasant smile, bowed, blurted out the typical farewell, and was gone.

"Jewel," Samuri called behind her, worried and confused. What had happened to Jewel? Why wouldn't she look up when it was only them?

"Pleasantness and safety," Para Patrick replied, pushing the door shut just as Samuri was about to rush past him.

Samuri's mouth gaped open in disbelief. A confused hurt shone from his eyes. Para Patrick put his arm around Samuri's shoulders moving him toward his cot.

"Jewel is doing what she must, Samuri, and doing it loyally. There *must* be a reason. On the outside she's not acting like the Jewel we know, but she is in there. Yes?"

Though Samuri had grown to trust Jewel deeply, lately nothing he cared about seemed safe. Where was Faithful One's help now?

"Yes Para Patrick, but what if I never see her again?"

Para Patrick was speechless. What was left to promise his young who he cared for more than his own life?

"Let's get to sleep. We need our strength, especially now." They hugged, then held on to each other, neither of them knowing what tomorrow would bring.

29
always

Bungalow seventy-six was bustling with activity the next evening. Para Chloe was to be there before the end of the next hourglass. Apprentice Dupree had sent a messenger with instructions for Para Patrick and Samuri. Para Patrick shuffled his cot out to the wall of the gathering room. Samuri replaced it with the new cot, shaking his head in disbelief the whole time.

Para Chloe would sleep on the new cot in her room. The Young Jewel would sleep on Para Chloe's old cot, just two meters away, if she *could* sleep. No one but Jewel was to be in Chloe's room through the night. Only Jewel knew exactly how to care for Para Chloe. And the Laws of Loyalty insisted Para Patrick and the Young Samuri must not be tired nor distracted at their tasks the next day. Apprentice Dupree was adamant about both.

A very sleepy-eyed Samuri and Para Patrick peeked in on Para Chloe the next morning. Neither had slept well because of Para Chloe's intermittent gasps and moans. Jewel smiled and whispered, "I'll let her know you looked in." So, they left for tasks reluctantly, as if this might be the last time they saw her.

As for Jewel . . . what could they say? The first two days Para

Chloe was back, Jewel rarely slept. She stayed loyally beside their dear para applying ointments, feeding her, and getting her to swallow funny liquids. Chloe's moans and garbled murmurings woke Para Patrick and Samuri countless times, but never for long. Each time Jewel rose swiftly and willingly, calming Para Chloe through the pain and the delirious thoughts. That was just the way it had to be in those first days.

Throughout the days and nights, Jewel softly chanted the words Faithful One had given to her. "The wind blows wherever . . . Oh, hide Para Chloe in the secret place of your presence and keep her safe." Jewel didn't need to understand the words completely, they were beautiful and powerful. Merely speaking them made Faithful One's nearness seem . . . nearer. More real.

The hardest part was the small pan, fitted down into the special cot for Chloe to relieve herself without getting up. Jewel felt incredibly embarrassed when it was necessary to clean Para Chloe, but she was sure this too was an important part of Para Chloe's comfort and healing. Twice, in the process, tears of humiliation came streaming down Para Chloe's face.

"Be brave, Para Chloe," Jewel said slowly, brightly, and with compassion. "You and I will be brave together. Okay?"

Para Chloe, eyes still closed, mumbled weakly, "Help me, Lord."

The words caught Jewel's attention. Was Para Chloe conscious? Was she aware Jewel was hearing her? And that word, l–or–d . . . Jewel thought she remembered markings that fit with that. What was it? Could it be another name for Faithful One? Jewel was stunned.

Oh, Faithful One. What do I do with this?

What if I'm right? This was too wonderful to hope for. *But what if I'm wrong?* That was too risky to pull Ri into.

Immediately that sweet, strong, tree-cave peace filled her. For now, she'd leave it safe in Faithful One's care and wait until she knew without a doubt.

Each day held new breakthroughs. Para Patrick and Samuri

burst through the door after tasks like fidgety juniors on their way to Celebration Day. Their intense, pale blue eyes, so much alike, held the same questions. *Is she okay? Can we see her today?*

If Para Chloe was awake, Para Patrick and Samuri wiggled cautiously past all the baskets of ointments and supplies to sit on the floor. They squished together on the same side of Para Chloe's cot while Jewel stood in the doorway to help if needed. Those moments were the highlight of the day for both Para Chloe and Jewel. But Para Chloe was exhausted within a hundred grains of the hourglass, simply from trying to pay attention to them.

Samuri and Para Patrick were incredibly gentle with her. Their strong hands touched her face as lightly as a feather, wanting to comfort her but afraid of bumping her and causing her more pain. Slowly she improved until they could sit with her for a full hourglass, telling her stories of the day and laughing.

Who could have imagined such a bungalow was possible? Jewel couldn't get enough of it, the tender look in their eyes, their quick laughter, and their intense concern. They insisted Jewel tell them every detail of Apprentice Dupree's daily report. They practically begged for a way to be helpful.

The first two weeks, Apprentice Dupree came after midday snack to check on Para Chloe's progress, and to help with anything Jewel needed. Para Chloe's needs and remedies changed daily. Dupree brought extra pillows and showed Jewel how to prop Chloe up bit by bit.

Jewel saved Para Chloe's sitting up for times when their whole bungalow was together. The smallest improvements were celebrations. When Para Patrick was gradually allowed to take on some of Para Chloe's care, Jewel and Samuri gave the paras that time to be alone.

The weaving room became Samuri and Jewel's getaway. The outer door had been built doubly-wide to get looms through it. So, they sat in the big open door where Jewel could breathe the fresh air and gaze into the woods but still hear Para Patrick if he called for them. *And* they talked.

It was the best ever to talk after all their time apart, and to talk freely with no fear of trouble. But Ri chose his words with caution. Could Jewel handle the worst news about the Woods Shop? He would have to tell her sometime.

"I've been training your replacement," Samuri said seriously, yet with a gleam in his eyes. "Looks like you're here for a while."

"Why didn't you tell me?" Jewel's eyes lit up with curiosity.

"Um, I wasn't ready. I thought we both needed a few more days." He double-winked at her, and she clapped her hands excitedly.

"Who? Tell me about . . . her? Or him?"

"It's . . . Daro." Ri spoke gently, hesitantly like a para softening the harsh blow of bad news, which was exactly how he felt. "Town Master Cree assigned him to the Woods Shop."

Jewel flinched like she'd been slapped. No wonder Ri had waited to tell her. Now she wished she could go back and not know. Jewel searched the treetops shaking her head, fighting back her first wave of anger in weeks. How cruel of the Township to give Daro her tasks! Were they trying to get Gran Para Brody and Samuri in trouble?

As if Samuri could read her mind, he assured her. "Don't worry Jewel; I manage. I do my best to be pleasant and loyal. I'm extra careful about being safe in every way. Of course, I am still furious about how he treated you but getting back at him . . . that would only get me in trouble and make it worse for all of us."

What Samuri didn't say was how empty the shop was without her, for him and for Brody. From the start Brody blamed himself for what Jewel went through. The day after the chase Brody was almost sick with regret. The next day the Young Daro came.

That day Brody had grabbed a tool and stomped through the shop pounding on counters, muttering angrily. "Brody's not goin' ta have some . . ." Brody caught Samuri staring at him and sulked away ashamed how close he'd come to venting his vengeful thoughts and words.

Samuri had worried Brody would actually hurt Daro and be

reassigned. Ri had to stop that from happening. He had to protect both Jewel and Brody now, and the best way was by keeping Daro close. So, Samuri told Brody the part about keeping Daro with them to protect Jewel and left out the rest.

"If Daro's with *us*, we can keep him away from Jewel." That changed everything for both Samuri and Brody. Of course, it meant Ri had to work even harder, but he was figuring it out.

Jewel shook it off and perked up. "Definitely. The last thing we need is for *you* to be in trouble. *And* listen to this. I have a report, too. A pleasant one. You'd *never* guess."

Jewel went on to explain that Town Master Cree had asked Apprentice Dupree when Para Chloe could weave again. The apprentice wasn't sure, but thought it would be from six to eight weeks until Para Chloe's casts could be removed. After that Para Chloe's wrists would be stiff for quite a while. Jewel paused, though not for long, stopping as if that were the end of the story.

"And guess what? Town Master Cree wants Para Chloe to teach *me* to weave. Of course, first she has to feel well enough to sit in the task room. Apprentice Dupree says we'll have to start with flags. But, who knows, maybe your para will design the first Scarf of Remembrance and let me begin the weaving."

Samuri's jaw dropped and Jewel was afraid he was upset with her. Then he took her hand and turned it palms up, exposing her rough, calloused hands. Ri scanned the shelves until he spotted Para Chloe's own small tin of specially made hazelnut, beeswax cream.

"Use this. Every day. By the time my para is ready to teach you, your hands will be as soft as the petals of a cosmos."

Faithful One's voice broke into Samuri's thoughts. *Now.* Samuri knew exactly what it meant. That one word was his answer to months of questions and waiting.

"I have something else to tell you, Jewel."

The change in Samuri's voice caused Jewel's brilliant, blue green eyes to light up like the first day he met her.

"Jewel, do you remember the new word Brody used to

describe the trees?"

Her eyes scanned the tall, swaying pines searching for the memory of it. She shook her head. No, she did not remember. Samuri was surprised.

"Brody said trees were like friends."

"Oh . . . f-r-r . . . ends. I think it reminded me of stories I'd made up, and I felt really close to Brody. But right away I thought of each tree's own pleasant name—pines, saplings, plums—I didn't want a new name for them. Then I forgot that word."

"What if the word had a different meaning?"

"Like what?"

"Like something a tree can't do. What if the word actually describes *someone*, not a tree? Someone who listens to you and knows what you need to hear. Someone you want to spend time with more than anyone else. Someone you can trust completely. *That's* a friend."

"Like . . . us?" She sounded doubtful at first, but then it burst out of her. "Like us! Ri, like us!"

"Yes Jewel, like us. The first day Para Chloe saw us in the yard she was so excited she accidentally called you my friend. But it's a very forbidden word, so of course it wasn't safe. You and I were small. My paras didn't know anything about your paras. My paras *wanted* me to have a friend and thought they could keep us safe." He laughed. Nothing about it had been safe.

"So, they decided to let me see you again *if* I was careful, *and* if I never said friend again. So, I didn't, but I never forgot it either."

Jewel pulled her knees up close to her chin, thinking of all the days and weeks she'd longed to find a word for what Ri was to her. All the hard times that had threatened to separate them rushed through her mind. But now . . ."

Ri took a deep breath. There was one more secret he'd been longing to share with Jewel. *Friend* wasn't just their word. Friend was on the marked pages of Faithful One's words. *I have called you friends.*

Samuri had sensed that *before* he discovered it in the markings, but having those exact words to look at whenever he wanted was like a Scarf of Remembrance.

"Jewel, I . . ."

Para Patrick's voice interrupted, calling out excitedly from beside Para Chloe's cot. "Samuri. Jewel. Para Chloe wants to sit by the loom for a minute. Come help me move her."

"Friends." That was all Samuri had time to say. But he sealed it with a double wink.

Jewel sandwiched her mouth and nose between her hands, her expression of indescribable joy. Her eyes met Samuri's eyes, and her hands parted the slightest bit to let her heartfelt vow bubble out. "Friends . . ." She winked back at him. "Always!"

There was a rush in the treetops as several winged-creatures swooped into Samuri's yard and back out again, trilling, "Always, always, always."

Then Samuri and Jewel shouted, "Let's go!" and raced through the bungalow together.

A Note From the Author

In their story, Samuri and Jewel gain courage and strength from the words of Faithful One. But Faithful One is not just a character in this book—He is the One, True God, and He is waiting to guide and help you through His words to us in the Bible!

Below are Faithful One's words to Samuri and Jewel and where to find them in the Bible. Remember that Faithful One will often give you a special verse for your life or certain situations. How wonderful it is that His words are so easily accessible in our world!

Like Samuri and Jewel, may you always be listening, watching, and waiting for Faithful One's words in your life.[1]

"Call to me and I will answer you and tell you great and unsearchable things you do not know." —**Jeremiah 33:3**

"The wind blows wherever it pleases. You hear its sound, but you cannot tell where it comes from or where it is going." —**John 3:8 a&b**

"I have called you friends." —**John 15:15b**

"In the shelter of your presence you hide them from all human intrigues; you keep them safe in your dwelling from accusing tongues." —**Psalm 31:20**

"That person is like a tree planted by streams of water..."
—**Psalm 1:3a**

---

1   All verses are taken from the New International Version of the Bible.

acknowledgments

"They knew each other's secrets and dreams and kept them safe in a place called friendship."
—*Tender Hearts Greeting Cards*

I never imagined how many friends God would bring into my path to help keep my secrets and dreams safe. Thank you, from my heart, to each of you who walked beside me on this Samuri & Jewel journey.

Faithful One, Creator and dearest friend of all, without you there wouldn't be a book. You showed me Samuri & Jewel, brought me the most incredible scenes, brought the friends I needed when I needed them, and stayed by my side through the best and the worst. There aren't enough words to thank you, but I know you hear my heart. Friends . . . Always!

First, to my husband, children, and grandchildren—thanks for the laughter, prayers, adventures, and great books you share with me. And for your help, now, with this book. You are my favorite friends, my life-long dream come true.

Bob, my dear, dear husband, and an extraordinary grampa! Your delicious cooking, long walks, moments with the Lord, family activities, and constant confidence keep me going. And those wrens! My heart still jumps every time I see them!

David, brilliant lyricist and composer, dear encourager, and loving son. You were the first to call me an author. You chatted with me for hours and shared beaucoup resources until I was brave enough to own it. I'll always cherish those times when few knew I was writing, but you already treated me like an accomplished author. (And then, you saved the map!)

Kendra, one of my dearest readers and my golden standard when I edit. I love our chats and our sweet times over tea. Going to the Buzz with you is a favorite.

Mary, what a surprising journey! Who knew we'd be mother-and-daughter dystopian authors? The stars shimmer more brightly and hum louder now that we can share our author joys, sorrows, and foibles together. And I think we shine brighter, too. I'm so grateful to have you beside me on this dangerous author journey, Lion Girl.

Josh, our official "anti-stress" tech support. I'm so grateful for your willingness to help keep our devices running smoothly. Thanks for being such an encourager about the book.

Jonny, there's nothing like getting to work with my own son on the cover project, especially since you had such a good understanding of my heart and of the earthy, mysterious world of this book. Thanks for finding an authentic painting and gifting it to me. It will always remind me our fun times working together and of your sweet, supportive heart.

Pietze, you laugh that warm laugh-of-knowing-hard-times that didn't beat you. Then you give me a big hug and say, "Everything will work out, Mom." And suddenly, life seems brighter, more hopeful.

My First Readers. Addison—aww, my first youth reader and the first to love the hero and his girl as much as I do. Thanks for your insightful, chapter by chapter, feedback—it made tough decisions, much easier. Hugs, and best ever pleasant feelings.

Xander and Nathaniel, you were the next two. What great

talks we had about the book. Xander, thanks for stepping out of your normal genre—I'm glad you were surprisingly pleased. Nathaniel, thanks for your ongoing enthusiasm and prayers, and . . . for the animals! How could I miss animals? (Just wait, book two is going to beat New Jersey all to pieces!)

Other readers, young and young at heart—Amy Straley, Suzanna G., Elly M., Dean, Heidi, Rhea, Lilly, Alexandra Yu, Jennie, Hester, Renee, M.E. Duffield, and Amy Grimes.

Collaborative Artists and Additional Tech Support! Heidi Morgan and my husband, Bob, sketched scads of illustrations before we settled on the interior design. Then Heidi spent hours upon hours on that fabulous Township map. Bob brought those beloved wrens to life on his first try, and then repeatedly sketched the compasses until they were just what we wanted.

My son, Jonny, did vision casting and found the mysterious painting for the cover's background. Faille Schmitz added a captivating aura to the mystery of the forest with her choice of font, fireflies, and the lovely hand-painted dragonfly.

We Are Leo and Matthew Clark, Jesus often brings your songs to me to break into my heart when nothing else can.

My techy friends the Free Website Guys and Derick Brown (Xander's dad). What a blessing for non-techy me to have your kind expertise just when I needed it!

Special note! Heidi's heart for this book went far beyond sketching what I ask her to. From the moment she read Samuri and Jewel, Heidi had a vision for it as if it were her very own. She has been my sounding board, prayer warrior, cheerleader, and sweet friend.

Others who stood with me in trying seasons were . . . Suzanne Murray's Tuesday Prayer Group who were first to champion this book in prayer. Amy Straley, whose words of God's truth and whimsy cheered me in the lockdown. Clinton Moore, who helped me hear the Lord's voice again in a confusing season. Ben and Beth Hackbarth's example taught me greater tenacity and tenderness. Suzanna Gallagher's timely texts meant more than she can know. The prayers and presence of Lisa Schell's Called Collective Group held me up in the darkest moments of 2023. Adrianne McFarland remembered me and pointed me to Colorado Prays.

My spunky, faithful praying friends, literally from plains, cities, and mountains, ocean to ocean. Just now, I imagined us sitting together, listening to heaven tell tales of the battles you fought in prayer and the awesome unseen victories won for me, for the book, and most importantly for its readers. Then we all jumped up, threw our crowns high in the air like graduation caps, and shouted as they landed in a glorious heap around the throne!

Special thanks to our church families, prayer groups, and pastors for all their support and love.

To Roger and Yvonne, for years of friendship, encouragement and prayers. I cherish the beauty and hope you have brought to my life.

Thanks also for writing help from . . . Lindsey, my first professional editor to "see" S & J. You met my inexperience with links, the kindest sort of honesty, and wonderfully detailed encouragement for the long path ahead of me. Marianne Hering, your lighthearted attitude, and your challenges to write more intensely have been a great support.

Kori Frazier Morgan from Inkling Creative Strategies. Step by step you get it, get me, the book, the struggle, and the joy. You always fight for me, encouraging my faith and my skills, while also challenging me to refocus and calm down. Thank you.

Doncheskis, thank you for your grins, giggles, food and never-ending open doors.

Duffields, the Township could have certainly used your heart of justice and celebration.

Aunt Max and Uncle Bill, who adopted this awkward, only-child, city-dweller into the busy summers on your farm. Here's to harvest moons, a table full of laughter and hired hands, prayer before meals, and the Bible by your chair. Those surely shaped some of this author I have become.

My mom, who wove her way into the lives of many, and especially mine.

Finally, there's all those who touched my life and this book in brief moments or silent heartfelt prayers—but aren't written here. I pray God's presence will remind you how genuinely special that moment was in the midst of this chaotic world, to me, and even more so, to Him.

P.S. Addison, Nathaniel, David, and Kendra! I loved the name Samuri (rhymes with sky) from the moment the Lord brought it to my mind. Then just when I was afraid I must give it up, you shared the brave and true nature of that name. I'm truly grateful.

About the Author

Kimily Kay, longtime adventurer, friend of youth, and storyteller now presents her first novel, *Samuri & Jewel: The Forbidden Friendship*. Kimily has always been on the lookout for intriguing books of wonder, friendship, quest, and faith. When her children were young, she gathered them together to spend evenings curled up in their country home reading aloud. If a storm-tossed night blew out the electricity, she made-up stories for them by candlelight. As her children grew, the enthralling storybooks and novels she chose were joined by family escapades on camping trips and short-term youth missions.

Though writing a novel was never on Kimily's radar, the Lord was preparing her all along. When Samuri and Jewel suddenly appeared in her mind's eye, she knew she had to tell their story. Like her characters, Kimily loves friendship, courage, frothy hot drinks, long hikes, lakes, and secret places with God.

Visit www.kimilykayduffield.com to learn more about Kimily's writing and adventures.